# The Gifting

# Praise for The Gifting

"Set in a not-too-distant future that feels frighteningly like home, this novel immerses readers within the heart of Tess's fear from the very first chapter. This is not, however, a novel of horror. Guaranteed to leave you breathless, *The Gifting* is an eerie merging of Gothic-like dystopian mystery and YA romance within a pulse-pounding supernatural thriller. Expect to lose sleep over this book! A must-read addition to any YA reader's collection, this one's a keeper!"

~Serena Chase, *USA Today*'s Happy Ever After blog, author of *The Ryn*

"Chilling from start to finish! K. E. Ganshert delivers an exciting young adult fantasy that's just as fun as it is riveting. THE GIFTING will keep you turning pages in an effort to unlock the mystery of this unsettled world."

~Addison Moore, New York Times Bestselling Author

"K.E. Ganshert brings a fresh new voice to the dystopian romance scene for young adults. Ganshert will wow her audience with captivating prose, a well-paced plot, and just the perfect amount of swoon!"

~Heather Sunseri, author of the Mindspeak series

# THE GIFTING

## BY K.E. GANSHERT

Edited by: Lora Doncea
Cover Design by: Okay Creations
Interior Design and Formatting by: BB eBooks

*For Ryan McGivern, the best big brother a girl could ask for. Without your crazy outside-the-box thinking, I'm pretty sure this story never would have taken flight.*

# CHAPTER ONE

# BIRTHDAY WISHES

According to science, humans have no souls. There is no afterlife or guardian angels or ghosts or spirits or anything at all supernatural. Our world is purely physical. The government has systematically removed God from society. He is no longer mentioned in the Pledge of Allegiance, no longer written on our money, no longer found in our Constitution or acknowledged in any of our political gatherings.

My father thinks this is a good thing. He believes the human race has caused enough damage in the name of religion. We are better off this way, more evolved, and anybody who thinks differently is a fool. He adamantly, wholeheartedly agrees with science. But I'm not as convinced. Because if science is right, then I'm crazy.

And crazy is dangerous.

Seventeen candles flicker on the cake, illuminating a portion of our kitchen. A pocket of warmth expands inside the room. One that has nothing to do with the cake or the people in front of me. The feeling doesn't originate inside of me at all. It radiates from beyond the border of the light's reach, pulsing in the dark. Something shimmers beside our refrigerator and for the briefest of moments—before that beautiful shimmering thing disappears—I feel terrified and brave all at once.

I blink and it's gone. The only thing hovering near our refrigerator is empty air. The temperature returns to normal, but my heartbeat does not. It thuds in my ears. My younger brother Pete yawns and shakes dark hair from even darker eyes, looking like he'd rather be anywhere else but here—at my lame, four-person birthday party. Dad stands with his arm wrapped around my mother's waist. She clasps her hands beneath her chin and nods encouragingly. "Go on, Tess. Make a wish."

So I ignore my brother and fill my lungs with oxygen and wish for the one thing I want most, the one thing that is constantly elusive.

*I wish I could be normal.*

I blow toward the candles as hard as I can, but the room does not go black. One small flame dances on a wick, mocking me.

## Chapter Two

# The Incident

It's August on the panhandle of Florida and I can't get warm. The icy chill that woke me in the night refuses to leave. It hovers nearby when I get ready for my first day of junior year, and it follows me into the kitchen where Dad reads the morning newspaper.

There was an earthquake in California, the second one in a month, another riot broke out at a fetal modification clinic in Chicago, a drive-by shooting in Tallahassee, which is like, twenty minutes from where we live, and the unrest in north Africa continues to escalate. Dad thinks it's only a matter of time before the U.S. gets involved. Dad thinks if we don't get Egypt under control as soon as possible, we'll have World War III on our hands. I think he should read the newspaper to himself. But he insists Pete and I know what's going on in the world.

I grab a carton of orange juice from the refrigerator. "Do you think the Chief of Press ever wants to off himself?"

Mom frowns. "Tess."

"What? The news is seriously depressing." I take a swig of o.j.

Mom's frown deepens. To her, the habit is disgusting. To me, it's economical.

The paper crinkles as Dad flips to the business section. "You gonna join me at work on Saturday, kiddo?"

"You have to go in this weekend again?" Mom takes the carton from my hands to pour some orange juice in a glass. When she's finished, she gives me the cup and returns the carton to the top shelf of our fridge.

"I need to get this account finished by Monday." Dad peers at me over the top of his paper. "Would love your help."

"Yeah, sure." While most kids my age hang out with friends on the weekends, I go to work with Dad. It's the way we bond. I probably know more about security systems than all of his employees at Safe Guard's west Florida branch combined.

Mom gives Pete and me a goodbye kiss on our cheeks and tells us to have a great first day. The icy chill follows me to school and remains while the principal of Jude High welcomes all 300 of us to a new year. It follows me into Mr. Greeley's classroom, too. He teaches Current Events, a course every high school student in the country is required to take, because apparently, the government agrees with my dad. Ignorance is unacceptable.

Mr. Greeley calls attendance over the familiar, excited chatter that marks the first day of school. Somehow, I can never figure out how to become a part of it. So I slouch in my seat and doodle mindless swirls on the cover of my folder while Missy Calloway flirts with Dustin O'Malley, a red-headed soccer player with a face full of freckles. Dustin isn't very cute—but he's confident and funny and is pretty much the reason why Jude's soccer team won state last year, so all the girls forgive him.

He crumples a gum wrapper and throws it at Missy. The foil ball tangles in her bleach-blond hair. She half giggles-half shrieks in that *stop-it-but-really-don't* kind of way and tries to throw it back. The foil ball lands on the corner of my desk.

Sydney Lauren—whose lips are never the same color—leans forward and pokes Dustin in the back with her pencil. "Psst."

He twists around.

"I'm having people over tonight. Nothing big. Just a small back-to-school get together."

I tuck my hair behind my ear to peek at Dustin, but my elbow knocks into my notebook. It falls to the ground. I have to turn all the way around to pick it up and when I do, Sydney raises her eyebrows at me. "You should come too."

The only reason I'm ever invited anywhere is because girls think if I come, my brother will too. And girls really like Pete, even though he's a skinny sophomore.

"So ...?" Sydney's eyebrows creep higher up her forehead. "Are you gonna come?"

"It's a school night."

"And?"

I can feel Dustin and Missy staring. "I—uh—already have plans."

Sydney shrugs. "Well, your brother should still come. Tell him I insist."

"Yeah. Okay." The last time I went to a party, I kept seeing stars in the periphery of my vision, as if I had some sort of concussion. I ended up coming home two hours before curfew. My mom was actually disappointed. I turn back around and resume my doodling. Only somehow, the mindless lines have turned into a form—one that resembles a monster with a forked tongue and horns, one I swear I've seen before—and for reasons I don't understand, I have the overwhelming urge to throw the folder away. Or tear it in half. I don't want that thing or the memory of it anywhere near me.

A collective giggle ripples through the class.

When I look up, Mr. Greeley is staring at me over the top of his clipboard. "Teresa Eckhart?" It's obvious it's not the first time he's called my name.

I clear my throat. "It's Tess."

"Speak up please," he says.

The class giggles again.

"I go by Tess." My voice escapes like a mouse.

∾

While most parents wouldn't let their fifteen- and seventeen-year-old children go to a party on a school night, my mom practically shoves us out the door.

*How are you going to make friends if you never go anywhere, sweetheart?*

I want to tell her that particular ship has long since sailed. We've lived in the small town of Jude, Florida for two years now. Since my dad is some bigwig for one of the nation's wealthiest security companies—a thriving industry thanks to the escalating crime rate—we move a lot. Part of his job requires planting new branches across the United States. He gets them going, helps them grow, and starts all over again somewhere else.

Mom never complains about the moving, so long as Dad finds a house that is at least fifteen minutes away from the city. According to her, any place with a population over fifteen thousand is too dangerous for children. Plus, she thinks if Pete and I go to smaller schools, we'll have an easier time fitting in. What she doesn't realize is that smaller schools also make it easier to stand out. Especially if you're me.

Anyway, I don't want to be here, in the balmy heat outside Sydney Lauren's home. In fact, I'd rather be anywhere but here. Before I express any of this to Pete, he rings the bell. Two seconds later, Sydney swings the door open. She wears neon purple lipstick and a mesh tank top that is completely perfunctory. As she squeals and flings her arms around my brother, I'm distracted by her lime green bra. I would never, in a million years, have the guts to wear that outfit.

"You're right on time!" She grabs Pete's hand and pulls him inside. "We just got out the Ouija board."

Pete laughs. "Ouija board? I didn't know those still existed."

"You have to know where to look." She wags her eyebrows. "I told Rose that this house was built on an Indian burial ground and she doesn't believe me."

Sydney lives in a peach-colored stucco home straight out of the twentieth century. Hardly haunted house material. Still, my stomach squirms. The law prohibits the selling of items that perpetuate belief in the supernatural. The thing is, forbidding teenagers to dabble in anything supernatural only guarantees that they will.

She leads Pete over to the small crowd lounging around a coffee table. There are five juniors. Two seniors. A bowl of candy, a bag of pretzels, and a half-empty bottle of Smirnoff. Pete squeezes in on the couch and Sydney sits on his knee like the two are a couple. Elliana—a girl with an eyebrow ring and fluorescent colored bracelets covering both of her wrists—shoots daggers at Sydney.

I feel sick.

Despite taking two Excedrin Migraine pills, a headache pierces my left temple. Clasping my hands in front of my waist,

I watch Missy set up the Ouija board while everyone else laughs and clowns around. Nobody has noticed me yet. Which means it's not too late to turn around and leave. As soon as the thought occurs, Missy spots me in the doorway. "Hey everybody, look who's here. It's *Teresa*." She raises a plastic red cup in my direction. I'm pretty sure she's not drinking water. "Aren't you going to come in? We're about to have a séance."

"Yeah, we're gonna talk to some dead Indians."

"The politically correct term is Native Americans, Syd." Dustin pops a handful of M&M's into his mouth.

I peek around the doorway. "Are your parents home?"

Everybody laughs.

Right. The vodka.

"Aw, is *Tewesa* scared the ghosties will get us without any gwown ups around?"

"Give it a rest, Missy." Sydney tosses the Ouija board box aside. "Will you hit the lights, Tess? I'm pretty sure this works better in the dark."

I swallow, but my throat sticks together. Everybody waits for me—Tess the Freak—to unglue my feet from the doorway when what I want to do is crawl under the doormat and disappear. No, scratch that. What I really want is to throw off my headache and my painful shyness and join in the laughter and fun. What I really want, more than anything, is to be a part of this group. So I ignore the erratic galloping of my heart and flip off the lights.

Sydney hops off Pete's knee and pulls the drapes across the large picture window. The swinging vertical blinds chop apart the waning daylight.

Dustin wiggles his fingers at Missy. "Oo-oooo-ooo!"

She punches his bicep. "Cut it out, jerk."

I follow Sydney, eager to be closer to the group. Despite being seventeen, darkness still creeps me out. The clamminess spreading across my skin doesn't help. I take a deep breath and tell myself that fear is irrational. Ghosts are not real. And even if they were, the Ouija board is made by Parker Brothers. Not exactly black market paraphernalia.

Elliana snuggles closer to Pete's shoulder and wraps her arm around his elbow. "Are you going to save me from the big bad evil spirits?"

Even through the semi-darkness, I can see Pete's crooked, half smile—the one girls go gaga over—and a surge of jealousy stabs my gut. How can he sit there so at ease? How can two people born from the same gene pool end up so incredibly different? For crying out loud, we don't even look the same.

Sydney kneels next to Pete's legs. "Okay, so I think we all have to put our hands on this pointer-thing."

"It's called a planchette."

Everybody looks at Elliana.

"Don't ask me how I know that."

"Don't we need candles or something?" Missy asks.

Rose—a senior with beautiful ebony skin and a killer volleyball spike—wraps her long leg over the arm rest of the love seat. "You can light all the candles you want, the only thing this board can do is teach J.R. the alphabet."

J.R. tosses an M&M at Rose. She catches it and pops it in her mouth.

"Hey, you better watch it or you're going to piss off the Indians," Dustin says.

The banter is lighthearted, but the hair on the back of my arms prickles. I can't bring myself to laugh with the rest of them. All I can think is that I really, really want to leave.

*Physical, physical, physical. Dad says the world is purely physical ...*

Missy sets her cup on the coffee table. "I think we should hold hands."

"Jeez, Miss, if you wanted to hold my hand so badly, you should have just said so from the beginning." Dustin gives her a lighthearted thwack with a pillow. "We don't need a séance for that."

Missy flicks her hair. "You wish."

Sydney puts her fingers on the pointer, the planchette. Whatever it's called. And I have the same feeling I had in Mr. Greeley's Current Events class, when that monster stared up at me from my folder—a coldness that won't go away. A coldness so deep I can feel it in my bones. I fist my hands in my lap.

Dustin and Missy put their fingers on the planchette too.

"I cannot believe we're doing this," Rose mutters.

"Shhh!" Sydney sits up straighter and closes her eyes. The room fills with laughter and ... something else. A presence that makes my breath come so quick and so shallow, I worry I might be having a panic attack. I glance at Pete and Elliana flirting, at Rose sticking her tongue out at J.R., and I can't figure out how they don't feel it.

Sydney wears the kind of expression that says she's trying hard to act serious, but a smile makes the corners of her lips twitch. She clears her throat and waits for the giggling and whispering to cease. "Who is with us in this house?" she asks in a low, spooky voice. Dustin and Missy giggle. "We'd like to speak with you."

I tell my heart to calm down. I tell myself I'm being a spaz. I tell myself I will never, ever fit in if I can't do a stupid séance with a group of teenagers on a Parker Brothers Ouija board.

But then something moves in the corner of the room, near the hallway, and I squeeze my eyelids shut.

*It was just my imagination. It was just my imagination …*

"We invite you in." Sydney's voice has turned into an exaggerated moan. I peek at her through squinted eyes. "Tell us who you are."

The planchette moves across the board. Missy takes her fingers away.

Elliana nudges Dustin with her foot. "Very funny, O'Malley."

He holds up his hands. "It wasn't me."

The room plunges into ice. I wrap my fingers around my throat and squeeze my eyes tight. This isn't real. None of this is real. But then the whispers come. Ghost-like voices that turn my blood cold. Visions slam through me—horrible, awful, terrible images—worse than any nightmare I've ever had. Visions of death and decay and gnashing teeth and man-made pits filled with cold, lifeless bodies. Visions of skinny, pale people wrapped in straitjackets, black mouths splitting their faces with silent, anguished screams.

Something brushes against my leg. I slap my shin. Something tickles my cheek. I slap at my face. But I do not—cannot—open my eyes. I refuse to face whatever is on the other side of my eyelids. The whispers turn into screams. Blood-curdling, heart-stopping screams. Like whatever is out there wants me to look. Demands me to look. As hard as I try, I can't make them stop. I can't make me stop.

The screams are coming from me.

## CHAPTER THREE

# TESS THE FREAK

I wake up to the hushed voices of Mom and Dad and another I don't recognize. My head pounds as I open my eyes to a blinding white box—white walls, white floors, white sheets, white bed. The brightness is so sterile and shocking, I throw my arm over my face.

*Where am I? What happened?*

"Her tests came back clean," the unfamiliar voice says. "We didn't find any traces of drugs or alcohol in her system."

"None?" My mom sounds deflated, like the no drugs or alcohol is bad news.

"No, I'm sorry."

*He's sorry?*

My temples throb around the response. Why would he be sorry? I slide my arm away and this time, I understand why the whiteness is so bright. Sunlight filters inside an open window. I turn my head on the pillow and spy my parents and a man in a white coat huddled together in the corner, near the door. My mom presses her fingers against her lips and shakes her head. "I don't understand."

"We'll know more when your daughter wakes up. We can hear what she has to say about ..." the doctor frowns, "the episode."

"My daughter is not crazy." Mom's words come out sharp and vehement. And with them, comes clarity. It floods back into place with a vengeance. The party at Sydney's. The Ouija board and the voices and the screams. My stomach churns. I should be afraid, maybe even terrified. But all I can feel is humiliation. Abject humiliation. Because what must I have done to end up in a hospital? The churning turns my stomach to rot.

"I'm merely following protocol, Mrs. Ekhart."

The doctor leaves and I close my eyes, feigning sleep. I cannot face my parents or their worry. I cannot face anybody ever again. I want to hide behind my closed eyelids forever. I want to avoid whatever repercussions lay beyond this bed. The seconds tick into minutes. The silence in the room crackles with tension.

"What are you thinking?" It's my father's voice.

"You know exactly what I'm thinking."

"I'm sure there is a perfectly logical explanation for what happened." These are classic my dad-isms. According to him, logic explains everything. And if it can't, he dismisses it altogether. His world makes no room for the unexplainable. "Tess is sensitive. We've always known that. She probably got spooked and the other kids exaggerated."

"You think Pete is exaggerating?" Mom's voice wobbles. "James, our son said she was hitting and scratching herself. He said she was screaming for something to get off her."

I sink further into the bed, fear expanding inside my lungs. Never mind the humiliation I will face upon returning to school, I could be committed for this. I could be locked up in a cell and never let out again.

"What do you want me to say?" Dad asks.

"I want you to promise me she'll be okay. I want you to promise that we won't lose her. I want you to promise that our daughter won't end up like your mom."

My heart pounds into the silence, joined with the erratic breaths escaping my lips. My grandmother is dead. She died of a heart attack years ago, when I was too young to remember. So what is my mother talking about? Why is she afraid I'll end up dead?

"Tess is not my mother," Dad says in a voice so low I have to strain to hear it.

"But we've always suspected—"

"That's enough, Miranda." The sharpness of his words slice through the air. "We can't talk about this. Not here."

I open one of my eyes. Dad has ahold of Mom's arm, their panicked expressions mirrored on each other's faces.

"It's not safe."

A chill ripples through my bones.

"She's going to have to speak with a government-mandated psychiatrist," Mom whispers. "Nothing about this is safe."

∽

News about my freak-out spreads like pink eye. Another disadvantage of these small towns my mom is so fond of. At school, Pete is guilty by association. No matter how cute the girls think he is, there's only so much high school students will tolerate. Apparently, having a whacked-out older sister isn't one of them.

So everyone except Elliana ignores Pete. She must have it bad to risk being ostracized by the entire student body. The two of them stick to each other like double sided tape.

Me? I'm not so much ignored as overtly avoided. Students hurry to the other side of the hall when they pass by, as if I have leprosy instead of an overactive imagination (this is the story I spun for the psychiatrist and I'm sticking to it). Part of me wants to run around touching people, just to see how they'll react. Instead, I hide behind my veil of dark hair and try to make myself as small as possible, which isn't very hard, considering my build.

None of this would be so bad if my nightmares weren't getting worse. Sleep offers no escape. Neither does home. As soon as I returned from the hospital, my parents sat me down at the kitchen table and asked me the same questions as the psychiatrist, only this time, they wanted the truth. My attempt at an explanation turned their faces to the color of ash. They don't bring it up again. Instead, they tiptoe around me like I'm made out of glass. Like the wrong word or the wrong volume will shatter me to pieces. Or maybe they're the ones who will break. Maybe I'm the one who's dangerous.

Their whispered conversation from the hospital clings to my thoughts like a stubborn dryer sheet. Jude High has its first football game tonight and Mom hasn't even tried talking me into going. She lets me hide in my room. I lie in bed, trying to make sense of my growing confusion. I understand their concerns about the psychiatrist. I understand why they warned me to be careful about what I shared. What I don't understand is why they're worried I'll end up like my dead grandma.

When my brain tires from trying to tease it all apart, I grab my worn copy of *I Know This Much is True* by Wally Lamb— one of the many banned books I've come to own—and thumb to the place I earmarked the night before. The book's about this dude with a schizophrenic brother. It's not good for me. It makes me wonder. But I can't stop reading. It's nice to lose myself in somebody else's messed up problems for a change, even if those problems are fictional.

I'm about to start another chapter when Pete pokes his head inside my room. For a kid whose life has been ruined all because I'm a freak, he doesn't hold a grudge. He doesn't walk around me like I'm made of glass. Instead, he's grown curious. Like all of a sudden, I'm the most fascinating person on the face of the planet. Apart from Elliana anyway.

"Hey," he says.

"Is dinner ready?" My family has had dinner together since the dawn of time. It doesn't matter if Dad has a late meeting at work. We will eat dinner at nine o'clock at night if it means eating together.

"Dad just got home."

"You going to the football game after?" I ask.

"Ellie's picking me up."

"Ellie, huh?"

He tosses a pillow at me. "Shut up."

"What? I think it's cute."

Pete plops on my bed. I close my book. It isn't normal. This. Us. Hanging out. We've never been close siblings. I love him. I'd do anything for him. He's the only kid close to my age who I can talk to without breaking into hives. But we're too different. And those differences have always created a wall between us.

"You can tag along if you want."

"No, I can't."

"Why not?"

"C'mon, Pete. You know exactly why not."

"So people think you're weird. Who cares?" This is why Pete has always been popular. He really doesn't care. He has this laid back way about him that doesn't fit the average fifteen-year-old. He can be in a room full of super popular seniors and his heart rate will remain completely steady. At times, it makes me want to judo chop him in the liver.

I hold up my book. "I'd rather spend the evening with Wally."

Pete rolls his eyes, then picks at my comforter. "You know, Ellie and I were talking …"

"About?"

"That night."

"Why?" The word comes out with jagged edges.

"We're intrigued." He continues his picking, then looks up with Dad's dark brown eyes. I inherited Mom's navy blue ones. "We Googled Ouija boards."

"Pete …" His name escapes on a sigh.

"No, listen, Tess. We found some really crazy stuff. Elliana thinks what you saw could've been real."

Now it's my turn for the eye-rolling. "Do you have any idea what Dad would say if he could hear you?"

"Who cares what Dad would say."

"I was tired, Pete, and I have an overactive imagination. That's all." Lately, I've been contemplating the possibility that somehow, I fell asleep during the séance. That would make the most sense. Especially considering my nightmares. It's a better option than being crazy. And it's definitely better than Elliana's theory. The thought makes me shudder. I don't want any of what I saw to be real. "Just forget about it."

The curious gleam in his eye doesn't bode well. But before I can convince him to drop it, the door opens and our parents walk in. Mom wears that false, familiar smile she dons every year or two, whenever she and Dad sit us down in the living room to tell us the news. I know what they're going to say before either utter a word. So does Pete. Because he flops back on my bed and groans.

We are moving.

## CHAPTER FOUR

# A NOT SO FRESH START

"**Y**ou want me to go *where?*" I can't help it. My eyes bug out of my head. I can feel them straining in their sockets as I stand among half-empty boxes in my brand new bedroom.

"It's called the Edward Brooks Facility," Dad says.

Beside him, Mom's hands engage in a wrestling match.

I pick up a box filled with books and set it onto my bed. Movers packed up all our stuff and in a matter of two weeks, we jettisoned across the country to Thornsdale—a small coastal town on the northern tip of California. I remove a stack of paperbacks and look out the window. We live in a gated community called Forest Grove. All the houses are ridiculous, including our own. The view from my bedroom is unreal. A panorama of rocky beach and towering redwoods and miles upon miles of misty ocean and cliffs. As I stare at a seagull gliding over the tide, a realization hits me right between my buggy eyes. "Is this why we moved?"

They don't have to answer my question. It's written all over their concerned faces. *Yes, this is exactly why we moved.*

I plop on the mattress, bouncing my box of books up and down. "I can't believe this."

We didn't move because Dad finished his work in Jude. We moved because of me and the Edward Brooks Facility and that thing that happened three weeks ago. My determination to fit in—to have a fresh start and make friends—fractures. It's kind of hard to act normal when your own parents doubt your sanity. "How do you know it's safe?"

Mom sits beside me on the bed and places her hand on my knee. "Because it's a private facility, sweet pea. One of the only ones left in the country. They are not required to report anything to the government."

Dad steps forward. "What your mother's trying to say, kiddo, is that you can be honest. You don't have to hide anything."

I stare down at the carpet. "You think I'm crazy."

"No, we don't." Mom squeezes my knee. "We just want to make sure you're okay. This facility is the best of the best. We think it'll help you … fit in."

Right. Fit in. Like that will ever happen.

"Maybe even get rid of those nightmares you keep having."

I look up into Mom's eyes. My eyes. We have all the same features. But somehow, the pale skin and the spray of dark freckles and the pointy chin and the upturned nose and round eyes that give us both a look of perpetual surprise are pretty on her face, mismatched on mine. "How do you know about my nightmares?"

She cups my chin and runs the pad of her thumb over the dark circles beneath my eyes. I try to cover them with makeup, but I don't do a great job. Makeup has never been my forte. "We hear you at night."

I release a puff of air. Maybe my parents are right. Maybe Edward Brooks—whoever he is—can help me be normal.

❦

For as I long as I can remember I've had a small patch of

eczema on the inside of my left wrist. I hardly noticed in Florida, thanks to the humidity. California weather isn't as kind. I scratch at it as I stand in front of my full-length mirror. Today is my first day at a new school. Mom thought going on Friday would make Monday easier. All I can think is that it makes Friday worse. I'd much rather stay behind and explore the beach and the forest and the cliffs that are my new backyard.

But my mother is adamant, so I push the wishful thinking away and check my reflection in the mirror. No dreams haunted me last night, which means my dark circles are faint. Yesterday, Mom took me for a mini makeover. I now have shoulder-length hair and—for the first time since kindergarten—bangs. The effect makes my navy blue eyes much less buggy. I wear a new pair of skinny jeans with a new pale pink camisole and a new champagne cardigan. I even have a new backpack. Basically, I am new. I am fresh. And for once in my life, I look ordinary.

I look like somebody who could blend in.

I take a deep breath, as if the key to confidence is an extra dose of oxygen. Nobody has to know about the séance or my nightmares or that I sometimes see and sense and hear things nobody else can see or sense or hear. Nobody has to know that I'm seventeen and still afraid of the dark. Nobody has to know that starting next week, I will have counseling sessions at the Edward Brooks Facility with a psychiatrist named Dr. Roth.

I can walk into Thornsdale High School and simply be Tess Ekhart, the very unextraordinary new girl. Who knows. Maybe I will find a way to fit in. I scratch the inside of my wrist until my eczema burns bright red.

Anything is possible.

## CHAPTER FIVE

# THE NEW KID

Majestic. There is no other way to describe the drive to school. Seriously. It's nothing at all like the flat, ho-hum commute in Jude. We are winding down a road with the ocean on one side and gigantic trees on the other. Briny air ruffles my hair. Everything is so green and beautiful.

Pete and I don't talk. Our momentary closeness in Florida vanished once he found out we were moving. He spent our final two weeks in Jude brooding or in his room with Elliana. I still can't believe Mom let him get away with it. I'm more convinced than ever that we do not have a normal mother. I mean, who does that? Who lets their hormonally-charged fifteen-year-old son spend unsupervised hours in his room with an older, more experienced girl?

Since coming to California, he's spent every waking minute talking to her on his cell phone. I can't believe Mom lets him get away with that either. It's not like Pete. But then, he's never left behind a girlfriend before and I'm pretty sure that's what Elliana was ... or is.

I peek at him from the corner of my eye and search for something to say. An apology maybe—for making him move away from Jude—but I'm saving my words. Rehearsing lines in my head. Things a normal teenager would say. Like:

*Oh hi, nice to meet you.*

Or ...

*My name's Tess. What's yours?*

Or …

*Yeah. We moved from Florida. It was a bummer to leave all my friends behind. But California seems cool.*

I'm not sure I can pull off that last one, but I tell myself I'll try. After all, this is almost definitely my final stop before graduation, and I'm determined to make these two years bearable. For me and my family.

The lady inside my GPS tells me to turn left, so I flip on the blinker, make the turn, and there it is. Our new school. It looks ritzy and big, even though Mom told me it only has 250 students, the majority of which—judging by the rows of polished Maseratis, Porsches, Mercedes Benz, and VW convertibles—come from well-to-do families like mine. As I pull into an empty parking stall, I wonder if anyone has a rich father named Dr. Roth or Edward Brooks.

Pete unbuckles his seatbelt and the two of us walk through pockets of students congregating by the door. I tell myself to mimic Pete's laid-back swagger, since he's the king of confidence. I tell myself I will not be his loser older sister anymore. I tell myself not to look scared as we make our way inside. I arrange my face into what I hope is a look of indifference—boredom—even though I'm far from either.

As soon as we step inside, a hum of excitement greets us in the locker bay. Red and gray posters of a fire-breathing reptile plaster the walls and the lockers. I am officially a Thornsdale Dragon. The entire student body is a mass of red and gray. Some wear football jerseys, some have painted faces, others have dyed hair. A poster on the door of the main office explains why.

Homecoming.

Tonight.

A groan rumbles up my chest. Pete and I are not only the new kids, we're the new kids on homecoming. My brother ignores my groan and pushes the door open. A cherry-cheeked lady with abnormally long ear lobes smiles at us from behind the desk. "You must be Teresa and Peter Ekhart."

"Pete," Pete says.

"Tess," I say.

Her smile doesn't falter. "Well, Pete and Tess, my name is Mrs. Finch and I have two ambassadors who will be showing you around over the next week or so."

Pete frowns. "Ambassadors?"

"Fellow students." As if on cue, the door opens and two students bustle in behind us. A very short, painfully-skinny boy with wire-rimmed glasses and pink ears, and a heavyset girl with a baby-face and warm, brown eyes. Her red loopy earrings, red sweatshirt, and matching leggings make her look like an apple.

"Oh, just in time," Mrs. Finch, the long-lobbed receptionist says. "This is Leela McNeil and Scott Shroud. Tess, Leela will be helping you find your classes and introducing you to teachers and students. Pete, Scott will be doing the same for you."

Pete towers over Scott by at least a foot. My brother is fifteen and already six foot two. He doesn't have the muscles to fill out the frame—not by a long shot—but you can tell one day he will. He hitches one strap of his backpack higher over his shoulder and takes his schedule from Mrs. Finch.

"Have a great first day, dear," she says.

Without saying anything to me, Pete steps out of the office. Leela watches him go with an all-too familiar look, her cheeks tinged the same color as Scott's ears. He scrambles after my brother with a slightly dazed expression—as if he's the new student and Pete is the ambassador.

Mrs. Finch hands me my schedule and I can't help but stare at her earlobes. They look like pulled taffy, only no earrings weigh them down.

"Thank you," I say and then follow Leela out into the noisy hallway. Pete and Scott are already gone.

"I'm so excited to meet you, Tess." Leela sticks out her hand. "We never ever get new students, so even though I applied to be an ambassador my freshman year, this is the first time I've actually been able to put my training to any sort of use."

We shake hands and I wonder what sort of training an ambassador has to go through. Firm handshakes? Friendly smiles? Leela has both of those nailed. She snags my schedule—not in a rude *gimme-it* sort of way, but in an *I'm-so-excited-to-see-if-we-have-any-of-the-same-classes* sort of way. It's kind of endearing. So is her subsequent squeal. "We have the first two periods together. And lunch!" Her eyes go a little wide. "Oh, but you must be super smart. Honors English and Honors Physics as a junior? Wow. I'm afraid we won't be having any of those classes together. C'mon, I'll show you your locker."

All my anxiety over what to say and how to say it disappears. Leela talks enough for both of us. Her words gush forth in a steady stream of chatter as we pass several clusters of students. So far, hardly any of them have noticed the new girl. They're all too busy jabbering about the "big game". I hear the phrase tossed around several times.

As soon as my bag and supplies are tucked away in my new locker, Leela leads me to our first class, which coincidentally, happens to be the same as it was in Jude—Current Events. As we walk, Leela tells me about her family. She has five siblings. She quickly adds that she's Irish Catholic, as if this ought to explain everything. I'm surprised she admits to it so openly.

"Do you go to church?" I ask.

People are allowed to believe whatever they want in the privacy of their homes. It's their prerogative and hey, if they want to put their hope in something that isn't true, then go right ahead. But churches have become a thing of the past, replaced by pharmacies and gas stations and liquor stores. The few that still exist are in serious disrepair. Why go when the object of worship has been reduced to another Santa Claus?

"No, there aren't any in Thornsdale. But my parents make us do our rosary before bed, even though I'm pretty sure they're closet atheists. It's more ritual than anything else. They do it because that's how they were raised."

I nod, drumming up images of religious folk standing on street corners, holding signs that say things like *Repent Now* and *The End Times are Here* and *Do You Want to be Raptured?* I had to look that last one up on the internet. I wonder if Leela thinks we're living in the end times. I wonder if she thinks the escalating crime and the influx of natural disasters are proof of our world's imminent demise. But I don't have the guts to ask.

"Mr. Lotsam teaches this class and let me tell you, he's crazy about the news. He gets this fire in his eyes, like it's the most important subject on the face of the planet, and sometimes he spits."

"Spits?"

"Only when he's really, really excited. He'll also be your history teacher. He never spits in history, but he does cuss."

"Cuss?" Teachers never ever cussed at Jude.

Leela bobs her head as we step inside Mr. Lotsam's class. Instead of desks, there are six tables arranged in the shape of a horseshoe. Leela leads me to one on the end. I sit down and watch as students file inside the classroom. I'm the only person not wearing red or gray.

When the bell rings, one last straggler slips inside and takes the seat to my right, bringing the subtle scent of fabric softener and a hint of wintergreen. I look over and my breath quickens. The straggler is a boy. Unlike his classmates, he wears a plain white t-shirt that shows off tanned, wiry arms and a frayed hemp bracelet tied around his wrist with three different colored stones—red, black, and green. His fingers are long and masculine, with worn nubs for nails. He has a straight nose and olive skin and unruly dark hair and the kind of build that reminds me of a mountain climber. Like his muscles come from practical use rather than pumping iron in a weight room.

Leela bumps my knee with hers and I peel my attention away, relieved to see I'm not the only girl staring.

The teacher—cussing, spitting Mr. Lotsam—stands from behind his desk with a gray soul patch and of all things, a thin ponytail. He wears a red button-down shirt and a gray tie and penny loafers.

I peek again at the boy next to me. He has a faded hunter green school bag strapped over the back of his chair and a notebook in front of him on the table. He rests his chin in his hand and twirls a pen around the tip of his thumb as a girl with long caramel hair and full, glossy lips flirtatiously nudges him with her shoulder.

Mr. Lotsam spreads his arms in front of the class. "I hear," he says, "that we have a new student in our midst."

Heat rushes up my neck. I want to duck under the table,

but I force myself to sit still, to act like I'm not about to pee my pants in front of everyone on my first day. Especially not in front of this boy, whose stare warms the side of my face.

"Leela, do you care to introduce us?"

Leela stands. "Everybody, this is Tess Eckhart. She just moved here from Florida. Tess, this is everybody."

I give a feeble wave, hoping with every fiber of hope in my body that Mr. Lotsam will not ask me to stand up and talk about myself.

"A pleasure to meet you, young Tess. I'm confident that all here will give you a warm welcome." He claps his hands and almost everyone swivels around in their seats. A few ogle a little longer, curious. I can see it in their eyes—the boys trying to figure out if I'm dating material, the girls trying to figure out if I'm a threat. I want to tell the girls not to worry and the boys not to bother, but it doesn't take long for their curiosity to wane without any help from me. "Since our classes are cut short today because of the pep rally—" the class hoots and hollers, "—how about we jump right in?"

The hooting and hollering turns into a groan, followed by rustling papers as notebooks open to fresh pages. Mr. Lotsam jots the words *Presidential Election* on the white board and the three candidates. This is the first time an independent has a legitimate shot at winning office and nobody can stop talking about it. I try to focus, but the side of my face remains warm. I swear the boy next to me is staring, but when I gather enough courage to peek through my hair, his attention is on Mr. Lotsam. The pouty-lipped girl beside him catches me checking him out and gives me the stink eye.

I quickly turn away and as I do, my elbow knocks into my pencil. The boy beside me goes from sitting like a statue to lightning quick, as if he had measured the proximity between my arm and the writing utensil and was waiting for the collision. Before I can react, he snags it up and hands it over.

*Whoa.*

His eyes.

They are the color of spring grass, fringed with the kind of eyelashes most girls would kill for. Or at the very least, pay money for. He stares at me as if I'm somehow familiar, and for the span of a millisecond, something like disbelief flickers in the grass green of his irises. He cocks his head slightly, a small furrow divoting his brow.

"Th-thanks," I stammer.

He gives me a slow nod before the girl on his other side jots something on his notebook. He shifts away, his mouth turning up at the corner, and writes something back. It doesn't seem possible, but even the way he moves his pencil is enticing. I find myself wishing his notes were to me, or that I could at least read them. The girl keeps the string of back-and-forth writing exchanges going until the bell rings. Then she strikes up a conversation and they walk out into the hallway together. I stare after him. I really can't seem to help myself.

Leela gives me a nudge with her elbow. "You've been Luka-ed."

"What?"

"It's a term some of the senior girls made up. His name's Luka Williams." Leela fans her cheeks. "A gorgeous specimen, isn't he?"

Understatement of the year.

"He moved to Thornsdale at the beginning of freshman year. All the girls are in love with him. All the guys want to be him. Even the jealous jocks."

We filter out of the class with the rest of the students. "Jealous?"

"Luka can run circles around them and their varsity letter jackets."

"What do you mean?"

"He's the best athlete in school. He can throw a football way farther than Matt Chesterson. You should see him in gym class."

"Who's Matt Chesterson?"

"Our annoyingly arrogant quarterback. Which is so beyond ironic, seeing as our team didn't win a single game last year."

We turn a corner and Leela takes a drink from the drinking fountain. "We have Ceramics next. Guess who else is in the class?" She wipes the moisture from her bottom lip and gives me another friendly nudge. "His initials are L.W."

I ignore the jab, and the giddiness expanding inside my chest. It's a silly feeling. If ever a boy was out of my league, it's this one. "Why isn't he on the team?"

"His mom is one of those super overprotective types. He's an only child. Nobody really knows what his dad does for a living, except it must be something important because they are loaded. And I mean, *loaded.* They live in Forest Grove, which, if you haven't heard about already, you will soon enough. It's a gated community. I'm not even kidding."

The heat in my ears creeps into my cheeks.

"You've already heard of it?"

I shrug.

She blinks. "Do you *live* there?"

"My dad works for Safe Guard."

Her eyebrows inch up her forehead. "As in Safe Guard Security Systems?"

I nod.

"Wow."

Yeah. Wow. I don't bother to tell her he stands on one of the top rungs of that particular corporate ladder.

There's a stretch of awkward silence, where we are walking side by side, but I don't know what to say. I hope my living in Forest Grove doesn't make Leela think differently about me. I can't imagine she has anything against rich people, considering all those cars in the parking lot. I think I saw a Lamborghini. We may live in Forest Grove, but my parents would never be that pretentious.

"I'd love to see what it looks like in there," she finally says.

I jump on the words. "You can come over if you want. After school."

"I'd love to!" She smiles big and waves me along. I follow her into a stairwell, down a flight of steps into the basement, past floor-to-ceiling windows which reveal an indoor swimming pool, and inside our second classroom. This room is bigger, with dusty, laminate flooring, a hodge-podge of tables, and several pottery wheels. It smells like must and chlorine. "Hey, maybe we can go to the game together. We'll probably get demolished, but you'll never find a student body with more school spirit."

Football games. I hate—no, I *loathe* football games.

"Come on, it'll be fun," Leela urges.

I can hear my mother's voice asking the question. *How will you ever fit in if you spend all your time hiding in your room, Tess?* I take a deep breath. "Sure. That'd be nice."

It doesn't seem possible, but Leela's smile grows bigger and I decide I really like this girl. We toss our bags on an unoccupied table. "So, how old is your brother?" she asks.

"He'll be sixteen next month."

She looks like she wants to ask more, but pinches her lips together instead. It's not until I'm working the bubbles out of a hunk of clay that I see him, dodging bits of eraser playfully tossed his way by a pretty blonde. Then, for no reason at all, his attention flits to me, so suddenly I'm caught off guard. For the briefest of moments, we look at one another—his stare open and curious, mine startled, until I come to my senses and drop my gaze, beyond embarrassed to be caught gawking. For the rest of class, I keep my eyes down on my project, attempting to regulate my heart rate. I don't dare peek at him again.

## CHAPTER SIX

# DO YOU SEE WHAT I SEE?

I have six more classes after Ceramics—Trigonometry, Physics, Study Hall, Honors English, and World History. Lunch comes in the middle and I'm beyond grateful to have it with Leela. Pete, too, although he chooses not to sit with us. I feel guilty. I hate that I've made my brother's life miserable. But then I spot Luka at the table next to Pete's, and I'm easily distracted.

He sits with a mixture of girls and boys. Miss Pouty Lips from Current Events and the clay-throwing girl from ceramics, a bulky boy with a very square head and a few others.

"You're staring again."

I quickly look away.

Leela smiles and cracks open her Coke. "Don't worry. It just means you're human. And female." Her attention wanders to my brother, who sits with Scott. The kid's ears are still pink. Poor Mr. Shroud seems to suffer from the same blushing problem as me.

I open my chocolate milk. "Who are the girls sitting next to him?"

"The short-haired blond from ceramics is Jennalee Fisher. The girl from Current Events is Summer Burbanks." Leela takes a bite of a French fry. "They pretend to be friends, but they secretly hate each other."

"Why?"

"Because they both want Luka."

I swallow, thinking back to the note-writing in first period and the clay-throwing in second. "Who does Luka want?"

"Neither."

"Neither?"

"They've given him plenty of opportunities, but he doesn't ever take them."

Summer is gorgeous. Jennalee is well above average. Surely he's at least somewhat interested. I pluck my apple off my tray and twist the stem, counting each revolution until it snaps off. Four spins.

Leela leans over the table, as if Luka might be able to hear us over the clamor of cafeteria chatter. "Everybody worships him, even the teachers. But he's not cocky about it, like most of the guys on the football team. Sometimes I get the impression that the popularity embarrasses him."

"Who's he bringing to the homecoming dance?"

"I don't think he's going. He's kind of mysterious like that. Nobody ever really knows when he's going to show up for things."

I brave another look at his table. Jennalee and Summer talk and joke and laugh with the others, but they keep one eye on Luka, as if waiting for the slightest opportunity to claim his attention while he peels his orange. I'm caught up by the effortless movement of his fingers when it happens. In the middle of his peeling, his eyes snap up, just like in ceramics, and for the second time in one day, he catches me watching him. I duck my head. Ugh. Could I be any more of a creeper?

"So ... are you and your brother close?"

I spend the remainder of lunch fielding Leela's questions about Pete, thankful for the distraction. I'm not very hungry, but I make myself eat my apple and half of my sandwich. I don't let myself look at Luka again, which requires significantly more self-control than I care to admit.

My Study Hall teacher—an old man with a hooked nose and a massive comb-over—not only makes me introduce myself, but interrupts halfway through, demanding that I speak up. I immediately fall in love with my Honors English teacher, who doesn't introduce me at all, but hands me a weathered copy of *Wuthering Heights* and tells me to get reading. By the time I get to my final class—World History—I'm feeling a bit checked out. Until I step inside and spot Luka Williams sitting at one of the tables. Three classes. We have three classes together. My nerves jump into overdrive, especially when Mr. Lotsam motions to the empty spot next to the boy who's caught me staring twice.

I slip into the seat as quietly as possible and try to pay attention as Mr. Lotsam jabbers about some war in France, but I'm much too distracted by my neighbor's presence—the fresh, clean smell of his clothes, the warmth that radiates off his body, the way he sits with his chin in his hand while everybody else frantically scribbles notes in their notebooks. By the time the final bell rings, I don't think I've learned a thing about the French war, but I have committed to memory the bored way in which Luka twirls his pencil around the tip of his thumb.

Everyone hurries to their feet—a mob of red and gray moving toward the gymnasium. Luka doesn't rush out with the rest of his classmates. He lingers beside me, which does funny things to my heart rate. I pretend to rummage through my bag until he scoots back his chair and leaves. My breath swooshes past my lips. I let myself be swept into the crowd, hoping Leela will be at our meeting place before me so I'm not standing all by myself.

Pep rallies make me nervous. Whenever Jude had them, each class would chant their graduating year as loud as possible while I stood there like an idiot, mouthing the words, clapping self-consciously, wondering what it would be like to let myself go and scream with the crowd. When I come around the corner and spot Leela standing by the drinking fountains, I almost melt into a puddle of relief. It's been a good first day. The best, actually.

No headaches. No weird feelings. No unexplained cold or warm presences. Just school and a friendly girl and a much-too-noticeable boy. All I have to do is get through this pep rally and I can officially categorize the day away as a success. My mom will be thrilled.

"How'd the rest of your classes go?" Leela asks as soon as I reach her.

"Pretty good." I consider telling her I have not just two, but three classes with Luka—it seems like the sort of thing girlfriends would tell each other—but I'm not sure how to get the words out. So we stand off to the side while students rush past, catcalling and shouting and whistling at each other. The sounds echo off the high walls. When the swell has passed, we become the caboose and filter into the gymnasium. It's the size of three basketball courts. Bleachers are set up on the far court and students sit in groups according to graduating class. The gym floor is empty except for a giant poster that says "Go Dragons!" A group of cheerleaders gather off to the side and the principal—a middle-aged man named Mr. Jolly—stands behind a podium, chatting with a gentleman wearing athletic shorts, a baseball hat, and a whistle around his neck.

Smaller pockets of students and faculty dot the court where

Leela and I stand. One wall is covered by huge windows that showcase a view of the swimming pool below. It's dark down there, but something flashes in the water and my pulse hiccups. I squeeze my eyelids shut and tell myself it was nothing. A trick of the light. A reflection off the water. I will not let this day be ruined, which is why I don't double check to make sure.

"I told Bobbi we'd go say hi before we sit down. I hope that's okay."

"Yeah. Of course."

Leela wraps her arm around my elbow and drags me through the crowd, away from the pool. It's not until we do a bit of weaving that I realize we're approaching the cheerleaders.

"Hey, Bobbi!" Leela calls.

Much to my surprise, Bobbi is a girl. A long auburn braid hangs over her shoulder and she holds a pair of pom-poms. She stands next to Summer—whose tan legs go on for an eternity in her cheerleader outfit. And between the two is none other than the boy who smells like fabric softener and wintergreen. He stands with one hand tucked into the pocket of his well-worn jeans and chews the thumb nail on his other. Our eyes meet, and I quickly look away, a swarm of butterflies unleashing in my stomach.

"Hey, Leels!" Bobbi has creamy skin and delicate features and an air of popularity that has me wondering how she and Leela are such good friends, but the thought feels mean so I bat it away. Why shouldn't Leela be popular?

Bobbi turns her cheerful attention to me. "You're Tess, right?"

I nod dumbly.

"Welcome to Thornsdale," she says. "Leela and I are cousins."

Ah. Cousins.

"Bobbi's a senior. She's on the homecoming court." Leela has that star-struck, idol-worship look in her eyes. Not all too different from the look she gave my brother in the office this morning. I can tell she is proud to be Bobbi's cousin.

"You coming to the game tonight?" Bobbi asks me.

I feel Luka's attention on me too, but I refuse to look at him. "Leela and I are going."

"I told her we're going to lose," Leela says. "I want her to have realistic expectations."

Bobbi gives Luka's shoulder a playful shove. "If this guy would join the team already, we wouldn't have a problem."

"That would mean your boyfriend would be out of a position," Luka says in a voice that comes out smooth and confident. Teasing, too. It's the kind of voice that gets listened to.

"He's not my boyfriend."

I glance then, and the butterflies bat their wings in unison, because he isn't just looking at me, he's studying me. Intently. I resist the urge to wipe at my nose or suck my teeth. Surely I have something on my face that is distracting him.

"Are you having a good first day?" he asks.

I nod, my voice box out of commission.

He cocks his head. "Where did you move from?"

"Jude." I clear my throat. "It's in Florida."

"Never heard of it." Summer picks at one of her nails, looking bored, and I notice with a twinge of satisfaction that her tan has a distinct orange hue to it.

"Not many people have. It's a small town."

"Can't be much smaller than Thornsdale. This place is so *boring*." She pins her sultry pout on Luka, as if he holds the solution to her boredom. "If somebody would teach me to surf, then it wouldn't be so bad."

I examine my shoes while Leela and Bobbi and Summer take over the conversation. Somewhere in the middle of homecoming dresses, a cold clamminess crawls over my skin. It's as if the entire gymnasium has dropped twenty degrees. I wrap my arms around myself, hoping the tightness of my grip will anchor me in place. Because what I want to do is run. Sprint far away from the gym and all these students and this feeling that is far too similar to the one I had that night three weeks ago. A shiver moves its way into my jaw.

This cannot be happening. Not here. Not now.

"Is California very different from Florida?"

I open my mouth to answer Bobbi's question, but past her, across the court, my brother stands apart from the crowd, outside the restroom doors. Only he's not alone. There is a hulking figure nearby—a man so pale he doesn't look human, his greasy hair hanging like curtains on either side of his emaciated face. "Who is …?"

Before the question takes shape, the hulking figure looks up and his eyes. The whiteness of them has me sucking in a sharp breath and taking a step back. He has no irises. No pupils.

"Tess?"

The man steps closer to my brother.

A scream builds in my lungs, but before it can tear up my throat, there's a blinding flash of light, so incredibly bright that I move my hand to shield my eyes.

I blink, expecting the gym to break out in screams, or at the very least, astonished gasps. Only nobody does anything. The students carry on as if nothing happened at all and when I look, Pete is alone. The man is gone.

Leela touches my forearm. "Tess?"

My heart beats in my throat. Nausea grips my stomach. I am going to be sick, all over the gym floor on my first day of school in front of my new friend and the most gorgeous boy I've ever laid eyes on. I swallow and try to tell Bobbi that California isn't as humid as Florida. I try to spit out something that will erase the suspicion I've aroused, but my eyes will not leave Pete. They refuse to stop searching for that man, as if at any second he will return and grab my brother and I will really have to scream this time.

A throat clears. It's a strong, attention-getting sound. "Can I get a picture?" Luka grabs his cell phone from his pocket, pulling everybody's attention away from me—a perfectly timed distraction.

The three girls gather, giving me a moment to collect myself. I blink and I breathe and I blink and I breathe and I wipe the sweat from my palms. I look at Summer with her long legs and Bobbi with her pretty face and Leela with her warm smile, their arms slung around each other as Luka snaps a few pictures with his phone.

A woman with teased, unmoving hair dressed in a pink velour track suit calls Bobbi and Summer over to the rest of the cheerleaders. My knees begin to shake. I am dizzy and weak, as if I've sprinted the 1500 meter. Leela talks to somebody off to her left, and Luka? He scrutinizes me beneath knitted dark eyebrows, his green eyes unfathomable.

❦

Leela takes my arm and pulls me toward the bleachers. "Luka is staring at you."

"He is?" I'd give anything for a big glass of ice water. All these bodies make the gym sweltering.

She looks over her shoulder. "Oh my goodness, he is *totally* staring."

I grab her elbow. "Don't look at him!"

She makes big eyes at me.

I tell myself it isn't true, but Luka's stare is like a beam of hot sun against my back. Did he notice my mini spaz attack moments ago? Does he think I'm a freak show? My temples throb as I follow Leela up the bleachers and Principal Jolly starts talking into the microphone. We find a seat with the rest of the juniors. I try to pay attention but my mind keeps replaying what happened. That strange man with the white eyes, the bright flash of light, Luka's photo session, as if he intentionally created a diversion so I could collect myself. I scan the gymnasium, searching for Luka or that man while Principal Jolly finishes his short speech and the cheerleaders rile up the crowd.

The football team crashes through the big paper poster. The students' cheers reach an unheard-of pitch and I resist the urge to plug my ears. Seriously, you'd think the San Francisco 49ers entered the gym. Somebody dressed in a red dragon suit does cartwheels across the court while the students count each one in unison. The higher the number, the louder the counting, until the dragon finally falls and Leela and the rest of the crowd erupts in laughter and whistles.

A lump builds in my throat because how will I ever be a part of this? A girl who is hospitalized after a séance, a girl who can't stand the dark, a girl whose parents want her to talk to a shrink at the Edward Brooks facility? A vision from *that night* flashes in my mind—all those people wrapped in straitjackets—and I wonder if my freak out at the séance was some sort of prophecy. Is that what my future holds—me cut off from society, locked up in a cell? I swallow the lump down and focus on getting through the rest of the rally so I can find Pete and get to the car and hide in my bedroom.

Leela clutches my arm. "They're going to announce the king and queen!"

Bobbi, four other girls, and five boys—two of whom wear football jerseys—parade out before the crowd while the dragon dances around them. Senior homecoming court.

"I really hope Bobbi wins!" Leela squeals, her fingers clutching her chin.

Nodding absently, I continue my search. I twist around and spot Luka, up toward the top of the bleachers, in the very back of the junior section. He bites his thumbnail while a kid with a buzz cut talks into his ear. Before he catches me staring for the third time in one day, I face front.

The drum line in the marching band pounds out a drum roll that knives my skull. Principal Jolly calls out Bobbi's name and Leela jumps and screams beside me. Then he calls out Matt Chesterson. One of the boys with a football jersey and hair shellacked with gel struts forward like a peacock and I remember what Leela said about Luka being able to outthrow him.

"They're going to the dance together," Leela shouts above the din.

Bobbi and Matt are given their crowns and the football team does a funny dance and the cheerleaders lead us all in a cheer and the rally finally ends. As the bleachers clear, I search for Pete, desperate for peace and quiet and my bed and the worn copy of *Wuthering Heights* that my Honors English teacher gave me.

"So," Leela says, "Are we going to your house?"

My heart sinks. I forgot all about my invitation from earlier. "I'm really sorry, Leela, but could we maybe get together some other time?"

Her face falls.

"It's just ... I don't feel so good." I cup my clammy palm over my forehead, thankful I don't have to act. I'm a dreadful actress. "My head kills."

"You do look pretty pasty."

I don't bother telling her that my face is always pasty. It's the natural color of my skin.

"Do you think you'll feel better by the game?"

"I don't think so."

Pete shuffles over and gives Leela a dismissive nod before turning to me. "You ready?"

I look at Leela apologetically. "Rain check?"

Her attention darts from my brother to me. "Monday?"

"Oh. I can't on Monday. I have a ... a thing." Dr. Roth.

A shadow falls across Leela's face. She's obviously skeptical about my *thing*.

I don't blame her. What plans could I possibly have being new in town? "What about Tuesday?"

The shadow lifts a little. "Okay. Tuesday. We can do makeovers."

"Yeah. Sure. Makeovers." I wave goodbye and follow Pete out of our new school. Once I step outside into the cool air, the heaviness on my shoulders lifts a little. "Hey, Pete?"

"Yeah?"

"Did you see anything weird in the gym?"

"Like a dragon doing cartwheels?"

The heaviness returns. "You didn't see anything else?"

He quirks one of his eyebrows. "Care to be a little bit more specific?"

*Oh, sure. Did you see a crazy-looking dude with white eyes and a blinding flash of light?* There's no way I'm uttering any of that out loud. And besides, if Pete didn't see it and the man was right beside him, then it couldn't have been real.

Fear twists in my gut. So much for a normal first day.

## CHAPTER SEVEN

# DREAMS

Over dinner, Mom peppers Pete and me with questions. I stick to monosyllabic answers and pick at my food. It's my turn to do the dishes. As soon as I finish, I escape to my room with every intention of reading *Wuthering Heights*, but my eyes grow heavy somewhere in the middle of the first chapter.

When I wake up, I'm no longer in my bedroom. I'm standing on the basement step of our old house in Jude, the one with the avocado-green walls and the musty, unfinished smell of cement floor as something—a zipper or a pen or loose change—clanks in the running dryer. I scratch at my eczema, but it does not burn. I don't feel it at all.

I must be dreaming.

Pete sits cross-legged in the center of the room, playing with the flickering flame of a candle lit in front of him. His fingers dance through the fire—as if his skin is immune to the burn—and my heart turns to ice because we aren't alone. The man from the gym stands in the corner of the basement, a hulking figure with those white, lifeless eyes. Goosebumps march up my arms, because I've dreamt about him before. This is not the first time he's visited my dreams—this man with the skeletal face. I try to speak, to grab Pete's attention so we can sprint away from this place, but like every other dream, I am immobilized. I cannot move or speak, and the candle engrosses my brother. He stares at it with a look of complete concentration, as if that flame holds every answer and untold secret in the world.

The man stretches out his arms and tentacles of black mist ooze from his fingertips, twisting and turning their way toward us. Pete looks up and stares—not with horror, but with a look of fascination, as if he can't decide whether to reach up and touch the black or crab walk quickly away. My body wants to lurch forward, but my feet are stuck and my tongue is frozen and the black swirls gather into a mass that grows bigger and bigger, as if it might consume Pete.

My body shakes. Why isn't Pete moving? Why isn't he running? Is he as stuck and helpless as I am? Will I have to stand here on this basement step and watch this thing swallow my brother whole?

The mass of black swoops lower.

The pressure clawing at my lungs tears up my throat and explodes out of my mouth. "Get away from him!"

The sound of my voice is so loud and unexpected that the white-eyed man does something he has never done before. As if I have startled him from his quest, he jerks his head and stares straight at me.

I bolt upright in bed, chest heaving, cold sweat trickling down my back as hazy morning light squeezes itself between the cracks in my blinds.

It is morning. I am in Thornsdale.

✆

I can't shake it—that dream. Even though it wasn't real, I pad down the hallway and peek inside Pete's room. He is lost beneath a bundle of comforters. Boxes are still scattered around his floor, as if refusing to unpack them might make our move less permanent. I have the oddest urge to go inside and sit on his bed and apologize for being such a burden of a sister.

Instead, I let out a long breath and close his door. The heavy feeling sticks with me as I brush my teeth and pull my hair into a ponytail and throw a hooded sweatshirt over my tank top and make my way down the stairs, where Mom and Dad chat in the kitchen while coffee percolates and eggs fry in a pan on the stovetop.

Mom sees me in the doorway first. "Good morning, sweetie."

I rub my eyes. "Hey Mom."

Dad offers me a smile and flips a page of the newspaper. I do not want to hear him read it out loud. I don't want to know about whatever bad things are happening out in the world. Not when enough bad things are happening inside my own head. "I'm going into work later today," he says. "Want to tag along?"

"Maybe."

Mom lifts the pan off the stove top. "How about some eggs?"

"Um, no thanks."

"You sure?"

"Maybe later. I think I'll go take a walk on the beach." As much as I don't look it, I love the outdoors and I really need to get out of the house. Away from their watchful, worried eyes. I walk to the cupboard and remove my favorite coffee mug—an extra big one with a bright red reindeer painted on the side. I fill it halfway with coffee and halfway with pumpkin spice creamer, slip on a pair of unlaced running shoes, and slide open the door leading out to our deck.

"Looks like rain," Mom says. "I wouldn't wander too far."

"I won't." I pull up my hood and step out into the foggy morning. The sun has already risen, painting the sky a whitish yellow, but the actual source of the light is lost somewhere in the fog. The heaviness that draped over my shoulders like a thick cloak falls away. I feel light, free, thankful for the ocean waves crashing against rock. I take a long sip of hot coffee and walk down the stairs to the earth. Seagulls squawk and the wind carries the distant sound of laughter from the shore as I make my way through a craggy path toward the beach. A boy in a wet suit looks out at the white-capped waves, a surfboard tucked beneath his arm. Something about his messy dark hair and the broadness of his shoulders makes me stop and duck behind a rock.

Luka Williams is standing in what might as well be my backyard.

I remember what Leela said yesterday, about Luka living in Forest Grove. I glance around at the other houses, wondering which one is his when a woman's voice calls over the waves. "Pancakes are ready, Luka!"

She stands on the deck to the left of my house—slender and tall with dark hair billowing about her shoulders. She waves at Luka, who tucks his board under his arm and jogs toward her.

I duck further behind the rock, my heart pounding erratically, because *holy cow*, Luka is my next door neighbor. Crouching low, I watch him make his way off the beach, into his back yard, until my hot coffee turns cold and my legs grow stiff from squatting. He stands on the deck with his mother, obviously in no hurry to get to the pancakes inside. Not wanting to be caught spying, I slink around my house, dump the coffee in the dying lilies growing up from the mulch, then slip inside the front door to the sound of my parents' hushed voices in the kitchen.

No sound or movement can be heard upstairs. Pete must still be sleeping, which is odd. He's usually an early riser. Back in Jude, he and Dad always went on Saturday morning jogs while Mom and I went to the local dojo for martial arts. It's something we've done together since the summer I turned ten. Dad insisted upon it. Apparently, it's important that we learn how to defend ourselves in such a violent world. I objected at first, thinking I would hate it. Thinking I'd be awful. To my surprise, I ended up being such a natural that our first sensei nicknamed me Tiny Ninja. I hope we'll continue our training here in Thornsdale. I could use the release.

Mom's voice rises, then quickly quiets.

Curiosity pulls me closer. I tiptoe to the kitchen door and press my back against the living room wall, feeling guilty. I should not eavesdrop on my parents.

"I think I should go wake him up," Mom says.

"Let him sleep, Miranda. He's a growing boy."

"It's not like Pete, sleeping in this late."

The paper crinkles. Dad has turned a page. "If the government doesn't put its foot down, these fetal modification protests are going to get out of control."

"I'm worried about him, James."

"He's a fifteen-year-old who had to leave his first girlfriend. He'll bounce back."

"You really think that's all this is? Puppy love?"

The phrase prickles. It always has. Not because I've ever been in love or because I think Pete was, but because every time I hear it, it sounds so condescending. As if young people aren't capable of the real thing.

"Of course. What else would it be?"

Mom doesn't answer.

Silverware and plates clink and clatter. The faucet runs.

"Pete's a solid kid. We just have to give him space." The newspaper crinkles again. "I'm not worried about *him*."

The water stops. I can almost see Mom turning around, placing her hands on the edge of the counter, tapping her fingernails against the marble top. "Are you sure we can't get a hold of your mother's file? You don't think her psychiatrist would give you a copy?"

I blink several times, startled by the sharp turn in the conversation. Her psychiatrist? My grandmother had a psychiatrist?

"I already told you, Miranda, that's impossible. And unnecessary."

"You just admitted to being worried."

"Of course I'm worried. Did you see our daughter this morning? Seventeen-year-olds should not have circles that dark beneath their eyes." He flips another page of the paper. "But that doesn't mean I think she's like my mother."

"I don't know. Sometimes I see ... similarities."

"Miranda." The name comes out like a warning.

"Would it really hurt to make a phone call?"

"And draw unneeded attention to our daughter?"

My body takes on a mind of its own. Before I even realize what I'm doing, I step out from my hiding place and gape at my parents. "What are you guys talking about?"

Their faces pale.

My mind races, spinning with confusion. "Grandma died of a heart attack. As far as I know, heart problems don't require psychiatrists."

Mom takes a step toward me. "Tess ... sweetheart."

But I shake my head and look at Dad. "Why did she need counseling?"

He sets the newspaper on the table next to his egg-smeared plate.

I attempt to reign in my helter-skelter thoughts. If Grandma had mental problems, how could they keep that from me—especially after what happened at the séance? "She didn't die of a heart attack, did she?"

Mom wrings a towel in front of her. "Honey, it's complicated."

"I'm smart enough to keep up."

Dad sighs, as if resigned, and ignores Mom's desperate head shaking. "She died in a mental rehabilitation center."

"She was crazy?" The question escapes on a whisper. I blink rapidly, looking from Mom to Dad as if they are strangers. "How could you keep that from me?"

Dad runs his palm down his face and stares past the sliding glass door, past the beach and the ocean beyond. "We kept it from everyone, Tess. Not just you. We didn't want that stigma hanging over your heads. Mental illness is frowned upon. You know that."

Yes, I do. Because I take Current Events. Crazy people are a burden to society. And we live in a time where burdens are not tolerated. Burdens make a nation weak. So they are removed, taken away. For everybody's own good. I've never thought to question the logic of it before, but suddenly I'm terrified. What if I become a burden?

Mom relinquishes the twisted towel and wraps her arm around my shoulder. I shrug her away, keeping my attention on Dad. "What was wrong with her?"

"She had frequent episodes of psychosis."

"Psychosis?"

"She saw things nobody else saw."

"Things?"

"She called them demons. Spirits." Dad laughs a humorless laugh and shakes his head, as if trying to rattle away the unpleasant memories. I can only imagine what he thought about his mother's claims. "When the illness reached its peak, she swore she could fight them."

Cold fear sinks like an anchor into the pit of my stomach. Mom tries to wrap her arm around me again, but I step away, a single thought echoing in my mind. One I cannot voice. One I can't even whisper. But inside, it shouts and rattles the walls of my soul. If souls exist.

Is psychosis hereditary?

## CHAPTER EIGHT

# PARANOIA

After absorbing the bomb my parents dropped in our kitchen on Saturday morning, I spend an hour in my room Googling psychosis. What I find disturbs me.

According to one site, psychosis is a loss of contact with reality that usually includes: false beliefs about what is taking place or who one is, which are referred to as delusions; seeing or hearing things that aren't there, which arc referred to as hallucinations.

It's the second one that gets me more than the first—seeing or hearing things that aren't there. I spend the rest of the weekend processing, curled up in an Adirondack chair on our back deck, inhaling the briny sea air, reading *Wuthering Heights*, pausing occasionally to alternately recall or push away the things I have seen and heard over the past several weeks that nobody else can see or hear.

Mom and Dad give me my space. Pete holes up in his room. And I find that as long as I stay outside, the heaviness is not so oppressive. I tell myself that my grandmother's insanity means nothing, changes nothing. I start to look forward to Monday, when I will see my new friend and the mysterious boy next door. I sleep relatively better on Saturday and Sunday. I experience no headaches or weird visions.

By the time Monday rolls around, I feel almost normal. The urge I have to ask more questions, to get more answers, ebbs with the tide. I don't need to know these things. Some people say knowledge is power, but in this case, I'm pretty sure knowledge is paranoia. And let's say for a minute that I am crazy. Paranoia will not help. So I stay far away from Google and I don't ask my parents anymore questions and I end up with a big lump of disappointment in my gut when Luka doesn't show up for Current Events on Monday morning. My hope dwindles even more when he is absent from Ceramics and disappears altogether when I catch sight of his empty seat during lunch.

Leela and the rest of the student body, however, are alight with the exciting afterglow of victory. None of them can stop talking about their unexpected win on Friday night. "I really wish you could have gone," Leela says, cracking open her Coke. "Matt threw this insane hail Mary at the end. When Marshall jumped up and caught the ball in the end zone, we were all going ballistic."

This is the third time I have heard the story, so I listen with half my heart, trying to think of a way to turn the conversation toward Luka without being obvious about my burgeoning infatuation. Thankfully, Leela makes it easy.

"And we all thought only Luka could make a pass like that."

I set my apple on my tray and clear my throat. "Was he at the game?"

"I stood by him in line at the concession stand at halftime. He remembered that my oldest brother got into a car accident last year and asked how he was doing, which is pretty amazing. Nobody else has asked. Anyway, he asked about you."

I cough. "He did?"

She nods emphatically. "He wondered where you were."

"What did you say?"

"That you weren't feeling well." Leela's cheeks glow. "First he stares at you at the pep rally. Then he asks about you at the football game. Do you know how many girls would love to be in your position right now?"

Yeah. My position. Crazy girl going to the Edward Brooks Facility. Somehow, I doubt that. I look over at his empty seat, as if Leela's bit of news will conjure him into the moment. Why would Luka ask about me? "I found out he's my next door neighbor."

Her eyes go wide as she stuffs a bite of her sandwich into her mouth, gives it a couple good chews, and swallows it down. "Are you serious?"

"I saw him surfing on Saturday."

Leela shakes her head, like she can't believe my luck. I can think of nothing natural to say that might continue the conversation, so it peters out. I chew my apple, searching for a logical explanation for Luka's interest. After all, I am my father's daughter. If he asked about me at the football game, it was probably leftover curiosity over the mini freak-out he witnessed at the pep rally. I'm sure he noticed it. Why else was he staring at me afterward? I take another bite of my apple. It's crunchy and sweet, but I don't enjoy it. I'm eating because I'm supposed to, not because I have any real appetite.

"So what's this thing you have after school?"

"Oh ..." I think fast, grappling for a believable lie. "I, um ... I take piano lessons."

Leela perks. "Really?"

I nod, hoping Leela is not a big piano person. I hope she doesn't ask if we can get together and pound out some music. Because the best I can do is "Twinkle, Twinkle Little Star" and even that's a bit choppy.

She looks across the cafeteria, toward Pete. "Does your brother play too?"

"No. Just me."

She opens a bag of chips. I eat the last of my apple. I can tell we both want to ask more questions, but neither of us do.

$\infty$

The Edward Brooks Facility is right outside my neighborhood. The tall, looming building sits on an actual cliff, a picture straight out of an Alfred Hitchcock film. Mom, who is a major history buff, explains how it used to be an orphanage. A long, long time ago when our country still had them.

Now it's a privately-owned treatment center for people like me. As I unbuckle my seat belt, Mom gives me a cheery smile and tells me everything will be okay. She reminds me that I can be honest with Dr. Roth. That it's safe. Then she squeezes my hand and I get out of the car and walk up the cement stairs, waiting for the thunder to crack and the lightning to strike and Frankenstein's doctor to yell, "It's alive!"

I struggle with the heavy front door and sign my name on a sheet of paper at the front desk and read *Rebecca* by Daphne Du Maurier (I finished *Wuthering Heights* on Monday) until a lady with yellow teeth calls my name and leads me down a long corridor into Dr. Roth's office. She doesn't say goodbye or smile. She just walks away and leaves me standing inside the room, staring at a man who sits in a cushy red chair. He wears a stiff-looking white shirt, a navy blue tie, and bifocals that slide down his bulbous nose. He smiles at me, scratching his mousy brown goatee. "Teresa Ekhart, I presume?"

"Tess." His office has no windows, but is somehow drafty,

and smells like an overpowering mixture of oranges and ammonia.

"Tess," he concedes, motioning to an equally-red, cushy chair beside him.

"I thought shrinks had couches."

He chuckles.

I sit and fold my hands in my lap, taking deep, steady breaths. I don't have to say anything. I don't have to do anything. He will ask questions and I can answer as vaguely as possible and maybe soon, my parents will stop making me come to this place that belongs on a Hollywood horror set.

Dr. Roth reads from a manila file, pushes up his glasses, and looks at me like one might examine an extremely interesting specimen beneath a microscope. I wipe my palms against my knees and scratch my earlobe. "Aren't we supposed to talk?"

"What would you like to talk about?" he asks.

"I don't know. You're the doctor. I'm the patient."

"I prefer client."

"Why?"

"Less of a stigma." He pulls at the whiskers of his goatee. "Don't you think?"

I nod at the file resting on his knee. Hasn't he heard of a thing called technology? "Your filing system seems a little outdated."

"Pen and paper doesn't crash. It's not nearly as accessible, either."

I eye the folder with a healthy dose of skepticism. "What does that say about me?"

"That you had a bit of a breakdown in Jude and the ambulance was called."

And I have hallucinations, but no need to admit to that. "Did you get that information from the hospital in Florida?"

Dr. Roth holds up the file. "This is all from your parents."

"Oh."

"Why don't you tell me about the séance?"

His question takes me back to the hospital, only instead of Dr. Roth, I am talking to a short-legged man in a white coat who doesn't smile, my parents' warning all too fresh in my mind. *Don't tell him anything, Tess.* I shift in the chair. "I have an overactive imagination."

Dr. Roth quirks one of his eyebrows.

"And I think I fell asleep."

His other eyebrow joins the first one. "Fell asleep?"

"The more I think about it, the more I'm sure that what I ... saw ... was a nightmare."

"Do you have very many nightmares?"

I plead the fifth.

"I'd like to know more about them—these nightmares."

I scratch my kneecap. I can't decide if I like Dr. Roth. He's warmer than the white-coated doctor in Jude, but there's a fascination in his eye that makes me uncomfortable. It's almost as though I'm a test subject instead of his patient, or client, or whatever he wants to call me. "They're just your standard nightmares."

"And that's what you think happened the night you were hospitalized? You think you had a nightmare?"

*No.* "Yes."

"Do you mind sharing with me exactly what you saw?"

I close my eyes, as if doing so might shut the images away, but they are seared into my memory—the dead bodies in ditches, the people in straitjackets. I give an involuntary shudder. "I saw a lot of death."

"Is this what you see in all of your nightmares?"

I think about Pete and the white-eyed man and the swirling mass trying to consume him. I think about the way my scream made the man stop and notice me. "Yes."

Dr. Roth purses his lips and jots something in my file.

"I haven't had one in a while." Two days to be exact.

He continues writing.

I shift in my seat. "Are you going to prescribe me medicine?"

"I'm hoping to avoid medicine."

"Why?"

He gives me a long, steady stare, then clasps his hands beneath his chin. "In many cases, medicine is extremely helpful. I'm not sure you're one of them. I think there are other treatment options we should try first."

I look around his office—at the cat clock on his wall and the framed degrees. I wonder if Dr. Roth has a wife or kids. I wonder what made him want to work here, in this facility, talking to people like me. I wonder if that file in his hand says anything at all about my grandmother.

He sets the folder aside. "You can be honest with me, Tess. This is a safe place."

They are my mother's words, but I have doubts. Something inside me warns against full disclosure. Something inside me is not sure Dr. Roth can be trusted.

## Chapter Nine

# ROUTINES

Luka is at school the next morning. He wears a darker pair of jeans, a pale blue t-shirt, and the same hemp bracelet. Hopefully, the thrill that runs through me upon seeing him is not as blatantly obvious on the outside as it is on the inside.

He sits beside Summer in Current Events, he works by himself on the pottery wheel in Ceramics, and does nothing at all in World History except stay quiet and chew on his thumbnail, but I'm positive I feel his stare several times throughout class. Only every time I gather up the courage to peek, he's looking at Mr. Lotsam. Which means I'm either suffering from a gigantic case of wishful thinking (I refuse to call it a delusion) or he's much more discreet than me when it comes to staring.

When the final bell rings, the zipper on my bag decides to stick. The classroom empties while I tug at the stubborn metal tag.

"Need help?"

The recognizable voice makes my heart stutter-step.

Luka stands on the other side of the table, distractingly perfect, and I curse myself for being such an easy blusher. "Um … sure," I say, scooting the bag over.

He unsticks the zipper on his first try and hands me my bag with a half-smile that does nothing to relieve the warmth growing in my cheeks.

"Thanks," I mumble.

"So you weren't at the game on Friday."

I stand and shrug my bag straps over my shoulders, not entirely sure how to respond. Was he disappointed by my absence, or is he still trying to figure out my odd reaction at the pep rally? Surely it's not the former. The former doesn't make any sense. Why should someone like Luka be disappointed by my absence?

"Leela said you weren't feeling well." We exit Mr. Lotsam's class side by side and I scratch at my patch of eczema. It burns, which means I'm not dreaming.

"I had a headache."

"That's too bad."

I have no idea how to respond to that either.

"Do you get headaches often?"

"Unfortunately." We come to a four-way intersection in the hallway. Luka stops. So do I, desperate to say something—anything—that might be the slightest bit interesting. "You're my neighbor," I blurt and the heat actually spreads to my forehead. I didn't know foreheads could blush.

"Yeah, I know." His half-smile turns into a whole one. "I saw you on Saturday morning. By that rock."

Oh my goodness. I officially want to melt. Disappear. Vanish into thin air like a puff of smoke. Luka saw me spying on him on the beach Saturday morning?

He cocks his head and there's something in his eyes. It's the same something that was there on Friday, when he picked up my pencil in Current Events. Before I have a chance to give that something a name, a huddle of boys down the hall whistles. "Hey Williams!" the square-faced kid from Current Events calls. "You have to check this out."

Luka hooks his thumbs beneath the straps of his backpack. "You should come to the next game," he says, then turns around and makes his way toward the boys. Several of them give me a lingering once-over before refocusing on whatever they think Luka has to check out.

I shuffle away in a mindless stupor, replaying what just happened. Leela meets me at my locker. Her stream of chatter as we walk through the parking lot allows me to mull over my encounter with Luka. Did he purposefully wait for me after class? Does he really want me to go to the next football game or was he being polite? When we reach my car, Leela's chatter stops abruptly. Pete is leaning against the bumper. He climbs into the back. Leela squirms in shotgun, leaving me to wonder why girls always fidget in front of the boys they like.

When we arrive at my house, my mother is a complete embarrassment. She's made cookies and has milk, like we are in kindergarten. Thankfully, Leela takes it in stride. In fact, Leela and my mom become fast friends. The two pummel each other with questions and jabber back and forth like long lost BFFs. By Leela's third cookie, Mom is absolutely beaming and offers to give her the grand tour of our massive home. Cue more embarrassment. I'm already self-conscious about the size of our house, especially given Leela's reaction to living in Forest Grove. Parading her through the hallways, up the stairs, and into each room makes my self-consciousness explode into a full-out complex. But Mom feeds off my friend's enthusiasm, going into more and more detail with each of Leela's *ooh's* and *ahh's*.

After the torture ends, we head to my bedroom and paint our toes with the nail polish Leela pulls from her backpack— bubble gum pink for her, lime green for me. She darts glances out into the hall, where angry music blasts from Pete's closed door. I keep the conversation on him, because if I don't, I will ask about Luka and I really don't need a reason to feed my growing obsession. Or call Leela's attention to it.

She joins us for dinner—Mom's homemade meatball sandwiches—and asks my dad all sorts of questions about his job. I can tell he's flattered. I keep waiting for her to mention that she's Irish Catholic, curious as to how he will respond, but she never brings it up.

Mom attempts to draw Pete into the conversation, but he is unusually broody, so she gives up and smiles at me with this look of tearful happiness in her eyes. I know exactly what she's thinking. Her daughter has a friend. A real live friend. I'm desperate to get Leela out of my house before Mom verbalizes her thoughts.

Once the meal is over and Leela has had another cookie, I drop her off at home, which is decidedly more modest than our own and not in a gated community.

As soon as I step back inside my house, Mom is there, raving about what a sweet girl Leela is and asking when she can come over again. I almost suggest that Mom invite her over. Maybe the two can have a slumber party. I bite my tongue and go up into my room and do my homework and for the first time in a long time, I have an uneventful night of sleep.

It becomes the first of many.

September melts into October and I discover that fall in Northern California is gorgeous, with mild, windy days and chilly evenings, perfect for bundling up and strolling along the beach. It is so much nicer than the unrelenting heat and humidity I endured in Florida over the past two years.

The more time passes, the more my fear over the word

*psychosis* recedes. Sure, I'm still sensitive to temperature fluctuations that nobody else can feel and there's a sense of heaviness in our house that seems ever-present, like it attracts more gravity than anywhere else, and I will occasionally spot a flicker of unexplained light or darkness in the periphery of my vision, but I attribute these to auras—a very scientific, logical explanation that comes with migraines. I know because I look it up. I have no hallucinations and I have no delusions, unless you count my growing suspicion that Luka Williams is keeping tabs on me.

He doesn't wait for me after class anymore, but when I go to the library during study hall, somehow, he's there too. When I'm out in the hallway in the middle of class—whether to get a drink or use the restroom—so is he. One time I went to the nurse to lie down because my headache was particularly bad, and I heard his voice in the office, speaking with Mrs. Finch. It seems too much to be a coincidence, but too preposterous to be true, so I keep any and all speculations to myself.

Besides the befuddlement that is Luka, I find it incredibly easy to slip into a routine. Mom and I find a local dojo and I advance to a bona fide black belt. We go to class on Saturday mornings and afterward, on the days I don't join my father at work, I sit out on our deck with the pretense of reading, but really I watch Luka surf, admiring the effortless way he navigates the waves. Sometimes I explore the cliffs and the woods. Sometimes I take long strolls along the beach, examining shells and rocks along the way.

When it comes to school, Thornsdale High is pretty much like every other high school in America. I only have to sit through a week of lunches in the cafeteria before I know all of the cliques. There's the popular crowd, which consists mainly of jocks and cheerleaders. They've mastered the art of looking down their noses at everybody else. Except for Bobbi. She is president of student council and bubbly and genuine, which makes her attraction to Matt Chesterson all the more perplexing. He's a major jerk. Sure, he's the starting quarterback and she's the head cheerleader. He was homecoming king and she the queen, but other than that, I don't get it. I think his personality fits much better with Summer, but Summer is way too obsessed with Luka to give anyone else the time of day.

Jared, the square-faced bulky kid who happens to be one of the football team's linebackers, is decidedly opinionated in Current Events and worships the ground Matt walks on. He also drools whenever Summer's around, which feeds her over-bloated ego. I'm not apt to dislike people, but she's a hard one not to dislike. She kisses up to Bobbi and puts on this sickeningly sweet act in front of Luka, but when those two aren't around, she's just plain mean. And bossy. Anytime she catches me looking at Luka, which is more often than I'd like, her pretty, spray-tanned face morphs into a mask of ugly. If only I could take a picture and show it to Jared.

The drama students hang out with the drama students and the band kids hang out with the band kids. Poor Scott Shroud tries sitting next to my brother at lunch for a solid week, which is a testament to his commitment as an ambassador. Scott is shier than me and a thousand times more brilliant. He's the only sophomore in my Honors English class. Eventually he gives up with Pete and moves to a table filled with other skinny, underdeveloped, socially-awkward boys. The stoners and the Goths intermingle more than any other groups, but maintain their autonomy.

The only two anomalies are a boy and a girl named Jess and Wren. I have no idea where they belong. Leela told me once that the boy—Jess—had a procedure his freshman year to get his tongue forked. The girl—Wren—is also in my Honors English class. She gave a very passionate presentation on the Salem Witch Trials and told everyone that her great-great-great something grandmother was burned at the stake and that sometimes, that same grandmother comes to speak with her in the dead of night. When our teacher told her that was enough, Wren started barking at her—like, actual barking—and she was sent to Principal Jolly's office. She has purple hair and wears a skull necklace and has a tattoo of a pentagram on her pale, skinny bicep and another of a symbol I've never seen before on the inside of her wrist. One day in class, I gathered up the nerve to ask her about it, but she looked at me like *I* was the crazy one. I can't help but wonder if she's ever been referred to Dr. Roth.

As far as me—I'm the quiet new girl who is largely ignored. And Leela? I am indebted to Leela. She is a lifesaver—my first real-life friend in well … ever. We hang out in our free time and she even convinces me to go to some football games. When I'm there, I never let myself look for Luka, despite his suggestion that I come. Surely he was just being nice. Searching him out would make me pathetic. So I stand next to Leela while she hoots and hollers, inwardly rejoicing whenever Matt throws an interception. The Thornsdale Dragons lose spectacularly to every team they play.

If not for my Monday visits with Dr. Roth and the headaches and the sensitivities I'm growing adept at hiding, my birthday wish would be entirely within the realm of possibility. Normalcy draws closer, dancing just out of reach—enticing and so very real.

Then Sunday happens.

## CHAPTER TEN

# HYPNOSIS

Leela is not big on hiking. She doesn't like the bugs or the dirt or really, anything outdoors. But the day is uneventful and my physics homework is a particularly heinous shade of dreadful and I find it impossible to get warm inside my big, drafty house, all of which makes the towering forest bordering my neighborhood irresistible. A variety of songs play from the iPod stand on my desk as I gaze longingly out my bedroom window and Leela digs in my oversized closet, making various outfits out of my hodgepodge ensemble of clothes. I have no idea how she does it, but everything she puts together—even items that don't seem like they should match at all—looks impressively fashionable.

I remove my pencil from my mouth. "Want to go exploring in the woods?"

Leela sticks her head out of my closet, eying me with a doubtful brow. "The woods?"

"Yeah. It'll be fun."

She comes out with a sequined top I never ever wear, looking at it longingly. "I wish we were the same size. You have amazing clothes."

Too bad I don't wear half of them.

"My mom thinks I should go on this new cleansing diet she read about in her latest issue of Health magazine. Maybe if I tried it I could fit into this top ..."

I scrunch my nose. Leela's mom is skinny and overdone. I always get the impression she's overcompensating for something and I hate the way she constantly comments on Leela's weight. "I think you look great how you are."

Leela's cheeks redden and she slips back inside my closet.

I sit up in bed. "Whadaya say?"

"About what?"

"The woods."

Leela comes back out again, this time without any clothes in hand. "I've heard rumors that the woods in Forest Grove are home to Sasquatch."

"You mean like ... Bigfoot?"

She nods, her expression solemn.

I can't help myself. I laugh and swing my legs over my bed. "All right, that settles it. Now we have to go."

"I'm serious, Tess. People have disappeared in those woods."

"We won't disappear, I promise. I've been in them at least a dozen times and haven't yet vanished. Now come on, let's go hunting for a big, hairy, imaginary man-thing."

Leela cracks a smile, which means I've won. I close my physics book with a thump, hurry out into the hallway, nearly plowing into Pete, who asks where we're going. I can tell Leela wants to stay and talk, but I give him a vague *out* and hurry down the steps, throw on my sneakers and a jacket, and lead the way outside.

It's damp. The sky overhead is thick with rain, but nothing falls. Leela talks about school and her siblings and this hot actor on a television show she watches as I stare at the dark windows of Luka's house and wonder what he's up to. The foliage underfoot is dense and green and wet and soaks a bit through my shoes.

"This is gross," Leela says, lifting her feet extra high into the air, as if this will stop the seepage.

I swipe a large stick off the ground and lead the way into the trees.

"Bobbi's having a Halloween party next Friday," Leela says a bit breathlessly, trying to keep up behind me. "She has one every year, but I've never gone before. Wanna go?"

I use my walking stick to bat aside a low-hanging branch and bite the inside of my cheek. Me and costumes? We don't get along so well.

"C'mon, it'll be fun. We can be the poor little kittens who lost their mittens."

I continue further up the path, my steps silent and quick, the gap between Leela and me widening. She stumbles over a root, but catches herself before falling. I stop and wait for her. "Aren't there three of those?"

"We can make Kiara come." Kiara is Leela's younger sister. A freshman and just as talkative as my friend. "She'll love it. We can dress up as cats and go around asking people if they've seen our mittens."

A crow caws from a branch right over Leela's head. She screams and ducks.

I laugh.

"Not funny," she says, putting her hand against her chest. "That scared me half to death."

I look up at the towering redwoods that climb into the gray sky overhead and use my stick to poke at a few nearby bushes. "I don't see any Yeti babies in here."

"You joke, but I'm not kidding. There have been bona fide reports." As if to prove her braveness, she takes a few steps ahead of me. "So what do you think?"

"About Bigfoot?"

"No, the party."

The idea is not appealing. Parties are about as high up on my list of favorite things to do as football games. But I've learned that when it comes to Leela, the stronger I object to something, the more determined she becomes to convince me otherwise. It's best if I don't say anything.

"Maybe Pete can come."

"Yeah. Maybe."

Twigs snap beneath our feet. I let Leela walk a couple bumbling steps ahead of me when a loud hiss stops me cold. Not more than ten paces up the path, there is a snake—a large, coiled, red-eyed snake. "Leela, stop!"

She freezes.

The snake slithers closer and stops right in front of my friend. I stumble backward, my heart lurching.

"What? Tess, you're freaking me out."

With paralyzed vocal chords, all I can do is point. She whips around, following the direction of my finger, but she doesn't move. Why doesn't she move? Has fear frozen her too? Is she going to stand there while the snake sinks its fangs into her? What if it's poisonous? The thing is huge.

Leela's shoulders relax and she turns back around with a smirk. "Ha, ha. Very funny. You saw Bigfoot."

"Snake," I manage to rasp.

"Oh my gosh! Where?" Leela's voice is shrill as she jumps over to me and clutches at the shoulder of my sweatshirt. "This is exactly why I don't like coming outside. Where is it?"

"Right in front of us!"

Leela jerks around, looking to the right, the left, behind

her, and then straight ahead, at the hissing, fanged serpent poised to strike. "Okay, you're freaking me out. I don't see anything."

How can she not see it? It's right in front of us, slowly slithering forward with those blood-red eyes. My heart beats against my eardrums. The snake rears back and I do the only thing I am capable of doing. I grip the stick in my hand and swing at the serpent with every ounce of strength inside of me.

"Tess!" Leela grabs my arm.

I wheel around. "Run!"

She stares at me with eyes rounder than I've ever seen. My attention flies back to the path, toward the snake I just whacked. Only nothing is there but another stick—slightly larger than the one I wield in my hand.

A stick.

I search the forest floor, unable to believe the snake is really gone. "Where is it?"

"Where is *what*?"

I do a full three-sixty. No way did a simple swing of my stick make that snake dart away. But when I come full circle, there's nothing. It can't be possible. Seconds earlier, a large frightening snake had been ready to sink its teeth into me and my friend. But all that's there now ...

Leela lets go of my sleeve. "Jeez, Tess, you never told me you were such a good actor."

"I wasn't acting. I ..." I blink several times, dumbfounded. "You really didn't see it?"

She shakes her head slowly.

Dread fills the empty space my fear left behind. And for the first time in several weeks, the word *psychosis* flashes in my mind. Seeing things other people don't see. Is that what just happened? Before Leela's concern turns into suspicion, I let out an uneasy laugh. "I thought that stick was a snake."

"Wow. You must really be afraid of them." Leela looks at the inanimate stick on the ground. It doesn't resemble a snake at all.

I'm suddenly very tired. Very cold.

"So why in the world do you like being outside so much?"

"I don't know." I drop the walking stick and shove my hands into the front pocket of my hoodie. "Do you mind if we go home?"

"You don't have to ask me twice."

We head back to the house, quiet at first, but then Leela starts talking about the pet snake one of her brothers had in junior high. Apparently, it got loose in the house once and her mom hyperventilated.

I have a hard time listening. Because that was no aura. I have no migraine. I either saw a huge, hissing snake that Leela somehow didn't see, or I just had a hallucination.

♾

The next day at school, Leela acts like nothing weird happened. Apparently, freaking out because a stick looks like a snake isn't all that unreasonable to her. She seems to have forgotten about the episode altogether. But I cannot. The scene is stuck on repeat in my mind. Over and over again through all eight periods, until the bell finally rings and I am released to go to my sixth appointment with Dr. Roth at the Edward Brooks Facility.

I sit in the red, cushy seat and jiggle my leg.

"Everything okay?" he asks.

My leg continues its frantic jiggling as I replay—for the

millionth time—what happened in the woods. Dr. Roth waits patiently. Finally, I stop my fidgeting and sit up straighter in the chair. "What would you say if you had a client who swore she saw a snake, but it turned out to be a stick?"

"That seems like an easy enough mistake to make. Sticks look a lot like snakes sometimes."

"What if that client told you she saw the stick slithering and hissing with fangs and red eyes and was about to strike her and one of her friends?"

He steeples his fingers beneath his chin. "You're positive it wasn't a snake?"

I nod.

Pushing his glasses up his nose, he leans forward. With each passing appointment, his interest in me has slowly waned. Now, however, I see a tenuous pulse of intrigue flicker to life in his eyes—like the twitch of a dying man's finger. This latest bit of news has resuscitated his interest.

"Does having hallucinations make me crazy?" I ask.

He raises one of his eyebrows. "Are you sure you didn't fall asleep?"

I don't miss the tone of sarcasm in his voice. He's referencing the séance, of course. Something we haven't discussed since our first meeting. Dr. Roth clearly doesn't believe my nightmare theory any more than I do. "For people who suffer with psychosis …"

"Psychosis?"

"It's just what came to mind." I grip the armrests on either side and pin my gaze on his framed degrees. I really don't want to watch the flicker of interest in his eyes turn into a flame, but I have to know more. I have to know what is happening to me. "Do they usually … are people with psychosis … are they aware of having it? Do they know what's happening to them?"

He doesn't answer. He simply sits there studying me until I'm boiling in my own frustration and my leg has resumed its jiggling.

"I'd like to try something with you, Tess," he finally says.

"What?"

"Hypnosis."

I scratch my patch of eczema. "Hypnosis?"

He gives a single, confident nod. "I think it will help."

But Dr. Roth is wrong. Hypnosis doesn't help at all.

## Chapter Eleven

# Genocide

That night, my nightmares return.

I'm standing in the middle of a crowd of people with angry faces, holding signs I cannot read. Babies cry somewhere off in the distance and standing before the angry mass is a man and a woman. The man wears a white coat and the woman, maroon scrubs. He has fine black hair and slanted eyes and she is petite and fair.

I don't know why I'm here—in this crowd.

But then I see something. The skeletal man with greasy hair and white eyes. He stands in the crowd, his spindly fingers spread wide, a dark web escaping from his fingertips, only instead of hovering over Pete, the web sticks to an expressionless man wearing a trench coat. He's like a marionette on a string. The web controls his arms and his legs, moving him away from the crowd, closer to the Asian doctor and the petite nurse.

When the man pulls a grenade from his coat pocket, my throat closes with fear.

I want to yell at him to stop—to shake off the black web and put the bomb away before people are killed. But babies wail and shock keeps me immobile, and before I can do or say anything, the man pulls the pin and there is an explosion of massive heat that sears my skin. I throw my arm over my eyes, but there is no fire. Just me. Sitting up in bed. Panting.

Sweating. Blinking. Thinking about Dr. Roth and his hypnosis. Wondering *why*, after weeks of no nightmares, I had one now.

As soon as I catch my breath, I throw off my covers and peel off my sweat-dampened pajamas. The red numbers on my clock tell me that I slept through the alarm. I slip into a pair of ratty jeans with holes in the knees, an Orange Crush t-shirt, and the same hooded sweatshirt I wore outside on Sunday—when I saw an imaginary snake almost attack my friend. I brush my teeth and rinse my face and pull my hair into a ponytail, all the while forcing the memory of that nightmare away. I will not attempt to figure out what it means. I will not let myself worry about it. People have nightmares all the time. They are simply brain activity in the midst of sleep. It's part of being human.

I hurry down the stairs and find Dad in the kitchen, reading the paper with a furrowed brow.

"Late this morning?" Mom says, dressed and pressed and beautiful as always.

"Slept through the alarm."

I squish my feet into a pair of unlaced Converse All Stars by the sliding glass door, grab a Pop-Tart from the cupboard, yell at Pete to get a move on, and we hurry out to the car.

At school, I fist my hands in my front pocket, trying to push away the sense of foreboding that has settled over my shoulders while Leela jabbers about Bobbi's Halloween party on Friday. When I step inside Mr. Lotsam's classroom, we grab two seats to the right of the horseshoe of tables, directly across from Luka. There's an empty seat beside him. For a brief moment, I imagine a confident version of myself taking the empty spot and smiling at him. I imagine a world where he is my boyfriend and I am his girlfriend. I envision us walking down the hall together, holding hands while everybody stares.

I blink away the daydream, hang my bag on the back of my chair, and pull out my notebook, prepared to resume our previous discussion about the growing population of immigrants and refugees in America. Students file in, filling up the chairs. Summer takes the one next to Luka. As soon as the bell rings, Mr. Lotsam breezes inside the class with a stack of magazines. He plops one in front of each of us and writes two words on the board.

Fetal Modification.

A collective groan overtakes the shuffle of notebooks and papers. One I silently agree with. I dread this conversation. People never agree. Our entire nation is up in arms over it because of a heated, indignant minority. The government-mandated pregnancy screenings and the dramatic increase of fetal modification over the past decade is one of the few news topics Dad doesn't even talk about at home. Mom told me once that when she went to school, inclusion was all the rage. I can't imagine. In all my seventeen years, I can count on one hand how many times I've encountered a person with defects. I look down at the magazine in front of me and the one in front of Leela. They are different, but both have relevant headlines.

*The Benefits of Government-Mandated Pregnancy Screenings*

*Anti-Fetal Modification Groups Picket at the White House*

My magazine has a picture of B-Trix on the cover, an internationally renowned pop star from England. All the boys are in love with her, all the girls want to be her. People legitimately hyperventilate at her concerts. Like, for real, need-a-paramedic hyperventilate. A couple months ago, she became the official spokeswoman for a pregnancy screening advocacy campaign. The commercials air so often, I can recite each one from memory.

Without saying anything, Mr. Lotsam points a remote control at the television mounted above his desk and a reporter talks inside the flat screen. Another fetal modification-clinic bombing occurred earlier this morning.

"Two people died in this explosion. Dr. Chang and Mindy Lucas."

The victims' faces fill the screen and every last drop of warmth drains from my cheeks. The babies crying. The people with signs. The web of black mist. The man in the white coat and the woman in scrubs. The grenade. The explosion. I stare, dry mouthed, at the television. At these two people—Dr. Chang and Mindy Lucas—and blink, as if blinking will make them change. As if blinking will make them not be the people from my nightmare.

As the reporter talks, it's as if I'm detached from my body, listening from the bottom of a well. Dr. Chang was forty-two years old with a wife and three children. Mindy Lucas was thirty-one and newly engaged. They died in my sleep and now they are dead in real life. I scratch my eczema, hating the burn, and search for an explanation. Like maybe I saw them before bed. Or maybe Dr. Roth planted this into my head as some sort of hypnotic experiment. But the explosion happened this morning.

Mr. Lotsam points the remote at the television. The screen goes black. "This is the fifth fetal modification clinic bombing this year. I think it's time we engage in a healthy class discussion."

Some students fidget, visibly uncomfortable. Some scoot to the edge of their seats, as if this discussion is long overdue. Most look indifferent. I look at Leela to see which category she falls into. She squirms and fiddles with her necklace. I glance at Luka. He wears an expression I've never seen him wear before. He is not bored or excited or uncomfortable. He is seething. In fact, he glares at those letters on the board as if they spell the most offensive swear word in existence.

Jared, his bulk too large for our small chairs, raises his hand, but doesn't wait to be called on. "If you ask me, it's smart."

Mr. Lotsam scratches his soul patch. "Elaborate."

"The pregnancy screenings." He flicks the headline on the magazine in front of him. "I mean, these kids would be born with severe birth defects. How is that fair to them or their parents? They wouldn't have any quality of life. Their parents would be wiping their butts when they're fifty years old."

A ripple of snickers follows the comment.

But I don't join. I'm too mesmerized with Luka, whose knuckles have turned bone-white. His anger gives him this air of danger that accentuates his appeal. It's a thought I'm sure Dr. Roth would love to unpack.

Five other hands raise into the air, including Leela's. Mr. Lotsam calls on her. Her fingers wrestle, reminding me of my mom, but I have to give her credit, because despite her nerves, she looks directly at Jared. "That's discrimination. Who's to determine the quality of life?"

"I think doctors are able to determine that, Leela." Jared says the words with a flat sarcasm that makes the class snicker again.

Summer sets her elbows on the table and addresses Leela. "You're just saying that because you're Catholic."

Leela's ears turn red.

My hackles rise. I shift forward in my seat. I've never given much thought to the pregnancy screenings or the fetal modification clinics, but Summer makes me want to open my mouth so I can tell her to shut hers.

"You're only regurgitating what your parents tell you," Summer continues. "How about having an original thought for once?"

"Let me guess," Luka says in a voice so low, it simmers. "Your parents are *pro* screenings?"

Summer's sneer melts away. Something inside me cheers.

"She brings up a good point though," Jared says, rising to Summer's defense. "The religious people are the ones doing all the bombings. This is exactly why the government nixed all the religion. Isn't killing *killers*"—he finger-quotes the word—"a little ironic?"

The conversation erupts. Kids interject and interrupt and Mr. Lotsam has to give several reminders to raise hands and disagree respectfully. Even the students who looked indifferent earlier have opinions—the majority of which seem to be in support of the government-mandated screenings. Apparently, I'm the only one without an opinion. Or maybe I'm too consumed by Luka to take the time to form one. A muscle ticks in his jaw as the conversation escalates, until finally he raises his hand and the entire class hushes. Even Mr. Lotsam looks curious, eager.

"Doctors are human. They make mistakes. Screening pregnant women and aborting—" Several students grimace at his choice of word. Aborting is no longer politically correct. *It puts a negative spin on a positive thing,* doctors like to say. "—every fetus they think may have a disability is genocide."

The accusation is so potent that Mr. Lotsam raises his eyebrows. "Genocide?"

Luka raises his eyebrows right back. "If you ask me, it's a modern-day holocaust."

"That's a bold comparison."

Luka doesn't back down. He doesn't reconsider. And beside him, Summer looks absolutely miserable. As if she wishes for nothing more than to take back her words. I can almost see the cogs in her brain working, trying to think of a way to get back into Luka's good graces. After so much chatter, the room is eerily quiet.

A Filipino boy—Max, I think?—who always wears a black leather jacket breaks the silence first. "The Nazis were killing people. These doctors are curing women of defective fetuses in the first trimester. That's hardly murder."

With that, the spell Luka cast breaks. The class breaks out into arguments again.

Mr. Lotsam holds up his hands. "All right, we definitely have opinions. Let's get on to our assignment and see if any of these opinions can be further shaped or perhaps even changed." He has us open up to the articles in our magazines and write down arguments for and against the pregnancy screenings. He encourages us to play devil's advocate. When we finish, we gather into groups of four and share our arguments with one another. Leela and I pair up with two others. I don't let myself look at Luka. I don't let myself hope that he might want to be in my group. I do my best to focus on the assignment.

But my mind has returned to last night's dream. I have no idea what to make of it.

## CHAPTER TWELVE

# MISTAKES

Luka broods through the entirety of Ceramics class. He sits at the wheel, shaping and reshaping wet clay into a beautiful vase with his strong hands, that same muscle ticking in his jaw. Nobody approaches him or attempts to engage him in a conversation. His brood is intimidating.

Leela and I murmur at a table about the intense discussion in first period. I can tell she is flattered that Luka rose to her defense, especially against somebody as popular as Summer. At lunch, Summer looks close to tears. She keeps darting glances across the table at Luka, whose mood has not improved. Study Hall and Honors English drag into an eternity. I jiggle my leg, impatiently waiting for final period when I will see Luka again. And Summer. I'm eager to watch the drama unfold. Just how *will* she win back Luka's favor? The moment the seventh-period bell rings, I jump out of my seat and hurry to Mr. Lotsam's room.

I sit down and open a notebook and start doodling, which keeps me from staring at the door like Summer, who's looking a wee bit desperate. She bites her lip and goes out of her way to keep the seat beside her open. When her eyes go wide, I know he's entered. I force my attention down on my paper, wishing my hair wasn't in a ponytail. I have nothing to hide behind.

"Is anyone sitting here?"

The smoothness of the voice makes my pulse hiccup. Luka

has a way of articulating his words so each sound is heard.

I look up from my doodling. "Um. Go ahead."

The legs of the chair scrape against the floor as he scoots it back to sit. I peek at Summer, who glares at me with such loathing, you'd think I just murdered her dog.

Jennalee comes in, sits on the other side of Luka, and twirls her hair. The bell rings and Mr. Lotsam announces that we need to partner up for a year-long project that will account for fifty percent of our grade. He claps his hands. "Find a partner and I'll explain what you'll be doing."

I consider excusing myself to the restroom. I hate when teachers make us choose partners, especially in this class without Leela. I don't want Luka to witness my lameness as everybody else in the class snags a partner and I'm left alone— the perpetual loser. My palms grow clammy. I want to put up my hood and hide my face in my arms. Forget religion, picking partners should be outlawed. So should captains in gym class. I'm always picked last, which isn't fair, since I'm fast and I can catch a pass, if somebody ever chose to throw me one.

Luka clears his throat. "Tess?"

My heart takes off, double time. When I look, he's staring at me with those striking green eyes, his head slightly cocked. "Do you want to be my partner?"

I point to my chest, not sure I comprehend his question.

His eyes sparkle with something—curiosity, humor, pity? Oh man, I hope not pity.

I swallow. "Uh. Sure."

Jennalee stares with insulting disbelief, her mouth ajar, while the rest of the class scrambles to find a partner. My limbs feel like dead weight. I'm not sure if I should move them or adjust them, but then I remember the way Leela fidgets in front of Pete and I make myself sit still while my insides hyperventilate. Luka wants to be my partner. Luka Williams chose me. I tell my heart to chill out before he hears the beating. This project comprises fifty percent of our grade and I'm smart. This is why Luka chose me. I shouldn't read any further into it.

He twists his hemp bracelet around his wrist. I think he might ask me something, but then Mr. Lotsam starts explaining the project and asks us to read a chapter from our history books and tells us we can talk quietly with our partners when we finish. I have no idea what the project is about. And the words I attempt to read make no sense whatsoever. But I stare at the pages, pretending to concentrate, until the majority of my classmates have put their books away.

Luka bites his thumbnail.

I search for something to say. Anything that might prove I can speak in semi-intelligible syllables. Nothing comes.

"You've been coming to the football games," he says.

Okay. So he's noticed.

"I waved at you last Friday but you ignored me." His smile is crooked.

My stomach drops in that way it does whenever I accidentally skip the bottom stair. I find myself wishing I would have worn a better outfit than this old sweatshirt and a ratty pair of jeans. Maybe even the sequined top Leela pulled out of my closet on Sunday. "I didn't see you."

"You were very into the game. Very focused. I was impressed." He twirls his pencil around the tip of his thumb, his smile fainter, but still there. "Most girls don't watch."

"Isn't that the point?"

He shrugs.

I scramble for something to fill up the silence. He beats me to it.

"So, you read a lot."

"What?"

"I see you out on your deck. You're usually reading. Sometimes you write, though."

"Oh. Yeah."

"What do you write about?" he asks.

Crazy grandma. Crazy dreams. The crazy things I see that nobody else can see—like snakes and flashes and men without pupils. Him. "Nothing really."

"Do you like your new home?"

"Um, sure. It's fine."

"You don't sound very convincing," he says.

His unwavering attention makes me feel hot and somehow, cold. I have to look away and in so doing, I catch Summer gawking at us. She's not the only one. "Thornsdale is as good as any other place to live, I guess."

He folds his arms over his backpack on the table in front of us. "Have you lived in many places?"

"Nine."

"Really?"

The bell rings.

Luka stands and hitches his backpack over his right shoulder. I wait for him to wave and leave, seeing as he's no longer stuck with me, but he stands there and waits. So I stand too, shrug on my backpack, and we walk out of class together. "That can't be easy on you and your brother, moving so much."

"You know I have a brother?" The question tumbles out before I can take it back. Of course he knows I have a brother.

This is a small school. Pete and I are the first new kids since him three years ago. Everybody knows I have a brother.

"Pete, right? Sophomore? Perpetual scowl? Kind of a loner?"

"He's really not."

"No?"

I shake my head and loop my thumbs under the straps of my backpack as we make our way toward the main locker bay. "I think he misses his girlfriend."

"Yeah, I guess that would be hard." We walk a few more steps. I'm all too aware of the tiny gap of space between his arm and mine. "Did you have to leave anyone behind?"

My cheeks turn warm. "You mean like a boyfriend?"

"Yeah."

I snort, like actually snort.

"No?"

"I don't think I'm girlfriend material."

"Oh, I don't know about that."

My stomach does that dippy thing again, because what does *that* mean? "I think he's still angry at me for the move. Pete—I mean. Not my boyfriend. Because I don't have a boyfriend." *Oh my goodness, Tess, close your mouth.*

"Angry at *you?*"

"Huh?"

"Why would your brother be angry at *you* for moving?"

My insides tighten. My attention flits from one wall to the next, as if an excuse might be etched on either. "I mean, not at *me*. He's just … looking for somebody to blame I guess."

Luka studies me like I'm an impossible-to-place puzzle piece.

"You seemed upset during first period today." I cringe as

soon as my mouth shuts. I really should not be allowed to talk in front of cute boys.

Luka steps in front of me, stops, and leans against the wall, his head dipped so he's more level with my line of vision. "Sore subject."

His nearness, his scent—both leave me unbalanced. "Wh-why?"

Some sort of internal battle wages war in his eyes, like he's trying to decide how much to say. I fight back an almost insuppressible urge to tell him that he can trust me with anything. Those words would be weird. Luka and I barely know each other.

"Are your parents against it?" I ask.

He looks over his shoulder, as if checking for eavesdroppers. The crowd of students has thinned into nothing. Even the gaping stragglers are gone. We are alone in the hallway. Everyone has escaped into the locker bay and then outdoors into freedom. "I'm an only child, but I wasn't my mother's only pregnancy."

The hairs on the back of my neck prickle. "What happened?"

"She failed her pregnancy screening."

"So she …?" The unfinished question dangles between us. I don't have to ask it. Luka doesn't have to answer it. Because of course she did. He just told me he's an only child.

"Eight months later she got pregnant again and the same thing happened."

I suck in a quick breath. Two failed screenings? I can't begin to imagine what that might feel like for a woman. She must have been so relieved to finally have Luka.

"Guilt tormented her after she terminated her first pregnancy."

I find myself holding back a grimace, like all my classmates did in first period when Luka used the word *aborting*. *Terminated* is every bit as frowned upon. It feels vulgar, somehow, and yet this boy throws out the words without hesitation.

"When the doctors gave her the same diagnosis, she decided to go against their advice."

"Against their advice? You mean …?" I am captivated by his stare. Stuck, even. The hallway could explode with fireworks and I wouldn't be able to look away. "What happened to the baby?"

"You're looking at him."

I blink. Several times. "But—"

"I'm healthy." He pushes away from the wall. "The doctor was wrong. He made a mistake. If she would have listened …"

I shake my head, the motion sharp and decisive. I do not want to contemplate a world without Luka Williams.

"That first pregnancy," he says, "haunts her."

## Chapter Thirteen

# A Fighter

As I walk through the parking lot in afternoon drizzle, I cannot get Luka out of my head. I am so absorbed with replaying our totally unexpected, intimate conversation after class that I don't process anything Leela says. She obviously has no idea Luka and I are partners for a project in World History, otherwise she'd be grilling me. I wonder how long her oblivion will last. Surely, among all the gawkers, one is bound to tell Leela that Luka and I were spotted walking and talking together.

I can't stop thinking about my nightmare and the debate in Mr. Lotsam's class and the things Luka *said*. If the doctors were wrong about him, could they be wrong about others as well? What does this mean about all the screenings that are happening right now—not just here in America, but all over the world? Are doctors curing women of perfectly healthy fetuses because of a glitch in the system? All the questions make my brain hurt.

By the time we reach my car, Pete is already there, earbuds in his ears. Leela waves at him and heads off to her car. When we get home, Mom asks about our day. I give her the shortest version possible, then lock myself in my bedroom under the pretense of *so much homework*. Only instead of cracking open any of my text books, I alternate between staring at my ceiling, writing in my journal, thinking about Luka, and trying to block out all the craziness that has conspired over the past two days.

I don't say much over dinner. Neither does Pete. Mom tries her best to draw us out of our shells, but eventually gives up and talks to Dad about the latest Safe Guard recall, which is always a headache. I do the dishes, retreat back to my room, and fall asleep somewhere in the middle of doing all the homework I should have done earlier.

That night, I have my first dream about Luka Williams.

The ocean is silent. It's as if somebody has pushed the mute button on nature's remote control. I'm standing on the rocky beach, staring out at the waves and there is nothing. No caw of seagulls. No crashing of waves. No spray against the rocks. No sound at all.

A soft lavender paints the sky overhead, but the sun is nowhere in sight—not in the west or in the east—so I cannot tell if it's morning or evening. And there, straight ahead of me, is Luka, wearing a faded pair of blue jeans that fit him perfectly and the same white t-shirt he wore on my first day of school. The silent wind ruffles his hair. Walking toward him, I feel brave, almost reckless, because this isn't real. I know that much without even having to scratch at my eczema. Oceans are not silent in the real world. I've lived by one or another long enough to be well-acquainted with their retinue of sounds.

In contrast to my buoyancy is his posture of alarm. He looks left, right, up, down, taking in our surroundings, as if at any moment the boogeyman will jump out and get us both.

"Are you okay?" I ask.

His eyes stop their frantic searching and he cocks his head

in that way I'm beginning to associate with him. "Are *you*?"

I look around—besotted by our gorgeous surroundings. Everything is brighter and more vibrant—the green of the trees and the granite of the cliffs, the briny sea air, the immensity of the silent ocean. It's as though turning off the sound has heightened everything else. "I'm *more* than okay, actually."

His posture relaxes, but only after painstaking hesitation. "Well, this is different."

Yes, it is. Incredibly different—instead of a nightmare, I'm in a dream I don't want to end. "But nice."

He nods slowly.

"I was thinking about you before I went to sleep. That must be why you're in my dream."

"I'm pretty sure it's my dream," he says. "Not yours."

"I don't think so." I sense something warm nearby, but I can't see it. Even so, its presence is this palpable, pulsing, undeniable thing—an invisible sun come down from the sky to share some of its energy. Or maybe it's not energy, but courage. Because a question I'd never in a million years have the guts to ask in real life escapes without any hesitancy. "Remember the homecoming pep rally?"

His green eyes smolder.

"Did you see something in the gym?" I ask.

"Did you?"

I nod.

So does he. "Me, too."

Even though this is just a dream, even though I'm totally projecting, my relief is intense and immediate. In dream world I am not crazy. "I see things like that sometimes. It's why we moved." The memory of the séance makes me shiver. It's an unwelcome feeling in such a happy place. "I'm going to the

91

Edward Brooks Facility because my parents think I'm crazy."

He takes a strand of my hair between his fingers.

I shiver again, only this time, the shiver is not due to fear. "Sometimes I wonder if they're right. Sometimes I think I'm going insane."

He steps closer. "You're not."

But his voice sounds far away and the rocky sand beneath my feet sinks. I'm sinking, sinking, sinking until the sound returns. Wind whips my hair about my shoulders. Gone is the beach and Luka. I'm standing on the Golden Gate Bridge. I know because of pictures, not because I've ever been there before.

A girl stands on the ledge—she can't be more than fifteen. Fear surges through me, because surely one big gust of wind will have her plummeting into the water below. That man stands beside her. The one with the pale skin and the greasy hair and the emaciated face. He taunts the girl. He whispers in her ear. "You are ugly," he says. "Nobody loves you. Nobody wants you. Everybody would be happier if you were dead."

The girl's mascara runs black down her cheeks as she scoots closer and closer to the ledge and suddenly, I am angry. Pissed off. Seething, even. Because this man has pulled me away from Luka and he speaks words that scrape too close to home. I do not want this girl to believe any of it. I do not want her to jump on account of lies. The anger that tears through me is fierce and hot and before I can stop myself, I lunge at the man's throat. Using every bit of strength, I tear him away from the girl and the two of us are falling off the bridge.

Falling, falling, falling ...

He wraps his cold fingers around my neck and smiles a smile that is terrifying. "I knew you were a fighter."

## CHAPTER FOURTEEN

# INTERROGATION

I t's the first time I've fought in a dream. You'd think I'd wake up empowered. Instead, I feel jittery and weak, like a diabetic in need of sugar. I saw Dr. Roth on Monday. He hypnotized me. And now I have had nightmares two nights in a row. It can't be a coincidence.

A faint throb pulses in my temples—the beginnings of a headache—as I shuffle into the kitchen, wearing the same ratty jeans from yesterday and a slightly more respectable purplish gray sweater.

"Your eyes look stunning in that color," Mom says.

I grab a bagel from the toaster.

She cups my chin and rubs her thumb beneath my eyes. "Still having bad dreams?"

My throat tightens. I'm so ready for this to be over. To outgrow these nightmares, if they are something I can outgrow. I pull away from Mom and pick up the butter knife next to the opened container of cream cheese while Dad crosses his ankle over his knee and holds the paper open wide. "Hard to believe it's been sixteen years since Newport."

Mom pours me a glass of juice and shakes her head, like she doesn't even have words. Dad reads snippets of the article out loud. For some reason, it settles me. Puts things in perspective. I was only one when the attack happened, when a terrorist group bombed the Naval Underwater Warfare Center in

Newport, Rhode Island, completely decimating an entire city. More people died than in Pearl Harbor and 9-11 combined.

Dad mumbles something about learning our lesson, then turns a page. "Looks like there was a close call last night on the Golden Gate Bridge."

A glob of white falls off my knife.

He clucks his tongue. "What can be so bad in this world that would prompt a fourteen-year-old girl to try and kill herself?"

I grab the paper out of Dad's hand.

Both of his feet come to the floor. "Tess!"

But I am not apologetic. I'm too busy ravishing the paper, looking for a picture. And there she is. April Yodel. Fourteen years old. The same girl from last night's dream. The same girl being taunted by the man I wrestled off the bridge. Apparently, authorities reached her before she could jump.

"Honey?" Mom pulls down the paper and looks me in the face. "Are you okay?"

Dad stands from his chair. "You're as white as a sheet, kiddo."

I hand the paper back to Dad with icy fingers, my body trembling like an earthquake.

"Tess, you're scaring us." Mom cups my forehead like she used to do when I was little, and the worst life had to offer was a fever. "Sweetie, you're as clammy as can be."

First Dr. Chang and that nurse at a fetal modification clinic and now this girl—April Yodel. What is going on? What is happening to me? I clap my hand over my mouth, then turn around and run up the stairs. I am going to be sick.

Mom tries to convince me stay home from school, but I insist on going. I do not want to sit at home by myself. I cannot give myself too much time to think about any of this. The more I can keep my brain occupied, the better. And despite my slipping sanity, I want to see Luka. I want to work with him today in History.

So I take two Excedrin and I force myself to eat some crackers. Still, my hands shake like I have Parkinson's. Pete stares at them the entire drive to school, like he doesn't trust me behind the wheel. He turned sixteen last week. Maybe he should drive. As soon as I get to my locker, Leela descends with a bagful of questions. Someone told her the news.

*You are partners with Luka?*

*You were talking outside the main locker bay?*

*What were you talking about?*

*How are you not more excited?*

When I don't answer coherently, she asks if I'm okay. I nod, focusing all my attention on getting to class and sitting down. Sitting down will be good.

We arrive before Luka. I rest my head in the crook of my arm and take deep, calming breaths. I don't let myself think about the dream or that girl. Instead, I focus on breathing. I tell myself I am a normal teenager with a normal crush on the cute boy in school. Then I smell fabric softener and wintergreen and any hope for calming breaths swooshes away. Luka has taken the seat to my left, his hair so messy it looks as if he spent the morning raking his hands through it. Only he's Luka, so he pulls it off. He glances at me, his jaw tight, something intense flashing in his eyes when ours connect. He looks like he's going to say something or ask something, but I curl my fingers around the back of my neck and let my hair fall like a curtain between us.

The bell rings.

Mr. Lotsam writes on the white board, the tip of his dry erase marker squeak, squeak, squeaking as he does. *Newport. 16 Years.* And that's when I see it. Darkness at first, like a mysterious shadow in the middle of the room, expanding and blackening, until all of a sudden, it's the same figure from last night's dream. The skeletal, frightening man with white, unseeing eyes. His mouth stretches into a sinister smile and without warning, he lunges at me.

I suck in a sharp, loud breath, close my eyes, and rear back in my chair—so forcefully I slam into the wall behind me. When my eyes pop open, the man is gone. My heart flutters like the wings of a hummingbird.

Leela stares. Luka stares. I'm pretty sure every single person in the classroom stares.

*Did I fall asleep? Did I have a nightmare in class?*

Without asking to be excused, I grab my backpack and hurry out of the room. I sprint down the hall. I don't wait to see if Mr. Lotsam or Leela come after me. I run out of the building and I get into my car and I drive to the Edward Brooks Facility.

I need to speak with Dr. Roth.

∞

"What did you do to me?"

Dr. Roth looks up from whatever he's working on at his desk.

I walk over to him, plant my palms flat on his desk, and glare. "I want to know what you did to me during hypnosis."

"I didn't do anything except bring you through a few relaxation exercises."

"That's it?"

Dr. Roth looks at me sympathetically and motions to the chair on the other side of his desk, not the red cushy ones we usually sit in. I wonder how many insane people he has diagnosed throughout the years.

"Why don't you have a seat, Tess. You can tell me what's going on."

I sit down and clutch my bag in my lap while he removes my manila folder from the file cabinet behind him and begins scanning the papers.

"Is there anything in there about my grandmother?"

His attention snaps up. "I wasn't aware you knew about your grandmother."

"I overheard my parents talking."

Dr. Roth doesn't say anything for a while. The silence gives me too much time to think. A thousand questions somersault through my brain. No matter how hard I try to make them sit still, they keep hurtling over each other. I don't know where to start. "You obviously know about her."

He nods.

"Do I have what she had?"

He scratches his goatee. "I'm not sure."

"My parents say she suffered from psychosis."

He stares, unblinking.

"Are they right?"

Dr. Roth takes off his glasses, rubs the corners of his eyes, then puts them back on.

"Do you trust me, Tess?"

I clutch my backpack in my lap, unsure. "I don't know."

"I need you to believe that everything we talk about here is confidential. I won't report anything to the authorities. I won't tell your parents. I won't even plug anything into the computer." He holds up the folder, a reminder of his archaic filing system. And its necessity. "If I'm going to help you, you have to let me. And the only way I can is if you're honest."

I rake my teeth over my bottom lip. "I think maybe ... I might be experiencing psychosis."

"Why?"

"Because I'm having hallucinations." Surely, that is what they are. They can't be real if nobody else sees them. "And delusions." Prophetic dreams? A cute boy keeping tabs on *me*? Really? Talk about false beliefs if ever there were any. I wipe my palms against my jeans and hug my backpack tighter. "The things I saw at that séance?"

He leans forward. "Yes?"

"I don't think I fell asleep." I scratch my patch of eczema and look down at my fidgeting feet. One Converse All Star rests on top of the other. Then they switch. And switch again. It's like they are somebody else's feet. "I also have dreams ..."

"Yes?"

"They come true."

A spark of excitement flashes in his pupils, but disappears so quickly I immediately doubt myself. He pulls at his goatee. "Could you elaborate?"

"I dreamt about an explosion at a fetal modification clinic and there was the next morning."

"There has been a lot of violence around those clinics lately. I'm sure many people are dreaming about clinic explosions."

"The two people who died were in my dream. I've never seen them before in my life. But the next morning, they were on the news."

Dr. Roth's face remains neutral.

"And last night, I dreamt this girl was about to jump off the Golden Gate Bridge and I … I stopped it from happening. She was in the paper this morning. Still alive."

I see the spark again, but he looks down at my file and jots something in his notes.

"Are you going to give me medicine now?"

He continues his scrawling. "How would you feel about a dream journal?"

"A dream journal?"

He sets down his pen, reaches inside one of his desk drawers, and pulls out a composition notebook—the kind we use in Chemistry and Physics. "When you wake up in the morning, I want you to record your dreams. Make sure to date each one."

I look at it skeptically. "And you think this will help?"

"Perhaps."

Pressing my lips together, I take the journal. I don't tell the doctor about what I saw in Mr. Lotsam's class. I'm not ready to divulge that yet. Dreams can be explained. Frightening creature-like humans that lunge at me in my waking hours? Logic cannot handle that. I thank him for listening. He tells me he will see me on Monday. I put the notebook in my backpack and shuffle out of the creepy, drafty facility.

When I open the heavy door, I run into someone.

That someone is Luka.

## CHAPTER FIFTEEN

# UNEXPECTED ENCOUNTERS

"**W**hat are you doing here?"

He steps back, his gorgeous eyes widening like he's seen a ghost. Like he can't believe I'm here. And then for a second, I see the same flash of intrigue in his eye as I did in Dr. Roth's. Of all the people I want to know about my visits to a shrink, Luka is the last. But he is here too. So does that mean ...?

"My dad owns the place," he says quickly.

My heart sinks. His dad? Luka's father owns the Edward Brooks Facility? My mind scrambles for an excuse, for some non-incriminating reason as to why *I* might be here. "I-I needed to-I, um ..." My mind fails. In my exhaustion, I am unable to drum up any sort of believable explanation.

His eyes soften. "It's okay, Tess. I won't tell anyone."

"I'm not crazy," I say.

"I never said you were."

A seed of suspicion germinates inside my chest. So his dad owns the facility. That still doesn't explain why he's here now, in the middle of the morning on a school day. "Why aren't you at school?"

"Why did you leave class so fast?"

I take a slight step backward. "Did you follow me?"

He steps closer. "What upset you in class, Tess?"

*Oh nothing much. Just a white-eyed man thing lunging at me.*

*Didn't you see it?* If not for my growing fear and Luka's dangerous curiosity, I would laugh. "I wasn't feeling well."

"So you ran out?"

"I didn't want to get sick all over Mr. Lotsam's floor."

He cocks his head. "And you came here?"

My cheeks blossom with heat. I don't know how to answer that one.

Frustration carves a deep furrow between his eyebrows. "You seemed really scared of something."

*I was,* I want to say. *I was terrified.*

But I can't tell Luka that. I can't tell him anything.

❧

I stare at the journal Dr. Roth gave me. It's half past midnight. My eyelids droop, but I pace inside my room. Dr. Roth wants me to record my dreams. I'd rather not have any. So I tell myself to stay awake. I realize the insanity of my plan. I will have to sleep eventually. I just don't want it to be tonight. I need a break.

A cool breeze ruffles my drapes and brings the scent of the sea inside my room. From my window, I have a clear view of Luka's house cloaked in darkness. I sit in the alcove and tuck my legs up to my chest, wondering which bedroom is his. Wondering why he showed up at the Edward Brooks Facility when he did. The more I replay the awkward conversation, the more convinced I am that he knows something.

But what?

Moonlight and the sound of breaking waves filters into my bedroom, reminding me of Connecticut. We lived there when I was six. Pete and I used to run up and down the shoreline on Sunday mornings, searching for shells and starfish that would wash up after the high tide. Life was so much simpler back then. When you're six, it's okay to be afraid of the dark. It's okay to have an overactive imagination. I didn't feel different yet. I was just a kid with a younger brother and an ocean at my fingertips.

My eyes grow heavier. I rest my head back against the wall and give into the weight. But then a light floods on and my eyes pop open. It's a sensor down below. It lights up the front of Luka's home and a shadowed figure slinks out the front door. I sit up straighter, all traces of tiredness gone. The figure looks over his shoulder—one way, then the other—then creeps into the dark.

It's Luka. I'm sure of it. Luka Williams is sneaking out of his house.

I don't give myself time to think. I don't give myself time to chicken out. I grab a zip-up hoodie off the floor and tiptoe quickly out of my room while jabbing my arms into the sleeves. I creep down the stairs as quietly and as quickly as possible, shove my feet into a pair of sneakers by the door, press the code on our alarm so it doesn't alert my sleeping parents, and hurry outside. I find Luka at the end of our block and take off after him—keeping far enough away that I can't be spotted, but close enough that I won't lose him.

Three blocks later, I come to my senses. This is not only extremely dangerous, it's insanely stalkerish. For all I know, Luka is sneaking off to Summer's house. And here I am, the freaky weird girl who goes to the Edward Brooks Facility, following him in the dead of night. But curiosity has trumped all reason. It propels me forward.

We come to the end of Forest Grove. Luka punches in the code and the gate squeals open while I hide behind a bush, my out-of-breath lungs screaming into the silence. The harder I try to reign them in, the worse they get. As the gate begins to close, I hurry to make it through, thankful for my silent feet, and fall back into shadow.

A couple blocks later, I see it—the Edward Brooks Facility.

It looms ahead of us in all its haunted-house glory, more intimidating in the dead of night than it's ever been in the afternoon. I take in all five stories—at the spotlights shining up the walls—and I wonder if there are crazy, deranged people inside. Like the ones I saw during the séance. Luka walks up the cement steps and I crouch behind the shrubs at the bottom, feeling like a female version of James Bond. He punches in another code—and I count out the time it will take to fly up the stairs and grab the door before it closes behind him. I won't have long and if I miss it, I'll be out of luck. Unlike Luka, I don't know the code.

I take a deep breath, preparing to bolt. One … two … three!

Luka opens the door and I sprint after him, catching the handle before the door shuts. I slip inside and let it close behind me, hoping he doesn't look back. He doesn't. He walks down the hall, like he knows exactly where he's headed. I tiptoe behind him, my shoulder blades pressed up against the wall, my heart beating like mad, my entire body pulsing with adrenaline. I've walked this path enough times now to know where we're headed.

He stops in front of Dr. Roth's office. I peek around the corner as he removes a key from his pocket and slides it into the lock. There's a loud click and the door squeals open. Luka disappears inside. I creep toward the office and stop in the doorway. Luka stands by Dr. Roth's filing cabinet. And he's reading a file.

Anger rises inside me—fierce and sudden. He has no right looking through files, especially if that file belongs to me. I step inside the room. "What are you doing?"

Luka whirls around, his eyes wide, and we stare at each other for an extended, silent, chest-heaving moment.

"Did you follow me?" he asks.

It's the same question I asked him earlier today. Or actually, yesterday. But he never answered then, so I figure I don't have to answer now. I step closer and my suspicions are right. The folder in his hand has my name typed neatly on the tab. My indignation swells. "That's my file."

He pulls it behind his back, as if hiding it will erase what I already saw.

"What are you doing with *my* folder?" I sound brave, strong, and for a second, I wonder if I'm dreaming. But I scratch my wrist and the spot burns. This is all very real. Luka. Me. Alone in Dr. Roth's dark office in the dead of night. "You have no right to read any of that. It's private."

"I know."

"Then what are you doing?"

He pushes his hand back through his hair. It sticks up in all directions, only instead of looking ridiculous, like I no doubt do, he looks sexy and disheveled. Frustrated, too. "I had to know what you told Dr. Roth today."

"That's none of your business." And how does he know I'm seeing Dr. Roth? I never mentioned his name. Surely there is more than one doctor in a facility this large.

"I know," he says. "But I was … curious."

Curious? *That* was his motivation? It doesn't make sense. None of it. Why would a boy like Luka go to so much trouble over somebody like me? Why would he be so interested? "This is not a normal response to curiosity."

His eyes flash. "No?"

"Breaking into a facility in the middle of the night and stealing private files? No."

He steps toward me. "Is it any worse than spying?"

I refuse to step back. I refuse to be intimidated.

"Were you watching me or something?"

My cheeks burn. "I was sitting at my window when I saw your sensor light come on."

"And you decided to follow me?"

"I'm not the one who's been caught committing a crime."

His jaw tightens.

"I don't understand why you'd go through all this trouble."

He shakes his head and pivots away. When he turns back around, there's a look of such desperation on his face that I'm momentarily flustered. He stares at me as if I have the power to save him. Me, Teresa Eckhart, a girl who can't even save herself.

He steps closer. We're standing as close as we did in my dream, only this isn't the beach and this isn't happening in my sleep. His eyes bore into mine and I can barely breathe, let alone think. "Why did you leave class?" he whispers.

"I already told you."

"The truth?"

My heart beats like a caged animal. I want to tell him, but I hardly know him. Who's to say Luka is trustworthy? Especially since he's here in the middle of the night with my file in his hand?

"You can tell me the truth, Tess. I promise to keep whatever secrets you have."

"How can I know that?"

After a beat, he walks to Dr. Roth's filing cabinet and pulls out another manila folder. He takes my wrist and places the thick file in my upturned hand. "Because I have secrets too."

I stare down at the name typed across the tab—Luka Williams.

"And I think we saw the same thing in Mr. Lotsam's class today."

## CHAPTER SIXTEEN

# REVELATIONS

O ur knuckles brush together and there's a spark of heat, like flint on stone. I slide my hands in the front pockets of my hoodie, unsure what to say. We walk side-by-side up the middle of the street. There's not a car or person in sight, but Luka's posture is erect, almost vigilant, as if he expects someone or something to jump out of the bushes and attack.

All of this has me very ... aware. Of my body. Of his. Of the night air on my skin. The subtle whisper of a breeze. His familiar scent. The sound of our shoes padding against the pavement. Being this close to Luka—listening to the smooth pitch of his voice as he answers my questions—does funny things to my body temperature.

"Do you think it was real?"

"I'm not sure." He squints at the sidewalk. "I always used to think I was crazy. But now ...?"

"Now you don't?"

"Now I don't know what to think. I've never met anyone who sees what I see."

I nibble my lower lip. "I don't get it."

"Me, neither."

"No, I mean, if you really saw what I saw, then why didn't you react? That man came right at us and you just sat there."

"I've trained myself not to react."

"Trained?"

"It's not safe to be crazy."

I think about my grandmother. When speaking with my parents, we never got around to how she died.

"A few months before we moved to Thornsdale," Luka says, "I overheard a conversation between my parents. About that pregnancy screening. I had no idea mine came back abnormal or that my mom had terminated a previous pregnancy. Supposedly, my parents took a big risk when they went against the doctor's orders. My dad had to pay a lot of money to cover things up. Make sure the records were erased from the system."

"Wait a minute. You mean women are *required* to proceed with treatment if the screenings come back with an abnormality? I always thought the decision was ultimately in the hands of the parents."

"Almost everyone chooses to abort. Mothers rarely decide to have the child."

*Abort. Child.* Luka is using language the world at large would not approve of. "But your mom did."

He nods. "At first, they assumed the test was wrong. I was a healthy baby. A healthy toddler. My dad considered suing. But then I started to see things nobody else could see and my parents reconsidered. Maybe the screening wasn't so wrong after all."

The blood inside my veins turns hot. "So what? Because you aren't perfect your parents regret their decision? They think people like us shouldn't be allowed to live?"

He stops, curls his fingers around my wrist, and turns me to face him. Moonlight reflects off his face. "If my parents regret any decision, it's listening to the doctors the first time."

"I—I'm sorry. I didn't mean to imply—"

"It's okay." He lets go of my wrist and we stand in the thick of an awkward silence. I wish more than anything I knew how to fill it.

Luka puts his hands in his back pockets. "Have you ever asked your mom about her pregnancy screening?"

"I've never thought to." But if my screening came back abnormal, I can't imagine my mom going against the doctor's advice. My parents are pretty by-the-book.

Luka glances over my shoulder, toward one of the manicured lawns within Forest Grove, then jerks his head for us to keep walking. "After I overheard that conversation, I knew it didn't matter if the things I saw were real or not. I had to find a way to hide it. It took a while before I could tell the difference between what everyone could see and what only I could see. Sometimes it's obvious—like at the pep rally and in class. Sometimes it isn't so clear. You have to look for tells."

"Tells?"

"Little things that tell you what you're seeing isn't ..." The furrow in his brow deepens. "Human."

"Like eyes that are all white?"

Luka gives me a slow, singular nod. "Once I was able to differentiate, I trained myself to ignore things."

The memory of what happened in Mr. Lotsam's class makes my shoulders deflate. I'm pretty sure I'll never be strong enough to ignore something like that.

"The summer before sophomore year, I told Dr. Roth the hallucinations were gone. My parents were relieved. Dr. Roth had his doubts, but his doubts didn't matter. I wasn't showing any signs of abnormality, so he had no choice but to dismiss me."

We walk a few more steps. "Do you trust him—Dr. Roth?"

"Sometimes I felt more like a science experiment than one of his clients, but I think he sincerely wanted to help. And thanks to my very existence, my father's passionate about keeping the government away from patient files. The staff at the facility knows this. Dr. Roth would lose his job in a heartbeat if he shared your case with anyone."

Maybe this should make me feel better, but honestly, all this talk about pregnancy screenings and governmental control and mental abnormalities sits like a dead weight on my chest. And really, how secure can the place be if a seventeen-year-old boy can break in?

Crickets chirp. The temperature is perfect. The night is beautiful, with stars and stars and stars freckling the black sky. Never in a million years would I envision me taking a midnight stroll with Luka Williams. But despite the perfection of the scene and the perfection of this boy, I can't shake the feeling that the world is about to come crashing down.

"This is going to sound crazy." He shakes his head. "Or maybe not, considering. But the reason I came to the facility yesterday is because of a dream I had last night."

I stop.

So does he. "You were in it. We were on the beach. And you told me you were going to the—"

"Edward Brooks Facility."

His eyebrows draw closer together.

"I had the same dream." I let out my breath. Run my hands back through my hair. "How is any of this possible?"

Clouds sweep in front of the moon and night darkens his face. I don't know why, but I have the distinct feeling that Luka is holding something back. Like he's not telling me the whole truth and nothing but the truth. He looks around again, as if he suspects we're being followed, then continues walking.

I follow after him. "What do you think it is—the things we see?"

"I have a couple theories."

"Like?"

"Do you believe in God?"

I dip my chin. "Do you?"

He shoots me a sideways smile. "I asked you first."

I twist my mouth to the side, forcing myself to consider the question. I don't want to be flippant, even if science and the government would scoff. Do I believe in God? I know how my dad would answer—ever the logical-minded atheist, a man who believes miracles are never truly miracles. Then there's my mom's sister, Vanessa, who despite everything, believes in spirits and reincarnation. There's those people on street corners, declaring the end times. And then there's the flash of light in that gym auditorium and a myriad of other unexplainable things I've seen since as far back as my earliest memories. "Honestly?"

"Always."

"I don't know."

We keep walking. I wait for him to elaborate, but we're getting closer to our houses. His isn't more than thirty yards away.

"Why—do you think God has something to do with this?" I ask.

"When I was a little kid, we went to church."

My eyebrows shoot up my forehead. I've never met anybody who's gone to a real church. Leela's the first person I've met that admits to having a religious background, and even they don't go. It seems so ... taboo. "Really?"

"My grandparents didn't approve. They thought my dad was putting us in unnecessary danger, but my parents were actually pretty devout for a while there. Sometimes, the pastor would talk about a spiritual realm."

"A spiritual realm? You mean like angels and demons and stuff?"

"I know it sounds weird, but it's better than my other theory."

"Which is?"

Luka looks at me, an entire sky worth of stars reflected in the depth of his eyes. "The doctors are right. We're both crazy."

## CHAPTER SEVENTEEN

# ANGELS

The next morning, I spend a good fifteen minutes staring at my dream journal, contemplating last night, unsure if I should record the events. Did it really happen—me and Luka and the Edward Brooks Facility? Or was it a really long, vivid, drawn-out hallucination? I decide to leave the pages blank and deflect Mom's questions about the strange brightness in my eyes.

I can't decide if the truth—that I snuck out of the house in the middle of the night and broke into a private facility with the boy next door—would freak her out or not. Most mothers, yes. Absolutely. Mine? For all I know, she could be relieved that I'm making friends. If that's what Luka is.

On the drive to school, I'm lost in a whirlwind of questions. If last night was indeed real, then how am I supposed to act in front of Luka today? Will he want to sit next to me in class? Will he want to talk about our shared dream again? Will he tell me more about this angel-demon theory of his?

As soon as I step inside the school building, Pete takes off toward his locker and Leela gives me a half-frantic, half-excited wave from the drinking fountain, races over and pulls me off to the side, away from the throng of students. "What happened yesterday? You just got up and left class and then Luka asked to go the nurse and didn't return until halfway through Ceramics."

As much as I want to confide in Leela, as much as I'm dying to tell her about Luka following me yesterday morning and then me following him last night and this bizarre connection we share, I can't. There is too much I still don't understand myself. So even though I'm a terrible actress, I do my best impersonation of dumb. "He left class too?"

"Yes! Right after you bolted. The whole class stared after you and then Luka raised his hand and told the teacher he wasn't feeling very well and would like to go to the nurse. Usually that never works on Mr. Lotsam. He doesn't let anybody out of class unless they're bleeding from the head or have a severed limb. But Luka's never asked to visit the nurse before and he looked so pale that Mr. Lotsam let him leave and then he spent the rest of the period trying to reign everybody in."

The bell rings—our five minute warning. With our shoulders together, we walk out of the locker bay. Leela, with her thumbs looped beneath the straps of her backpack and me with a note from my mom clutched in my hand. Given how yesterday morning started, she one hundred percent believed me when I told her I left school in the middle of first period because I was about to be sick. "He came back to Ceramics, though?"

"Yeah, but he seemed distracted. At lunch too. Rumors are buzzing. First he asks you to be his partner in history class— which you totally owe me a story about, by the way. And then you both disappear yesterday morning." Leela opens the door leading into the stairwell. I slip through and the two of us walk up the stairs while others pass us by. "People are saying he never went to the nurse. Jennalee's brother is a senior and was driving in late after a dentist appointment and he said he saw

Luka peeling out of the parking lot in his car."

I keep my face as blank as possible. "That's weird."

"So what happened to you?"

I hold up my mother's note. "I really was sick. My mom didn't even want me to go to school in the first place."

Leela plucks it from my hand and scans the short paragraph, her expression sagging with each successive word. "You didn't see Luka?"

I press my lips together and shake my head, a twinge of guilt stabbing my stomach. I hate lying to anyone, but especially Leela, my good friend—the girl who welcomed me into Thornsdale with opened arms.

Her posture droops. "Rumors are always more interesting than the truth, aren't they?"

If she only knew.

I'm quite positive the truth couldn't get more outrageous. Me and Luka at the Edward Brooks Facility at two in the morning? Me and Luka seeing things nobody else can see? Visiting each other in a dream? I'm still not sure how that worked. Still not entirely sure that in my desperation to not be crazy, I didn't make the whole thing up.

Mr. Lotsam's classroom comes into view and my insides squeeze tight with a strange mixture of misery and anticipation. I don't want to record last night in my dream journal, but I can't fight the sinking sensation that I will be. That last night was truly a deranged figment of my imagination. I've never been more uncertain, or hopeful.

When I step into the classroom, Luka is already there. Summer sits on the table in front of him, her feet on the chair to his left, successfully gathering his attention as she laughs and talks. The seat to his right is taken by Jared. Disappointment crashes through me. Not that I'd be brave enough to sit by him if that were an option. Still, a small piece of me hoped he might save me a seat. I find myself staring at Summer's cleavage. The view is no accident. She has flirting down to an art form and Jared is practically drooling. My shoulders droop to match Leela's as I follow her toward two open chairs, unsure if I want Luka to look at me in light of the perfect, creature in front of him.

He doesn't.

Not when the bell rings and not through the entire first period, even though I can do nothing but look at him. Summer catches me at one point and gives me a disgusted look that seems to say *in your dreams, honey.* By the time the bell rings, my heart hurts, I have no idea what we discussed in Current Events, and I'm convinced Summer's right. Only in my dreams do Luka and I have anything in common.

It's hard—as I walk with Leela to Ceramics—not to despair. I don't have any proof that last night was real. This morning, my hoodie was in the same place I left it after dinner. Nothing was out of place, not even the unlaced running shoes I supposedly slipped on to follow Luka in the dead of night. The one person who could provide the proof I want doesn't even acknowledge me. He looks completely unfazed and well-rested. Surely he can't be that good of an actor.

"Hey, you okay?" Leela finally asks, as we shuffle inside the dusty basement classroom.

"Still feeling a little off, I guess." I'm suddenly very grateful I didn't tell Leela anything. What a freak I am, believing a boy like Luka Williams would go through the trouble of sneaking out at night, breaking into a facility, all to read *my* file.

I hang my bag over the back of a chair. The teacher calls us over to the pottery wheel for a demonstration and I join the rest of the class. Someone moves to stand slightly behind me, a smidge to the left—unusually close. I glance over my shoulder and all my muscles tense. Because it's Luka. He's not looking at me. He doesn't even seem to notice me. But he's there, so close that if I were to lean back on my heels our bodies would touch. My scalp tingles at his nearness. I hold my breath and cross my arms and pin my eyes on the spinning wheel, even though the teacher's instructions are a muffle of indecipherable sound. My heart thumps in my ears, my throat, my wrists. It's like I have a hundred hearts placed throughout my body.

All of a sudden, the heat of Luka's closeness combusts into something infinitely hotter. So much so that for a fraction of a second, I think the kiln has exploded. I jerk my head around, toward the corner of the room, and see something—a ball of brightness. Luminous and terrifying and beautiful. I am about to stumble back, but Luka's fingers wrap around my forearm and hold me in place.

I'm frozen. I can't even look over my shoulder to see Luka's face. So I stand there, panic swelling, as the rest of the class stares with glazed, bored eyes at the teacher and the pottery wheel, unaware of this very not-normal thing hovering in the corner of the classroom. But Luka sees it. He must, otherwise why is he holding my arm, anchoring me in place? My knees shake. As much as I want to, I can't look away from the light. It's so bright that it's impossible to look away.

The ball of light moves out of the corner, toward me. I am terrified, like yesterday. Only instead of feeling threatened, I am enraptured. In awe. It takes everything in me not to fall to my knees.

Luka's grip tightens and he shifts his body so he stands in

front of me, like a shield, only I don't feel in need of protecting. Not from this. The light hovers in front of both of us, its warmth like the sun. My heart crashes against my sternum. I'm positive it will burst straight through the bone. But as quickly as the light appeared, it vanishes. And I'm left blinking and dazed.

My chest rises and falls as I look one way, then the other. Leela covers her mouth with a yawn. Jennalee picks at her nail mindlessly. A few students look genuinely interested in the hypnotic way our teacher's hands mold the spinning clay on the wheel. Luka lets go of my arm, but the heat of his touch remains. A million questions spin in my mind. They chase each other in circles, like a frantic dog after its tail. Our teacher finishes his demonstration and the class disperses. Without acknowledging me or the bizarre thing that happened, Luka claims one of the pottery wheels.

Dumbstruck, I follow Leela to our table. She talks as I poke at the hunk of clay in front of me and sneak covert glances at Luka. He is a master at the wheel. Just as good, if not better than the teacher. About halfway through class, Leela waves her hand in front of my face.

"Earth to Tess?"

My eyelids flutter.

She glances at Luka, then at the hunk of clay I have decimated in front of me. I don't even know what I'm trying to make. "You should probably be a little more subtle," she mumbles from the corner of her mouth.

"Huh?"

"About the staring." Leela's almost finished with her project—a ceramic lantern with lopsided walls. "I know Summer can seem nice at times, but she's really possessive when it comes to him. With all those rumors flying around about yesterday ... let's just say you don't want to get on her bad side."

I bite the inside of my cheek and will Luka to look at me. *Come on, give me something. Please. I'm freaking out over here.*

Nothing.

His eyes stay glued to the clay in front of him.

I scoot back from the table. "I think I'll go get a drink."

"Did you hear anything I said?" Leela calls after me.

"Yeah. Promise. I just need a drink."

I slip out of the classroom, slightly terrified the bright thing will reappear while I'm all alone. Its warmth remains like an invisible residue coating my skin, but the hallway is empty. Nothing but quiet and chlorine. I shuffle toward the restrooms and take a long drink from the fountain. The cool water does nothing to soothe my frantic thoughts. I take another drink and the sound of a closing door jars the quiet. I stand straight and whirl around. Jumpy.

Luka walks toward me, closing the gap between us with long, sure strides. I let out my breath and wipe away the wetness from my bottom lip. He stops in front of me, a divot creasing the space between his dark eyebrows. "Are you okay?"

I don't know. Am I? The warmth is still there, on the outside, like a cloak. But inside, my bones are cold.

"Tess, look at me."

I do what he says. It does nothing to de-frazzle my nerves.

"Are you okay?"

Caution keeps me silent. Because what if I imagined it all again? What if Luka didn't really see what I saw? What if he simply thought I was having some sort of panic attack and so he grabbed my arm in an effort to calm down the crazy girl who ran into him on the way out of the Edward Brooke's

Facility yesterday morning?

His divot deepens. "Tess?"

"Are—are you okay?" Great, now I'm turning into Dr. Roth. Answering questions with questions.

"I'm not sure. I've never ..." He shakes his head and curls his hand around the back of his neck.

"Never what?"

"I don't understand what's going on."

"What do you mean?"

"That thing." He jerks his hand toward our classroom. "It was almost as if it was trying to interact with you."

*That thing.* So he saw it. He really saw it. All my despair and fear and questions evaporate. I want to grab a hold of those two words and hug them close. "You saw it."

"Of course I saw it."

"What do you think it was?"

"I'm not sure."

"If you had to guess?"

"An angel."

A laugh bubbles up my throat and tumbles into the air. It sounds panicked. Slightly hysterical. "An angel? In our ceramics class?"

"Do you have a better explanation?"

I think about the bright light in the gym my first day of school. And other instances, too. Ones that can't be explained by science or logic, no matter how adamant my father is that the world is not supernatural. "If your theory is right, then that means everyone else is wrong."

A student walks toward us. Luka takes my elbow and pulls me off to the side, then scratches the back of his head until the kid passes. When he does, he leans in and whispers, "Just because a lot of people believe something doesn't make it true."

Swallowing, I look away from his eyes, glance at his lips and settle on his nose. Safer territory. There is nothing sexy about a nose. Scratch that. There's nothing *distractingly* sexy about a nose. "Okay, so let's say it was an angel. Why couldn't anybody else see it? Why was it even there in the first place?"

A muscle ticks in his jaw—in, out, in, out, like a heartbeat. "I don't know," he finally says.

"This is crazy."

"I know."

"Up until twenty minutes ago, I didn't even think last night happened. I thought it was a dream."

Luka quirks his eyebrow.

I scratch my wrist. "For all I know, right now is too."

"You must have very realistic dreams."

"In first period, you acted like nothing happened. You ..." I trail off, unwilling to admit how much his dismissive attitude hurt.

"I'm a good actor, remember? I've been doing it for years and I didn't want to draw attention to us." He stands so close, I can see specks of pine-needle green in his eyes and smell the cool mint in his breath. "I'm real, Tess. This isn't a dream."

"Dream Luka would probably say the same thing."

He takes my hand and puts it against his chest.

I might hyperventilate.

"You can feel my heartbeat. Would that happen in a dream?"

"I—I don't know."

Luka drops my wrist. "I think we should meet up after school. Get a head start on our history project."

The sudden departure from heartbeats and angels to school

projects spins me in a circle. "O-okay."

He pushes off from the wall. "My house or yours?"

"Yours." I blurt the word so fast that Luka cocks his head. I envision my mother and cookies and an embarrassing grand tour. I tuck a strand of hair behind my ear. "My brother's into angry music. We'd have a hard time getting anything done."

He smiles a crooked smile. "My house it is, then."

## Chapter Eighteen

# Anticipation

Trigonometry and Physics are painful. All I want is to fast-forward the day. I have so many questions for Luka. So many things I could tell him. And then there's the memory in my palm—of his heartbeat and the warmth of his chest. All of it pings around inside my brain, making concentration impossible. Still, I force myself to take notes, because the last thing I need is plummeting grades.

By the time lunch rolls around, I am a fidgeting mess. Leela and I find a table with our trays and in my search for Luka, my attention snags on Pete. He's not sitting alone today, like he has over the past several weeks. He's sitting with two others—fork-tongued Jess and barking Wren. Not exactly a happy crowd.

Leela slides into a seat, her eyes glued to the same table. "Why is your brother sitting with them?"

"I have no idea."

My brother looks darker, almost gothic in his black shirt and jeans. Discomfort squirms in my stomach, but doesn't stick around for long. Not when I spot Luka across the cafeteria. Summer sits close to him, jabbering in his ear. As if sensing my stare, he looks up. Our eyes lock and in the span of our connected gaze, a sharp pain stabs my head. Like a lightning bolt splintering through my brain. Wincing, I press my fingers against my temples and look down at my tray.

Ouch.

When I look back up, he's still staring, his head cocked, a funny look in his eyes.

I spend Study Hall at the library, Googling crazy things like spiritual realm and angels and demons and evil spirits and good spirits and ghosts and Ouija boards and prophetic dreams—which apparently, have happened to various people throughout history. When I'm finished, I delete my search history, head to Honors English, and listen to the class engage in a heated debate over whether or not Fitzgerald attacks conventional ideas about masculinity in *The Great Gatsby*. Even though it's one of my favorite books, I cannot engage.

As soon as the bell rings, I speed walk to History. I find a seat toward the back and make an awkward, self-conscious attempt to save the spot beside me by placing my backpack on the chair. A girl takes the seat to my left and Beamer asks if he can sit where my bag is. I'm not really sure Beamer is his real name, but it's what everybody calls him. He has blonde highlights and wears skinny jeans that sag halfway down his butt and expensive-looking V-neck sweaters. He floats somewhere between the jock crowd and the hipster-crowd.

I'm too chicken to tell him no. So he sits beside me and fills the space between us with idle chatter while I give him the occasional nod or grunt, my attention fixed upon the door. When Luka enters, his attention flickers to me, then to Summer, who wiggles her fingers at him from across the room. Seriously, how does someone turn a wave into something seductive? Letting out a long, resigned breath, I fold my arms over my backpack and give Beamer the courtesy of some eye contact, but he stops talking.

I follow the direction of Beamer's stare. Luka stands behind me.

"Hey Beamer, do you mind if I sit there?"

"There's plenty of empty seats, bro."

"I know, but Tess is my partner. I think we should sit together."

The entire class stares.

So much for remaining inconspicuous.

Beamer looks from me to Luka, hesitates a few agonizing seconds, then stands up and moves a few seats down. Luka slides into the seat beside me and I'm not entirely sure, but I think he scoots his chair closer. I put my elbow on the table and Luka puts his elbow on the table too—so close our skin almost touches. I tell myself this is a coincidence, that Luka doesn't honestly care about being close to me, he's only happy that he's not crazy. Still, I do not move my elbow. I keep it in place.

Luka gets out his notebook to take notes—something I've never seen him do before—and in the process, his forearm touches mine. I don't move. I don't reach for my pencil. I sit like a statue, unwilling to break the contact of his warm skin against my own.

Mr. Lotsam explains that we won't have much partner time in class. The majority of our project will need to be completed outside of school—as homework. I bite the inside of my cheek and stare straight ahead, while Mr. Lotsam writes the word *Holocaust* on the board.

"I want to hear what you know about it." He focuses his attention on Luka, no doubt thinking about the comparison he made in Current Events a couple days ago, about fetal modification being a modern-day Holocaust. But Luka doesn't raise his hand. He keeps his arm right where it is, touching mine. For the remainder of the period.

When the bell rings, he leans close and whispers, "See you soon." His breath tickles my ear and before I can respond, he slips out of class. Across the room, Summer scowls. I can't bring myself to care. Or heed Leela's warning.

"What's your deal?" Pete stares at my thumb, which taps the steering wheel.

"Nothing."

"You're speeding." Pete eyes the speedometer. "You never speed."

"I'm eager to get home."

"Why?"

"I'm ... meeting someone."

Pete shakes his head disgustedly. "Is it that Williams kid?"

"How do you know?"

"I overheard some seniors talking in gym class."

I turn off the winding road onto Linden Avenue, which brings us to the gates leading into Forest Grove.

"I don't like that kid."

I scrunch my nose. "Why not?"

"He's full of himself."

Full of himself? Matt Chesterson is full of himself. Luka, no way. Those are about the last words I would use to describe Luka. "Pete, you don't even know him."

He slouches in his seat as the iron gates slowly open. "It's a feeling."

"Well, I have a *feeling* about the kids you're hanging out with too."

I drive into Forest Grove, my mouth suddenly dry. Luka's

car is parked in the driveway. He is home. Waiting. For *me*.

"Since when do you hang out with the popular kids?" Pete asks, unbuckling his seat belt.

I pull into our driveway. I have no idea how to respond. I don't even care to. For once in his life, Pete is being the pestilent younger brother, a role he has never played. A piece of my brain knows I should ask him what's going on—the change in clothes and the loner attitude and the awful music. But I'm too anxious to get to Luka. "Since when do you have a problem with popular kids?"

Pete shrugs.

I roll my eyes, open the car door, hurry through the cool fog, and step inside our house. Mom is there, as always. I can't think of a time she hasn't been. Ever eager to ask us about our day, about our friends and classes and how we are doing. Usually it isn't a big deal. Usually I don't have much to report, but today is different. Not only do I have something to report, I really don't want to report it to her.

Pete slinks in behind me and lets Mom kiss his cheek. "How was your day, sweetie?"

"Not nearly as interesting as Tess's," he says.

I shoot him daggers.

Mom gives me an interested, sideways look. "Oh?"

"She has a boyfriend."

"He is not my boyfriend."

Despite my denial, Mom's eyes go bright. Pete heads up the stairs, leaving me alone with the nosy parent. "Who's he talking about?"

"It's nothing. I'm going next door to work on a school project."

"Next door? To the Williams' house?"

I kick my shoes off into the closet. "You know them?"

"We met a few weeks ago. Mrs. Williams came over to welcome us to the neighborhood. Are you really doing a project with their son?"

"Yeah."

"Wow." Mom follows me up the stairs. "He's a hottie."

"Mom!"

"What? Isn't that the lingo you kids use these days?"

My cheeks grow warm. "Please never use that word again."

She follows me into my room. "So tell me about this project you're working on."

"We have to research genocides throughout history and give a presentation on it."

"Cheery."

I stand in front of my full-length mirror and run my hands down the front of my sweatshirt, wondering what it would be like to be sexy like Summer or pretty like Bobbi or even cute like Jennalee. I consider putting on eyeliner or eye shadow or mascara. Anything that might make me less average. But what if Luka notices? What if it looks like I'm trying too hard?

"You look beautiful, honey."

I dip my chin at Mom's reflection in the mirror. "You have to say that."

"Yes, but I really mean it." She puts her hands on my shoulders and squeezes. "Have fun at Luka's."

I take a deep, rattling breath and try to return her smile.

## CHAPTER NINETEEN

# CONFESSIONS

The short walk over to Luka's doesn't give me enough time to gather my courage. I find myself wishing he lived on the other side of the country instead of next door. In all my seventeen years, I've never worked alone with a boy before. At the library in groups, sure. But never one-on-one.

I hike the strap of my backpack over my shoulder and step onto his front stoop, inhaling deeply through my nostrils. I can do this. I can work on a history project with Luka. If the topic is broached, I can talk to him about insane, impossible things—like spiritual beings that aren't supposed to exist. I shake my head, wondering if psychosis would be the better scenario. At least then medicine could solve the problem. But angels and demons that nobody else can see but me and him? There's no solution that I've heard of.

I glance at my house, then back at Luka's door. How long before he regrets asking me to be his partner? How long before he realizes the girl with the frozen tongue is an idiot? I lick my bottom lip and stare at the doorbell. Why is it so hard to reach out my finger and push a stupid button?

The door swings open.

I step back and almost stumble off the step behind me.

Luka stands on the threshold, his hand on the door, his head cocked, his eyebrow quirked. "I was starting to wonder if you were ever going to knock."

"You were watching me?"

"Maybe." He opens the door wider—a nonverbal invitation to step inside.

The foyer is large and tall with a hanging chandelier that looks like it came straight out of the nineteenth century. The house is warm and quiet. I look past Luka toward a kitchen that is different from our own.

"Looking for somebody?"

Oh, just an angel. Maybe some evil spirits. Perhaps a parent. I bite the inside of my cheek. This is all so preposterous.

"You rarely say what you're thinking."

I pull my gaze away from the great room and look him in the face.

"I can tell you have a million thoughts racing through your head, but you keep them to yourself." Something like amusement sparkles in the green of his eyes. "You're very mysterious."

Me? Mysterious? I think painfully shy is more accurate.

"My mom does Zumba on Thursdays. She won't be home until dinner. Can I get you anything? Water? Chocolate milk?"

"Chocolate milk?"

"Your drink of choice at lunch."

Heat creeps into my cheeks. "Water's fine."

He disappears into the kitchen and I'm left standing in his tall, empty foyer with dark polished floors and textured, copper-colored wallpaper. My attention follows a wide-set staircase up to the second floor. A family portrait and school pictures of Luka through the years hang on the wall in gold, ornate frames. We don't live in one of those neighborhoods where every house is a slightly different version of every other. We lived in one like that in Illinois for about a year-and-a-half and Mom was perpetually pulling into the wrong driveways. The houses in Forest Grove are all unique and old—mansions from the early twentieth century.

A can cracks open behind me. I swivel around.

"Pretty embarrassing," he says, raising his Mountain Dew toward the portraits.

"My mom does the same thing." Only unlike Luka's flaw-less transition from adorable boy to striking young man, mine are filled with awkward years. The winner being seventh grade, when no girl should ever be photographed. My hideous haircut is forever memorialized in a frame in our hallway. "Mine are more embarrassing though."

"I doubt it." Luka hands me my water. "Want to go up to my room?"

"Um …" Gulp. "Sure."

He leads the way up the stairs, past several open doors, and into his bedroom. It's large and not at all like the typical teenage boy room—at least not at all like Pete's. He has no posters on his walls or dirty clothes on the floor or unidentifiable smells. The room is tidy with warm, brown walls, a large window that overlooks the ocean, a desk with an opened laptop, a dresser with an attached mirror, a queen-sized bed with a navy blue comforter, and an insanely huge bookcase that covers an entire wall. Several pictures are pinned to a bulletin board—not of girls or friends—but a couple of the ocean and one of his parents. There's a water glass on his nightstand, a pair of glasses, and an intimidating book titled *World Dictators: Past and Present*.

"You like to read." It's a nice discovery.

He stands in the doorway looking uncertain, as if he's awaiting my approval. "A little."

I walk over to his nightstand, run my hand over the cover of the thick book, and raise my eyebrows.

He shifts on his feet. "I like history."

I twist the cap off my water.

Luka sets the Mountain Dew on a coaster on his desk, pulls out his computer chair, and sits on it backward. He nods toward his bed. "You can sit down if you want."

Positive he can hear the lame thumping of my heart, I take a sip of water and sit on the very edge, trying hard not to think about the fact that I'm on his bed. The air feels charged, like it does whenever a storm rolls in and lightning is about to strike. I wonder if Luka can feel it too. I twist the cap back on the water bottle and clear my throat. "So where should we start?"

He folds his arms over the backrest of his chair. "I have a confession."

I look up from his hemp bracelet, momentarily dazed by his face. Seriously. It's like staring at a picture of a Calvin Klein model.

"I don't want to work on our history project."

The water bottle crinkles in my hand. I set it beside the glasses on his nightstand, trying to imagine what he might look like in them, then slide my hands beneath my knees. "I did some research during study hall. About your theory."

"Find anything interesting?"

"There are people out there who believe in it—a spiritual realm." The two words sound silly when I speak them out loud. Sillier even than when I read them on the computer screen in the library, paranoid somebody might come up behind me and read my Google search. "But I couldn't find anything about people who are able to see it."

Luka wheels his chair closer. "I keep thinking about what

happened today, in Ceramics. I've never seen anything like that before."

"I thought you said you have."

"I don't mean what we saw. I mean what happened."

My forehead scrunches. "I don't understand."

"It was trying to interact with you. And then yesterday, in Lotsam's class. It was almost like that thing was trying to provoke you. Like it wanted you to react. Every time I replay it in my head, that's what I come up with."

His words settle between us. I'm not sure what to do with them, so I leave them untouched. Perhaps I'll come back to them later. "I have a question."

One corner of his mouth lifts. "Just one?"

"It's about our dream."

"Okay."

"How did that work, do you think?"

He shakes his head. "I wish I knew."

"Has anything like that ever happened to you before?"

He averts his gaze, but in the split second before he does, I see something guarded flicker on his face. He swivels away to take a drink. When he turns back around, his expression is unreadable. "Has it to you?"

I scratch the inside of my wrist, trying to decide if I should tell him or not. Especially since he's not being forthright with me. I can tell he's holding something back. I just wish I knew what. "Remember the clinic bombing?"

"Sure."

"This is going to sound crazy."

"Crazier than angels in Ceramics?"

"Right." I let out a shaky laugh, loosening up a bit. "I dreamt about the bombing the night before. Two people died in my dream. Then the next morning in Current Events, I learned that the bombing actually happened and the two people who died in my dream were on the news, reported as dead."

I pause, waiting for his reaction. He stares at me attentively and waits.

"The next night ..." I shake my head. "This is totally weird."

Luka scoots even closer, so much so that his knees are on either side of mine. "What?"

"When we visited each other in our dream?"

He raises his eyebrows, urging me to continue.

"What happened to me?" I have to know what he saw.

"You sank into the ground. I tried grabbing you, but I wasn't quick enough. Where did you go?"

"All of a sudden, I was on the Golden Gate Bridge. And the freaky man in Lotsam's class? He was taunting this girl, trying to get her to jump. I wrestled him away from her and we fell." I think about the cold words spoken—about me being a fighter—but can't bring myself to say them out loud. I don't even know what they mean.

"You wrestled him?" There's a hint of amusement in the question.

"Is that hard to believe?"

"It's just ... you don't look like the wrestling type."

"Hey, I'm a black belt." And I was strong in the dream. It was only later, when I woke up, that I felt weak and drained.

"Really?"

I lift my chin. "Really."

Luka laughs. "Okay, so what happened next, Karate Kid?"

"I woke up. And that same girl was on the news. She was

about to commit suicide, but the police got to her in time. She didn't die."

Luka's teasing from a second ago has disappeared. His eyes search mine with an intensity that makes my skin break into goose bumps. "Do you think they're real—the dreams? Prophetic or something?"

"I don't know. Maybe."

My shoulders sag. "You've never had dreams like that? Dreams that actually come true?"

He doesn't answer right away. The longer he waits, the more I regret telling him. Maybe he's finally realizing that between the two of us, I am a whole different brand of crazy. "I've had one," he finally says. "It's recurring."

Hope blossoms in my chest. "Like mine?"

"Not exactly." He wipes his palms along the thighs of his jeans. "Your first day of school wasn't the first time I've seen you."

"You saw me when we were moving in or something?"

"No."

Confusion settles in my brow.

He takes a deep breath. Like *here goes nothing.* "I've dreamt about you."

"Yeah, that night—"

He shakes his head. "Before that night."

"Before?"

"For as long as I can remember. I've dreamt about this girl with dark hair and fair skin and big, navy blue eyes and freckles across her nose."

The hair on the back of my arms stands on end.

"And then you showed up in class and … it was you. You're *her.*"

"What happens in the dream?" My voice escapes in a whisper.

"That man in Lotsam's class? There's a whole army of them. They are strong, impenetrable. But there's another army too. An army of these bright beings, charging ahead, and you're leading them."

"Me?"

He nods. "You're fearless. Brave. But you're in danger, too. So out in the open and the soldiers of the other army are targeting you. In the dream, I'm fighting them. Trying to get to you. Screaming for you to run. It's like your life is the most important thing. Like if you die, then so will everything else."

The weight of Luka's words sits between us.

He leans forward, his chest against the back of the chair, so close my knees touch his seat. "I've spent my life looking for you. Everywhere. At stores, restaurants, malls, in the newspaper, on TV shows. When you showed up in Current Events, I couldn't believe my eyes. I still can't."

I can't seem to get a handle on my breathing. It's too fast, too loud.

"When we met on the beach in our dream, it was the first time your life wasn't in danger. But then you disappeared and I thought ..."

"You thought something bad happened."

"Yeah."

My attention drops to my feet. I wish I knew what was going on. I wish I understood this connection between me and Luka. I wish I could go to the library and check out a book titled *Seeing the Spiritual Realm, Prophetic Dreams, and Dream Sharing: All You Need to Know.* Somehow, I don't think that book exists.

"Tess?" Luka's voice is husky, close.

I look into his eyes.

"I'm glad you're here, in Thornsdale."

"Me too." Despite all the unanswered questions, having someone to share the craziness with makes the burden so much lighter.

There's a knock on the door.

Luka scoots away, leaving my legs cold and numb.

"Luka?" A slender woman with dark, shiny hair pulled into a ponytail leans inside Luka's bedroom. She and Luka share the same straight nose, the same full lips, the same olive colored skin. Only this woman has dark, suspicious eyes. Not Luka's green warm ones. She's dressed in yoga pants and a tank top. "Who's this?"

"Tess Ekhart. She moved in next door. Tess, this is my mom."

Her smile is tight, pinched. "Nice to meet you."

"You too."

Mrs. Williams turns toward Luka. "We're going to have dinner in thirty minutes. You should probably wrap things up. And leave your door open, please. You know that's the rule when girls are over."

*Girls.* I blush at the implication. How many girls has Luka had over?

When she leaves, a tinge of pink stains Luka's cheeks.

I'm suddenly claustrophobic. I need to get away from this boy who makes thinking impossible. After everything he told me, I need to go on a hike. Gather my thoughts. Glancing at his bedside clock, I stand, pull my backpack over my shoulders, and head to his door. "I should get going."

Luka comes out of his chair. "Tess."

I stop. Turn around.

"We should try to do it again."

"What?"

"The dream thing." He shoves his hands in the back of his pockets. "If we think about each other before we fall asleep ..."

"You think that's how it works?" The warmth in my face intensifies. If that's so, then he'll know I was thinking about him. But it also means he was thinking about me, too.

"It's worth a try."

"O-okay. Sure." Before he can offer to walk me to my house, I hurry out of his room, down the stairs, and out the front door.

## CHAPTER TWENTY

# DISCOVERY

With hands folded behind my head, I stare at my ceiling, impossibly awake. As if I'd just awoken from ten hours of sleep and chased an entire pot of coffee with a Red Bull, when in reality, it's past midnight and sleep over the past few nights has been fitful. My after-dinner hike did little to clear my head. I kick off my covers and walk into the bathroom. Even though I don't have a headache or a cold, I pop two Tylenol PMs into my mouth, take a swig from the faucet, and tuck myself back into bed.

As I wait for the medicine to take effect, my mind spins with all that has happened since the séance back in Jude. The terrifying voices and the disturbing visions. My parents' whispered words in the hospital. Moving here to Thornsdale with the Edward Brooks facility down the street and Luka Williams next door. I think about Dr. Roth. I think about Luka's mom failing both her pregnancy screenings. According to the government, he shouldn't exist. His mother should have been "cured" seventeen years ago. But she wasn't and now he's here, my only proof that I'm not crazy—a boy who claims to have had dreams about me before we even knew each other. Dreams about me leading an army.

What would Dr. Roth say to that?

My eyes grow heavy as my mind wanders to my grandmother. A woman who died in a mental hospital. Did she really suffer from psychosis? The last thought I have before I nod off into medicated oblivion is that I wish she were still alive. I wish I could sit across from her and ask her questions ...

I'm standing on the rocky beach in my backyard, a little weak in the legs. A little lightheaded. I blink a few times and he's there—sitting several paces away, arms draped over his knees, staring out at the waves, his perfect profile obscured by a thick fog. A thrill of excitement simmers beneath a film of lethargy that I can't seem to shake. I take a step toward him. The movement must catch his attention, because he turns his head, then quickly stands, wipes the rocky sand from his palms, and closes the short distance between us. "You're here."

I squint through the haze. "How long have you been waiting?"

"A while."

"I had a hard time falling asleep." I cup my forehead with my palm, wishing I could rattle away the fog in the air. It's as if it's seeping into my ears and clouding my brain. "I had to take two Tylenol PMs and then I started thinking about my grandma."

"Your grandma?"

I forgot to tell Luka about my grandmother. I open my mouth to explain, but before any sound escapes, he drifts away. I grab for him, but my hand hits nothing but empty air and I'm no longer on the beach. I'm in a room—white and small and barren, yet somehow, the fog has followed me. A woman lies in bed, her hands and feet bound, her long, white hair wild about her face as she strains and thrashes against the leather restraints.

"Help me." The woman turns her crazy eyes on me, her

voice not a shrill scream, but a rasp that raises the hair off my arms. "Please, help me."

I grab the shackles and pull, but they don't budge. I whirl around, desperate to get help—a doctor or a nurse, somebody with a key who can let this woman go—and come face to face with a man. He has the kind of plain, forgettable features that could make him one of a hundred other men. The only identifying feature is a jagged, white scar that runs the length of his right cheek.

He wears a pleasant, apathetic smile.

"Who are you?" I ask.

He takes a couple steps closer to the woman straining and thrashing in the bed. "That's the wrong question, Little Rabbit."

Little Rabbit? My eyes rove over his apparel—blue scrubs, white coat. He must be a doctor. Which means he must have a key. "You have to let this woman free."

"I'm afraid I can't do that."

"Why not?"

"Sadly, she's no longer my patient and it's important that I follow orders. Just as important as it is for you to be careful. You don't want to end up like her, do you?"

I cast an anxious glance at the thin, desperate woman. "Who is she?"

He steps closer, his head cocked, a smirk on his face. Like I am food and he is playing. "You mean you don't know?"

I look more closely at the woman. The color of her eyes, the slant of her nose, the shape of her chin. It's all terribly familiar. A gasp tumbles past my lips and I shake my head. She is an older, female version of my father.

"Oh, yes."

"But my grandmother is dead."

"Is she really?"

My attention darts back and forth from the woman in the bed to the man with the scar. "Am I like her?"

He runs his fingers along the sheet. "That's up to you."

"What do you mean?"

"You're keeping dangerous company."

"Dangerous company?" My thoughts whir. Whose company could I be keeping that could possibly be dangerous? Surely not Leela, and the only other person I've been hanging out with is ... "You mean Luka?"

"Continue, and your life will become a living hell." A smile cuts through his face. "Consider yourself warned."

The white room falls away and I am somewhere else. A man sits at a desk, slouched over, writing on a notepad in slow, sad strokes, the air so heavy with hopelessness and desolation that it seeps into my pores. He picks up a gun. A *gun*. But guns aren't allowed. It was resting by his note and now it's in his hand and he sticks the barrel into his mouth.

"No!" I make to leap forward. To stop him. But the man with the scar is there, standing beside me, and he holds my arm.

"Be careful, Little Rabbit. People will think you're going mad."

The gun explodes with a loud crack. It ricochets off the walls and rings in my ears and I jolt upright in bed, lungs heaving in the dark, sweat pouring down my back, those final words reverberating through my mind.

*You're going mad ... you're going mad ... you're going mad.*

I flip on my bedside lamp and grab the journal on my nightstand and write until my hand cramps, desperate to capture everything before it slips away. When I finish, the sky outside my window has gone from dark blue to a pale pink. I sit at my desk and jiggle the mouse on my computer and open a website with local news. Taking a deep breath, I poise my fingers over the keys. The tip of my ring finger presses the S, then my pointer finger reaches for the U, my middle the I, the other the C until the word sits in the search box.

*Suicide.*

Taking another deep breath, I hit enter and several news stories pop up. The one at the top is thirty minutes old. *Family Man Commits Suicide in small California town.* I click on the link and devour the story. A man, thirty-seven, unemployed. Married for ten years, with two daughters in elementary school. The police were called late last night when a neighbor heard the sound of a gunshot. His wife and two daughters—both in elementary school—were out of town visiting the mother's family. The police found the man, in his bedroom, dead, along with a note of farewell. There's a small thumbnail photograph of his face.

It makes me push back from the computer.

*You're going mad … you're going mad … you're going mad …*

I feel it. To the marrow of my bones. I throw on a sweatshirt and slippers and hurry down the stairs, wild and frantic. Mom pokes her head out from the kitchen, her hair rolled in curlers. "Tess?"

But I don't answer. I need air. I need Luka. I need to know what is happening. I'm about to tear open the door and escape into the cool, fresh morning air, but Mom grabs my arm. Her touch reminds me of the man with the scar and that old woman with the white hair and Dad's nose. "What's wrong?"

I whirl around. "Is Grandma alive?"

She doesn't have to answer. The truth expands in the blackness of her pupils.

∽

Cold eggs and overcooked bacon sit in front of me at the kitchen table. Mom—a constant swirl of motion—has not yet changed out of her robe or taken the curlers from her hair. Pete looks from me to Mom to Dad's empty seat while the clock on the wall ticks into the silence. First period has already begun.

I cross my arms, my confusion morphing into anger with each passing tick. I don't understand why this has to be a big family meeting. I don't understand why Mom had to call Dad, who left early this morning for work, or why she won't say a word until he arrives. She should have told me the truth in the foyer. It's more than obvious grandma is still alive. Pleading the fifth only confirms it.

A car door slams shut outside and the front door opens. Mom stops her frantic movements at the sink and walks out of the kitchen. I want to follow her, make sure they aren't coming up with more lies out in secret. But I know they will only send me away. So I curl my fingers beneath the bottom of the seat and ignore Pete, who only has me to stare at now.

Dad comes in first, loosening his tie. Mom follows, worrying her bottom lip. He scoots out Mom's chair for her to sit, then takes a seat with a loud sigh. When he meets my gaze, his face is as neutral as Dr. Roth's. "What makes you think your grandmother is alive?"

I raise my chin. "Does it matter?"

Mom and Dad share a look.

"It's obvious she is. If she were dead you would just say so.

Mom wouldn't have called you back from work."

Pete looks at all three of us with narrowed, interested eyes. If he were a rabbit, his ears would be cocked back. The thought reminds me of the man with the scar. Why did he call me Little Rabbit? And what did he mean when he said Luka was dangerous company?

Dad folds his hands over the table. "Your grandmother isn't well."

"Isn't? As in present tense?"

He nods.

Pete sits up straighter in his chair, his mouth open.

I shake my head, confusion completely replaced by a hot anger that courses through my veins. "Why did you lie to us? Why did you say she was dead? Where is she? What's wrong with her?" The questions come out in quick sputters, so close together it's as if they are tripping over each other's heels. I think about the old woman from my dream—her frail, wasted form shackled to that bed. I think about her raspy plea for help and her frantic eyes. "Is she safe? Is she—?"

"Calm down, Tess," Dad says. "She's in a facility."

"A facility?"

"Honey, we weren't lying about her suffering from psychosis." Mom twists and untwists a napkin with nervous fingers. "We weren't."

"Why? Why would you lie about her being dead?"

"We thought it was better this way."

"Better? How is this better? Tell me where she is. I want to go see her." I scoot back my chair, but Dad reaches out and stops me from standing.

"You can't see her, Tess. None of us can."

"Why can't we see her? Where is she? And what do you

mean, 'a facility'?"

Dad slowly releases my arm, his shoulders rising and falling with a resigned breath. "She's in a home for the mentally unstable."

"Where?"

"Oregon."

"For how long?"

"Fifteen years."

"Against her will?" I glare at him, then Mom. Tears pool in her eyes, but I don't care. I never imagined my parents to be cruel or uncaring. Yet my father has had his own mother locked up for fifteen years?

"She was delusional, Tess. She had very incoherent thoughts. Nothing she said made sense. She was admitted to a hospital for almost a year. The doctors diagnosed her with paranoid schizophrenia. Your mother and I would visit. She seemed to be improving. But then ..." Dad folds his hands again and shakes his head.

"Then what?"

"Then she escaped. I was away at work and she showed up at our home while your mother was at the doctor for Pete's two week checkup. A babysitter was with you. Your grandmother showed up and tried to take you. Thankfully, your mom got home before she could. She had you in her arms and she was babbling like a madwoman. We had to call the authorities. Your mother was terrified she was going to hurt you."

Dad's story hits me like a glass full of ice water to the face. I sit there, in shock, blinking dumbly. My grandmother tried to kidnap me? Why? None of it makes any sense. "I don't get it. Why did she want me? What did she say?"

"It doesn't matter. She had crazy thoughts in her head. She

was unwell. By the time the police arrived, she didn't even know where she was."

I look at my brother, who stares at me in the same way he stared at me back in Jude, after the séance—a glimmer of intrigue in his dark eyes.

"After that, she was admitted into an institute for the mentally insane. We visited a few times, but our visits made the psychosis worse. Every time we saw her, she would ..." Dad's voice trails off. He stares at some spot over my shoulder, his expression far away.

I lean over the table. "She would what?"

"It doesn't matter. She was completely lost by then. The doctors discouraged our visits. When she knew we were coming, she would refuse her medication and her condition would accelerate. So we followed the doctor's orders and stopped coming. We never told you or Pete about this because it wasn't your burden to bear. And anyway, it doesn't matter. There's nothing any of us can do."

"Doesn't matter?" I push back my chair. "You didn't see her the way I saw her. She was locked up like a prisoner. She was terrified."

Mom's face pales. "See her? Honey, what are you talking about?"

"She was in my dream last night." Mom and Dad exchange worried, skeptical glances. Pete's mouth gapes even wider. "You don't understand. She was locked up. She was trying to get out, but she couldn't."

The doubt on their faces makes me want to scream. It's like I'm slipping away, dropping off into some unknown oblivion, and they are just sitting there watching it happen.

"You don't believe me."

Mom reaches across the table and puts her cold hand over mine. I want to jerk away from her touch. "Sweetheart, it was a dream."

"No, it wasn't." The words escape through clenched teeth. "It was real."

Dad rubs his jaw. "Tess …"

"I'm not crazy."

"We don't think you are." Mom looks at Dad, then at me. "We're just worried. And confused. We thought things were going well for you this past month. You've looked so happy. Leela's a great friend. And Dr. Roth seemed to be helping."

"It was. He was. It was good. But then …" A headache forms in my temple. I close my eyes and dig my fingers into my hair. "I don't know."

"We'll talk to Dr. Roth. I'm sure there's some medicine you can take."

"Medicine?" The word escapes like a pathetic squeak.

"If there's something that can help you with these nightmares, then there's no shame in taking it, sweetheart."

My shoulders sag. Maybe Mom's right. Maybe medicine is the only way I'll ever get a shot at being normal. It's obvious that something is not right in my head.

"This is a hurdle, kiddo." Dad cups his large hand around the back of my neck and gives it a reassuring squeeze. "Not an impenetrable wall. We'll get over this. You're not going to become my mother. We won't let you."

"Dr. Roth is the best," Mom says. "He'll know how to handle this."

Dad nods. "We don't want you to worry."

He says it like the choice is simple. Like all I have to do is put it out of my mind and go about my day. Only they don't know. They didn't see my grandmother and they didn't see that man sticking a gun in his mouth. They don't know that what happened in my dream happened in real life. They don't know anything.

## CHAPTER TWENTY-ONE

# A RUSE

I walk to Ceramics with a late slip in hand. When I step inside, there isn't the usual chattering or wandering energy as students work on various projects. Instead, everyone sits at tables, heads down, pencils scratching against paper. There are a sum total of two tests in Ceramics and I forgot that today happens to be one of them.

Our teacher stands behind his desk, so absorbed in the glazing of his latest masterpiece that he doesn't notice me in the doorway. But Luka does. He stares at me with his wiry muscles coiled, as if ready to spring like a lion across the length of the room. His green eyes burn with questions. Swallowing, I shuffle over to our teacher on wobbly legs and hand him the late pass. Without looking up, he nods at the stack of tests. I take one off the top, looking from the empty seat next to Luka to the empty seat next to Leela. I'm not brave enough to take the former, so I pretend not to notice his intense stare-down and walk over to my friend, who watches me with wide, eager eyes.

Before my backside makes contact with the stool, she leans close and whispers, "I've been going crazy. I called you a million times last night but you didn't answer."

I look over my shoulder, then whisper back, "My phone was on silent."

"You have to tell me everything that happened. You were

in Luka's house! What did you talk about? Were you nervous? What does his room look like?"

Our teacher clears his throat loudly and gives Leela and me a high-browed stare. I give her a helpless shrug, secretly thankful to be caught. I have no idea what to tell her.

"After class." Leela mouths the words, then turns her attention to the test.

My stomach tightens as I jot my name on the top of the paper and try to focus on the questions, but they are a blur of incoherent lines and loops and curves. While I fill in bubbles and write answers that can't be correct, I try to think of something—anything—to tell my friend. But nothing comes. So I stall. By the time both sides are meticulously filled, class is thirty seconds shy of ending. I hand in my test, the bell rings, and when I turn around, Luka stands behind me with my bag.

He puts his hand on the small of my back and ushers me out of class. I manage a quick glance over my shoulder. Leela stands with her mouth open, watching us leave. As soon as we're out in the hallway, he pulls me toward the wall. Students shuffle past, all of them looking at us, some more discreetly than others.

"I waited for you in my driveway all morning, but you never showed." He leans closer, bringing with him the clean, fresh scent that is him. "What happened? Where've you been?"

The chill that's haunted me since that man put a gun in his mouth ripples up my spine. I cross my arms as Leela walks out of class. I try to muster up the energy for a friendly smile. She clutches her books to her chest and hurries past, but not before I catch a glimpse of hurt in her eyes. She thinks I'm intentionally leaving her out.

"Tess, you're killing me."

My attention zips back to the boy in front of me, waiting for an explanation I'm not sure I've found yet. His attractiveness doesn't bring any coherency to my erratic thoughts either. "Last night, in …" I look around, checking for eavesdroppers. We're about to enter into a very strange conversation. "Our dream. What happened to me? Where did I go?"

"I don't know." His voice is low, for my ears only. "One second you were in front of me, the next you weren't. But I could hear things. It sounded like you were struggling, like you were fighting to escape something. And then you weren't in class this morning."

I look into the green depths of Luka's eyes. "I wasn't the one struggling."

"Who was it?"

"My grandmother." I press cold, clammy fingers against my temples. I still can't believe she's alive.

"Your grandmother? Wait a minute, you mentioned her. Right before …"

A group of seniors walks toward us, their pace slowing like cars at the scene of a crash. They obviously don't get it—me and Luka. Their skepticism oozes into the air.

Luka leans even closer, so much so that his breath tickles my neck and tingles my skin. I close my eyes, wishing everything but him and the feel of his nearness would disappear. "We can't talk about this here. I'll find you at lunch."

By the time my eyes open, he is already gone.

$$\infty$$

I step out of line with a tray of my usual—apple, sandwich, chocolate milk—and catch Leela waving from our table. Uncertain as to whether I should join her or not, I wave back.

Then Luka's hand presses firmly against the small of my back. "Follow me," he whispers.

So I do. Because if I don't dispel all the junk expanding inside my head, I will explode. I just wish me not exploding didn't have to hurt Leela. Her face clouds with confusion as I give her a helpless shrug and follow Luka past his friends. Summer and Bobbi and Matt and the others stare at me like I've grown a beard or a third ear. I can feel the entire room's eyes on me as we find a table on the periphery of the cafeteria. Luka pulls out my chair and takes a seat beside me, his back to the student body, which ogles with equal parts curiosity and disbelief.

My attention snags on Pete, who sits at the same table as yesterday, with Wren and Jess, the school freaks. Only instead of sitting in silence, their heads are bent together. Pete's lips move and I have this unexplainable sinking sensation. Pete and I didn't debrief after this morning's impromptu family meeting. Surely he knows that the things we learned are strictly confidential. But when he finishes whatever he's saying, Wren leans back in her chair, a disturbing, enigmatic glow to her cheeks.

A surge of heat rises in my chest. I would like nothing more than to go over there, grab Pete's arm, and yank him away. He doesn't belong with those two. Instead, I swallow the impulse and look down at my tray.

"You okay?" Luka asks.

"Besides the fact that I'm going crazy? Sure."

"You're not going crazy." He folds his arms on the table.

"My grandmother was crazy. It must skip a generation."

Shaking his head, he cracks open his Mountain Dew.

I glance past him, at our classmates. "Everybody is staring."

"Let them," he says, opening my chocolate milk and setting it in front of me. "And while they stare, why don't you tell me about your grandmother?"

"She suffered from psychosis." My voice is lifeless and dull.

"I take it you didn't know this?"

"Not until we moved to Thornsdale. For as long as I can remember, my parents have always told me that she died of a heart attack when Pete and I were really little, but last night I dreamt about her."

"And that means she's not dead?"

I pick at a fray in the knee of my jeans, battling uncertainty. The man in my nightmare warned me against hanging out with Luka. And now here I am, spilling my guts. I don't know who to trust anymore. "Luka, can I trust you?"

He draws back. "Why do you ask that?"

"You didn't answer the question."

"Of course you can trust me." His eyebrows pinch together. "Tess, what's going on?"

"There was a man in my dream last night. He said you were dangerous company."

"Dangerous?" Luka's eyes narrow. "Who was this guy?"

"I don't know. He was with my grandma. I think maybe he was her doctor or something. After I left the beach, I was in this white room and there was this old woman who looked like my dad. She was restrained to this bed, only she was trying to get free." I squint, trying to recall the details. "And the guy was there. I don't really remember what he looked like, except he had a scar on his face. He told me if I wasn't careful, I'd end up like her."

A muscle ticks in Luka's jaw. He looks angry.

"Then all of a sudden I was somewhere else. In a house

with a man."

"The one with the scar?"

"No, somebody else. He was really sad and he had a *gun*."
It was the first time I've ever seen one so up close. People aren't
supposed to own guns. "He stuck it in his mouth and he ..." I
close my eyes, wishing I could blot out the memory. "He
pulled the trigger. That same guy committed suicide last night.
I looked it up on the computer and his picture's the same. He
lived on the other side of town. He had two kids and a wife."

Luka sits very close and very still, his expression unreadable.

"Then this morning, I found out that my grandma has
been alive all this time. My parents have been lying to me all
these years. Supposedly, she tried to kidnap me when I was a
baby and now she's locked up in some mental hospital." A hot
lump expands inside my throat. How did my world turn
upside down so quickly? Is it really possible that last week, I
was a nobody eating lunch with Leela? Now I'm talking about
impossible things with the most sought-after boy in school, an
invisible target on my forehead. I dig my fingers into my hair.
"I know you see what I see, Luka. But how do I know you
aren't another delusion? How do I know I'm not sitting here at
this table, talking to myself?"

"I'm real, Tess. You can touch me if you want." He extends
his hand, palm up.

I stare at the offering, doubtful it will do much to settle my
nerves. Or get rid of the stares. "I bet that's the kind of thing
people suffering from psychosis tell themselves."

Luka pivots so his chair faces mine, reaches under my seat,
and pulls my chair closer. My eyes widen. "You aren't suffering
from psychosis."

I let out a long breath and catch Leela picking at her food, her shoulders devoid of their usual perk. I wish more than anything that I could tell her the truth. I need someone to confide in. "I wish I could tell Leela."

"That's not a good idea."

My insides deflate. Luka is right, of course. "What am I supposed to tell her, then?"

"About what?"

"This." I motion from him to me. "Us. She's going to ask."

Luka chews on his thumbnail, as if considering. I take an unenthusiastic drink of my chocolate milk, trying to think of a believable explanation, but my headache makes thinking impossible. "You could tell her we're dating," he says.

I laugh.

"What?"

"Nobody will believe that."

"Why not?"

"Because ..." My cheeks catch fire. He needs to go look in a mirror. Boys like him do not date girls like me. The student body would have an easier time believing there are angels in Ceramics. "It's not believable."

He opens his mouth, but before he can say whatever it is he was about to say, Matt and Jared plop down at our table. Luka leans back in his seat, away from me while Matt plucks the apple off my tray and takes a bite. "What's up Williams? Too cool to sit with us now?"

Jared motions toward my chips. "You going to eat those?"

"Go ahead," I say.

"Summer glared at you the entire lunch period." Matt takes another bite out of my apple, specks of juice spitting from the flesh as he does. "I thought her head was going to pop off. It wasn't attractive."

"Summer's always attractive," Jared says, opening my bag of chips.

Matt tips his chin at me. "Better watch out, new girl."

"She has a name," Luka says.

I peek at Leela. She dumps her food in the trash and hurries out of the cafeteria, keeping her head down the entire way.

After school, I find Leela in the locker bay. As soon as she sees me, she slams her locker shut and hurries away. I hurry after her. "Leela!"

If she hears me, she doesn't stop.

"Leela," I call again, weaving my way through students, trying to close the gap between us. "Leela, will you wait?" I grab her arm and she spins around, her expression a strange mixture of hurt and hard. I let go. "Hi," I say lamely.

"So you're talking to me now?"

"Of course I'm talking to you."

"You sure that's smart?"

"What do you mean?"

"I mean, now that you're in with the popular crowd, are you sure you want to be seen with somebody like me?"

"I'm not *in* with the popular crowd. And even if I was, that wouldn't change the fact that you're my best friend."

Her face softens a little at the declaration. She bites her lip. "You were sitting with three of the most popular boys in the whole school at lunch today. I think that makes you a part of the crowd."

"I was sitting with Luka. Matt and Jared didn't sit with us until the very end."

Leela crosses her arms and continues her lip nibbling. "I tell you everything, Tess. You even know how I feel about your brother, which is embarrassing. But that's what best friends do. They tell each other everything."

My insides go all perky and warm. So Leela agrees—we are best friends. I've never had one of those before. The urge to confide in her grows, but Luka's warning is fresh. And the memory of his suggested cover-up makes my insides go from warm to hot. Dating Luka? Nobody's going to believe that.

"I feel like you're keeping secrets from me," she says.

"I don't want to."

"Then tell me what's going on. What happened yesterday when you went to his house? And what were you talking about at lunch today? You both looked so ... intense."

I sigh. "You wouldn't believe me if I told you."

"Try me."

"Luka and I—we're sort of ..." Crazy. Nuts. Suffering from psychosis. Sharing the same dreams. Seeing white-eyed demons in pep rallies and angels in ceramics class and somehow, in a crazy universe that makes no sense at all, this makes him interested in me. "Together."

Leela's jaw drops.

Heat mounts in my cheeks. "See."

"Oh no, I totally believe you. He hasn't been able to keep his eyes off you since your first day of school. He watches you like a hawk."

"What? No he doesn't."

"Yes, he does. And I'm not the only one who's noticed either. Why do you think Summer's always scowling at you?"

"Because she's inclined to scowl at people?"

Leela's eyes are bright and wide. Any trace of hurt has evaporated. "I cannot believe this! Luka's never dated anyone.

And now you two are together?" Her expression falters. "Why aren't you more excited about this?"

I hook my thumbs beneath the straps of my backpack. "I am."

She looks highly skeptical.

"No, really. I am. It's just ..." I sigh, wishing I could join Leela in her enthusiasm. Wishing this wasn't a ruse. Wishing I really was the new girl who gained the impossible-to-get attention of a cute, popular boy. "I found out that my grandmother's sick. That's why I was late this morning." This, at least, isn't a lie. My grandmother—wherever she is—is very, very sick. "Luka's helping me process."

"Oh, I'm sorry."

I shrug off the condolence. I don't want to talk about this anymore. Or answer any questions about my grandmother's sickness. I need a subject change. "Hey, why don't we go to that party tomorrow? The Halloween party. You still wanna go?"

"Are you kidding? Of course I want to go!" Leela wags her eyebrows. "Maybe your boyfriend wants to come, too."

I let out a nervous laugh. "He's not really my boyfriend."

"That's what *together* means, doesn't it? Oh my gosh, is he a good kisser?"

"Leela."

A far-off, dreamy look clouds her eyes. "Do you have any idea how lucky you are?" She blinks several times, as if realizing something important, and grips onto my forearm. "Or how much trouble?"

"Trouble?"

"Summer is going to kill you."

Really, Summer is the least of my worries.

## CHAPTER TWENTY-TWO

# PARENTAL CONCERN

I 'm annoyed with Pete on the drive home from school.
Something about his presence beside me in the car and the
sullen way he stares out the window scratches against raw
nerves. I grip the steering wheel, unable to erase the gleeful
look on Wren's face after Pete told her whatever he told her
during lunch. I don't like his choice of friends. I don't like the
way he's been pouting. And I don't like his unfair judgment of
Luka, either.

He must be equally annoyed with me, because the second I
turn into the driveway, he flings open the door and climbs out
before I'm able to shift into park. I turn off the car, step
outside, and pull my backpack over my shoulders, squinting
against a hazy, bright sky. I slam the car door and follow Pete's
fresh trail into the house.

Mom stands in the foyer, staring nervously up the staircase.
Obviously Pete has blown her off too. I can hear his retreat up
the final stair, the slam of his bedroom door, followed by the
loud blast of angry music from his stereo. Seriously, how long
are my parents going to let him get away with this?

Mom turns to me. "Are you okay?"

"I'm fine, Mom. I just need some space." I walk into the
kitchen and grab a Coke, unsure when I'll be able to get over
the fact that Mom and Dad lied straight to my face. In this
very kitchen. I asked them about grandma that first Saturday

and my dad looked me in the eyes and told me she was dead. If they could lie about that, how do I know they aren't lying about other stuff too?

Mom follows me. "I'm worried about you, sweetheart."

"If I were you, I'd be more worried about Pete."

Mom's forehead wrinkles. "What do you mean?"

"*What do I mean?* Seriously? Mom, all he does is lock himself in his room and listen to music he never used to listen to. And now he's hanging out with these total freaks at school." Mom's face fills with alarm. A small sliver of satisfaction works its way through my frustration. I don't care that I'm ratting out my little brother. If Mom and Dad aren't concerned about his behavior, then maybe it's time I make them concerned. "I wouldn't be surprised if he were doing drugs."

Mom's eyes widen.

I slide open the door. A breeze sweeps into the kitchen, and along with it, the briny smell of the sea and the sound of rolling waves. Mom stands beside the refrigerator, looking unsure as to whether she should press me for more information or go confront her angst-ridden teenaged son. Pete must win the battle. The drug-mention on my part was effective. She pivots on her heel and makes a beeline for the stairs, to Pete's room, no doubt.

Good.

Let him be the freaky, troubled child for once. I will pretend I'm the well-adjusted girl with a best friend and a boyfriend. I step outside, walk to the edge of the deck, set my Coke on the banister, and let the crisp ocean breeze hit my face. Closing my eyes, I take a deep breath and try not to think. I focus on clearing my head of everything until all that exists is the sound of the sea and the freedom of the outdoors. The day's tension slowly rolls off my back.

"How'd it go with Leela?"

My eyes fly open.

Luka stands on the edge of his deck, the side that is closest to mine, his elbows resting on the banister.

Peace scurries away, replaced instead by embarrassment and nerves and a thrill of excitement. "Have you been out here this whole time?" I call over.

"Maybe." The breeze tousles his hair. "Did Leela believe you?"

"I think so." Heat gathers around the collar of my shirt as I think about her question—*is Luka a good kisser.* I'm fairly certain I will never know, but my imagination can't help but get a little carried away. "I promised her I'd go to that Halloween party tomorrow."

"Bobbi's?"

"Yeah."

"Care if I tag along?"

I raise my eyebrows. "You want to go?"

"That's what couples do, right? Go to parties together."

My stomach breaks out in a round of impromptu somersaults. And in the middle of the gymnastics routine, a groan escapes.

"What?"

"I'm not a big fan of costume parties. I never know what to wear." Or how to wear it without looking foolish.

"You could go as a crazy person. I'm sure Dr. Roth has a straitjacket you could borrow."

I laugh. It feels good. Great actually—being able to joke about everything. "Or I could just go as Tess Ekhart."

"Lame." His tone is teasing.

"What are you going as?"

"Dr. Roth. I can be your shrink."

A sobering thought cuts my smile short. What if I freak out again? Luka doesn't know about the séance. He has no clue that the last party I went to didn't work out so well. I fiddle with the tab of my Coke can, a slow trickle of fear and doubt filling up the space behind my sternum. I shouldn't have promised Leela something that has a very high chance of turning into a disaster.

"Hey, you okay?"

"What if something is there?" Like the man with the white eyes or the ball of light from Ceramics? Or worse, the army from Luka's dream.

"I'll be there, Tess. I won't let anything happen."

The door behind him slides open and his mother comes out. Her attention flits from me to her son and the disapproval that sets across her shoulders is impossible to miss. I straighten from the railing and self-consciously run a hand through my hair. It's weird. I've never been the kind of girl guys introduce to their mom. But let's say for a second I was. I always imagined I'd be the girl mothers would love. Luka's mom doesn't love me at all.

"I'd like you to come in for the evening, Luka," she says.

Luka slides his hands into the pockets of his jeans. "Mom, you remember Tess."

She gives me a forced smile and a stiff nod.

"What time's the party tomorrow?" Luka calls over.

"Seven, I think."

Mrs. Williams watches both of us.

"Seven o'clock, then. Want to meet in my driveway?"

"Sure." It feels like a lifetime away.

"See you then." He smiles one last time, then steps inside his house, completely missing the cold look his mother gives me as he goes.

⌒⌒

Pete sulks in our living room on Friday night. When Mom and I return from our martial arts class Saturday morning, he's already resumed his position. He broods the entire day away. Dad doesn't let him retreat to his room. Apparently, Mom had a talk with Pete after my tattling session, which explains why the bulk of his dark mood is directed at me, but I can't bring myself to care. I'm going to a party tonight and not just with Leela, but Luka Williams too.

Despite my better judgment, I tell Mom. Not about the Luka part, because I'm sure the excitement of that news would spin her head right off her body. I simply tell her I'm going to a party. Which is why, despite Pete's glowering, she is downright giddy. It's also why she has retrieved a box of old Halloween masks and accessories and costumes from the attic.

Most are too small, even for me. Somewhere in the middle of trying on an old pair of Tinkerbell wings, Leela calls and convinces me to be a kitten. She and her younger sister need a third. After I hang up, I throw on a black sweatshirt and black pants while Mom digs through the box and finds a headband with cat ears.

A few minutes later, she sits on the toilet lid, fiddling with a wand, watching as I check my reflection in the downstairs bathroom.

"Are you sure you don't want me to paint some whiskers on your cheeks?" Mom asks. "It'll make the costume complete. Every kitten needs whiskers."

"I'm good."

Mom twirls the wand. "Is Leela picking you up here or are you picking her up at her house?"

I bite my lip. I'll have to tell her eventually. "Actually, Luka's driving."

"Luka? As in, next-door Luka?"

"Mom. If you call him a hottie …"

Laughter bubbles out of her mouth—so light and refreshing I can't help but smile. She stands and puts her hands on my shoulders. "I'm so happy you're making friends."

The hope in her voice makes me sad. I wish more than anything that it was warranted. I wish I wasn't hiding anything from Leela. I wish Luka's interest in me had nothing to do with unexplainable dreams and shared visions. I wish I was a normal girl, crushing on a cute boy. But yesterday morning's conversation with my parents is a painful reminder that I am far from normal, so I push the wishes aside and return Mom's smile.

She looks out into the living room where Pete sits despondently on the couch. "Now if only we could get that brother of yours to snap out of it. I wish I knew what was going on with him." Mom sets her wand on the vanity, her eyes gaining a brightness that bodes ill. "Maybe you should take him to the party with you."

"Mom …"

"Honey, he took you to a lot of stuff in Jude."

No, he didn't. Mom forced me to go. Those are two very different things. Still, she's not the only one worried about Pete. As upset as I was with him yesterday, I don't like to see him so miserable. Plus, Leela would be in heaven if we showed up with my brother in tow. Letting out a sigh, I exit the bathroom, take the remote from Pete's hand, and turn off the television.

He glares up at me. "What are you doing?"

"Do you want to go to a Halloween party tonight?"

He laughs a laugh devoid of humor.

"C'mon Pete, it'll be fun." Not to mention, I'm almost one hundred percent certain Jess and Wren will *not* be there. Maybe Pete will meet some new friends. Or better yet, maybe he'll realize how wonderful Leela is.

Mom walks into the room. "Honey, you can either go to the party or sit in the living room with your father and me tonight. You're not going to your room."

His dark eyes flash. "Fine. I'll go to the stupid party."

"Great." With a glance at the clock, my stomach swoops. The big hand is two ticks away from the twelve. "Hurry up and grab a costume. We're meeting Luka in his driveway in two minutes."

Pete unwedges himself from the couch, rummages through the box, and grabs a set of glow in the dark vampire teeth. "Ready?"

"That's it?"

"Says the earless kitten." He sticks the teeth in his mouth.

Ignoring the jab, I walk to the door. Mom hands me my headband, which I can't bring myself to wear. She kisses our cheeks like she's sending us off to our first day of kindergarten and we step outside. As soon as the door closes behind us, I grab Pete's arm. "Will you be nice to Luka, please?"

He shrugs. Probably the closest thing to a yes I'm going to get.

I let go and walk toward Luka's yard. The last of the sun has made the sky in the west a deep pink, the east a navy blue. When I round a hedge, I spot Luka wearing cowboy hat, a shoestring neck tie, cowboy boots, and a pair of Wranglers. I only lived in Texas once. For eight months. We went to a rodeo for Pete's ninth birthday and I saw a bunch of cowboys. None of them looked as good as Luka does now. He stands with one leg crossed over the other, his thumbs looped beneath his brass belt buckle, leaning against his very nice, non-cowboyish car, staring off into his lawn with a divot between his brow.

Fiddling with the cat-ear headband, I walk toward him.

He tips his hat with a grin.

"Have room for one more?" I ask lamely.

"Sure." He meets me at the passenger door while Pete ducks into the back seat.

I put my hands in the front pocket of my sweatshirt. "My mom wanted Pete to come. I hope that's okay."

"Of course." He cocks his head a little, his stare moving from my feet up the length of my body, warming my skin. "Goth girl?"

I hold up my cat ears. "A little kitten. One of three."

He laughs. The sound is intoxicating.

"You pull off the cowboy look pretty well," I say, motioning toward his hat.

"When I was a kid, I wanted to be a real-live rodeo cowboy."

I look over my shoulder. Pete slouches in the back seat. "What changed?"

"I'm afraid of horses." One of the front windows in his house lights up. He reaches past me and opens my door. "We should go."

I duck inside and click my seatbelt into place. The car smells exactly like him—fabric softener and wintergreen. And for the first time since moving, I'm grateful for Pete. Because with him in the back seat, I won't be alone in the car with Luka. Even though Thornsdale is small, Leela lives on the opposite side of town.

Luka slides behind the wheel and starts the car. "We haven't officially met," he says over his shoulder. "I'm Luka."

Pete acknowledges him with barely more than a grunt.

"Adjusting to life in California?" Luka asks, reversing out of the driveway.

Pete shrugs.

"Classes okay?"

"*Peachy.*" My brother's voice is flat with a heavy dose of sarcasm.

I want to throttle his neck. Seriously, this is the best he can do? What is up with this delayed case of teenager punk-ness? He has all these walls up. Walls he's never had before. In Jude and every other city before, he was laid back, go-with-the-flow, everybody-loves-him Pete. Now he's dark and moody and sits with his arms crossed and his eyes down. I glance at Luka as he pulls past the gates of Forest Grove, wanting to explain that Pete's attitude isn't personal. That he's angry because I ratted him out and now he's forced to go to a party he doesn't want to go to.

Instead, I swallow and ask, "Do you know where Leela lives?"

"I have a general idea." His eyes meets mine and a thousand questions scroll through my mind. Is he annoyed with Pete? Does he regret his offer to go to the party? Or worse, does he regret our cover story? "Want to punch in her address?"

I plug it in and clasp my hands in my lap, wishing away the clamminess.

The lady in the GPS tells Luka to take a left hand turn.

My leg jiggles. I'm eager to get to Leela's. Perhaps she and her little sister, Kiara, will dispel the growing tension in the car.

GPS lady tells him to make another left.

Luka makes a point of catching my attention and winks, as if to reassure me that everything is okay. Or will be okay. It's a simple gesture, but it does wonders to soothe my jumpy nerves.

Eight minutes later, we're idling in front of a ranch home with a small, tidy lawn. As soon as the headlights hit the house, Leela comes out, followed by a smaller version of herself—Kiara, a freshman.

Leela stops midstride, her mouth a perfect oval and Kiara runs into the back of her. I can practically read Leela's thoughts. I never told her I was coming to pick her up in Luka's car. In fact, I didn't tell her Luka was coming at all. To her credit, she recovers quickly and the two hurry toward us. Leela opens the back door first, her eyes bright, a black triangle painted on her nose, whiskers on her cheeks. The second she catches sight of Pete, her face floods with color. I give my brother my best death stare over the seat.

*Be nice.*

If he sees it, he doesn't react.

Kiara dances behind her. "Get in, Leels. I'm freezing!"

Leela hesitates for a moment, then climbs in, careful to keep a nice gap between her leg and Pete's, squishing poor Kiara against the window.

"Hi Pete," Leela squeaks. She clears her throat. "Where's your costume?"

He smiles wide, showcasing his fluorescent yellow vampire teeth.

Kiara gives Leela a sisterly shove with her shoulder. "Be

careful, Leela, he might bite you."

It doesn't seem possible, but Leela's face grows a deeper shade of red.

"Where are your ears, Tess?" Kiara asks.

"And your whiskers?" Leela adds.

Luka reverses out of the drive and raises his eyebrows teasingly. "Yeah, Tess, where are your whiskers?"

## CHAPTER TWENTY-THREE

# THE HALLOWEEN PARTY

B obbi lives out in the country. The sound of music and laughter grows louder as we approach her house. Luka walks so close to my side our knuckles brush.

Cover up, cover up, cover up. This is all a cover up. Whatever connection we share is a natural byproduct of the crazy things we both see. Assuming anything else is only setting up my poor heart for some significant aches and pains.

"You okay?" His question tickles my ear.

I bob my head.

He presses his hand against my back. Even through the sweatshirt, I can feel the heat of his palm. I close my eyes. *This is all just part of the act, Tess.*

"If things get claustrophobic," he whispers as we step onto Bobbi's front stoop, "we can slip out and go for a walk."

I swallow, unsure what is more frightening—walking in the woods on the eve of Halloween, or being alone with him. Leela and Kiara step onto the stoop with us as Luka jabs the doorbell with his thumb. Two seconds later the Bride of Frankenstein answers, letting the sounds of the party escape into the night. The bass thumps through my chest. Bobbi wears a floor-length white gown that shows off her figure, a black beehive wig with streaks of gray, and a choker with neck bolts. Just like Luka in his cowboy getup, she looks amazing. Not at all ridiculous.

"You came!" She flings her arms around Luka, then Leela

and Kiara and even me. She points at Pete, her smile one hundred percent genuine. "You're Tess's little brother. I'm so glad you're here!"

Pete gives her a dismissive nod, then slinks past her into the party. I'm half annoyed, half grudgingly admiring. I would never have the guts to leave the safety of the group I came with to venture into a party by myself, especially friendless.

Bobbi opens the door wider and yells over the din, "Come on in!"

We step inside to a mob of monsters and witches and angels and superheroes, dancing and mingling in groups, most holding red plastic cups. I spot Matt in the crowd, dressed as Frankenstein, of course, and beside him Jared wears his football jersey. They stand by a keg in the corner.

"Make yourself at home," Bobbi says. "Keg's over there— but I'll warn you now, it's just Root Beer."

I exhale. A little too audibly.

Bobbi flashes me such a warm smile that I'm reminded of her relation to Leela. "Don't worry, Tess. My dad's the chief of police in Thornsdale. He would have me shipped off to boarding school if I threw a party with any type of illegal shenanigans. Both of my parents are upstairs." She points toward the kitchen. "Food's in there. Fire pit's in the back yard, where it's not so loud. People are actually bobbing for apples on the deck. Not my idea."

The doorbell rings again.

"You guys have fun!" Bobbi turns away from our small group and flings open the door, the perfect hostess.

Luka leans toward my ear. "You hungry?"

I'm not, but I nod anyway, eager to get out of the foyer. He laces his fingers with mine and my palm catches fire as he pulls me through the crowd. I look over my shoulder, motioning for Kiara and Leela to follow.

A smaller group of guys exit the kitchen as we enter. They slap Luka's free hand a high-five, eyeing me as they pass. Party food fills an entire counter—M&M's, chips, licorice, Candy corn. A large, opened cooler sits on the tile floor filled with ice, water bottles, Dr. Pepper, and Red Bull.

"I'm gonna go find my friends." Kiara grabs a handful of M&M's, pops a few of the candies in her mouth, and leaves.

Leela turns to me. "You have to wear your cat ears."

Luka pulls out the headband from my pocket. "I agree."

"I'd rather be Goth girl."

My protest must not be very convincing, because Luka fits the ears on my head. "You make a very cute cat."

His words steal my breath. So do his eyes.

"Aw. Are we interrupting a romantic moment?"

I blink and turn around. Summer stands in the doorway of the kitchen, wearing devil horns, a skimpy red dress, and an ugly sneer. "How cute. Two little kittens." Her eyes rove over Leela. "Well, one's little anyway."

Leela's cheeks go bright red.

I glare at Summer, a slow burn of fury working its way through my blood stream. I hate her for that comment. "And you're the devil," I say. "How fitting."

Luka coughs. I can't tell if it's an actual cough, or if he's covering up a laugh.

Summer's eyes flash, but then she struts into the kitchen. Jared trails behind her like a pathetic, lovesick puppy. She cracks open two Dr. Peppers and pours the soda into her cup, Jared's, and an unused one from the stack. She reaches behind Jared, pulls a flask from his back pocket, jiggles it in the air with a wicked grin, then puts her finger to her lips. "We brought the party," she whispers, mixing in a generous amount with the Dr. Pepper. Judging by the flush in her cheeks, this isn't her first drink.

She holds out the cup to Luka.

He rests his arm behind me on the counter. "I'm good."

She turns to me.

I shake my head.

"More for us then." She raises her cup to Jared. He taps his against it and takes a long drink.

"Looks like Jennalee's having fun with your brother on that couch over there," Summer says when she's done drinking.

I glance out into the living room. Pete lounges back on one of the cushions with his red cup of Root Beer, talking very intimately with Jennalee, who's dressed like a slutty nurse— almost as cliché as Summer. Their heads are bent close and whatever Pete says, Jennalee listens with rapt attention. I want to walk over and tear him away, especially when I catch Leela looking much more like a wilted flower than a kitten without her mittens.

"All sorts of unlikely people are getting together these days." Summer shrugs, like her words mean nothing, then leaves the room with Jared. I watch her and her legs and her gorgeous pout leave the room before pinning my gaze on Pete.

"That was pleasant," Luka says.

Jennalee stands and makes her way toward a crowd by the stereo. She whispers something to them. A few scan the party, then catch sight of me in the kitchen with Luka, their expressions openly curious, Jennalee's triumphant. The heat in my bloodstream gathers and swirls. I leave the kitchen and stalk through the bodies and don't stop until I'm standing in front of Pete. "What did you tell Jennalee?"

He looks up at me. "You and Mom want me to socialize. That was me socializing."

"Pete." I grind his name through my teeth.

He shoves off from the couch and brushes past. I want to stomp my foot, then go after him and force him to have a conversation. Enough ignoring the issue. If Pete's still upset about our move, it's time we hash things out. He's acting like a passive-aggressive teenage girl, which is so far from the Pete I know that my confusion almost drowns out my anger. As I stare after him, my attention snags on Jennalee. She tilts her head back and laughs with a new group of classmates. My uneasiness grows. I take a step back, as if doing so might make me shrink, or maybe disappear. Instead, I run into something hard. It's Luka. Leela stands behind him. The moisture in her eyes exacerbates my anger. Leela has been looking forward to this party for days and now because of a witch named Summer and an idiot named Pete, it's turning into a miserable night.

"What was that about?" Luka asks.

"I'm not sure." I narrow my eyes at Jennalee, unable to shake the feeling that she is talking about me. Great. So now, along with psychosis, I can add paranoia to the list.

Luka steps into my line of vision. "How about we get some air."

I look at Leela. "Wanna come?"

She glances from me to Luka, her chin wobbling. "I don't want to be the third wheel."

"Leela, you aren't a third wheel."

"I should probably go check on Kiara, anyway." She gives me a weak smile, then turns around and walks away with deflated shoulders.

I watch her go, cursing my brother. Why can't he see what an awesome catch Leela would be? Why do guys always go for the pretty face and the lithe body, oblivious to the ugliness inside? Luka takes my hand and maneuvers through the clumps of dancing, talking bodies while my nerves hop and tumble and skip. Some girls notice us, their attention flickering to our linked hands. Others don't. They go about as normal— laughing, playfully shoving, teasing, making eyes with the boys. Any sliver of confidence I might have had dissipates. Because I will never be like them. I will never be a part of this. I have no idea how to flirt. It's absolutely not in my DNA.

Luka guides me out the back door, where classmates hoot and holler and dunk their faces into a tub of water and apples. He leads us past the fire pit where several teenagers roast marshmallows and hotdogs. A girl in my Study Hall shrieks and runs away from a boy who holds something. A bug, maybe? My breath escapes in small white puffs as Luka brings me closer to the woods behind Bobbi's home and releases my hand.

I scold myself for feeling disappointed. There's no reason for him to continue the charade, not when nobody's around to see. Of course he would let go.

"There are some pretty cool paths through here," he says, stepping beneath the cover of the trees. A full moon shines overhead. Tree limbs break apart the light so that only parts of the path are visible. I keep my eyes trained on the ground, on the lookout for jutting roots or rocks. The last thing I need to do is trip and fall in front of Luka.

"Care to share what you're thinking," he says.

The pale moon illuminates half of his face. Night shadows the other half. It's a darkness I'm thankful for. Because it hides the heat rising in my cheeks. There is no way I'm going to tell him that I'm thinking about my lack of know-how in the flirting department. Or that my hand feels much too cold apart from his.

He sticks his hands in his pockets. "I can never tell."

I step over a stray branch and settle on a half-truth. Something I'm only partially thinking. "I feel bad for Leela."

"Why's that?"

"Because she's in love with my brother and he's being a total jerk." Dread puckers my insides when I think about the way Pete and Jennalee were talking on the couch. What could he have possibly told her to make her look at me with such unbridled interest?

"And?"

"And what?"

"What else are you thinking?"

"I really don't like Jennalee."

He laughs. "That's refreshing."

"What is?"

"You. Your honesty."

"I don't like Summer either." I think about her mean remark to Leela. *Don't like* is too tame. When it comes to Summer, I pretty much loathe her.

"A lot of girls pretend to like them." We take a few more steps, twigs snapping beneath our feet. "Can I ask you a question?"

"Sure."

"Why did your brother want to come tonight?"

"He didn't."

"So why did he?"

"It was between this, or sitting in the living room with my

mom and dad."

"Why's that?"

"I told my parents he was hanging out with Wren and Jess. I may have implied that he's doing drugs." The moon glints off a spider web dangling over the path. I bat it aside and keep walking. "All he does is lock himself in his room. He never used to be that way."

"What did he used to be like?"

"Reluctantly popular." I glance at Luka. "Kinda like you."

"What changed?"

"I don't know. He sort of had a girlfriend in Jude. He blames me for moving."

"Right. You said that before. The first time we talked, but you covered it up."

"It was my fault. I went to a party with him. They got out a Ouija board." I shudder. It's not something I want to remember, but the image of people in straitjackets and the gnashing teeth and the cold presence is impossible to forget.

Luka draws closer, his body warm. "What happened?"

"We did a séance and I freaked out. I guess. I don't remember that part. I just remember waking up in the hospital …" The wind brings chilly air up the path. It presses against my back and my neck. I can still hear my parents whispering.

*I want you to promise me that our daughter won't end up like your mom.*

*Tess is not my mother.*

*But we've always suspected …*

I stop in the middle of the path. "What do you know about Wren and Jess?"

"Not much."

"Has Wren ever gone to the Edward Brooks Facility?"

His lips curve into a crooked smile. "Contrary to what you might believe, I don't make a habit of snooping into other people's files."

"Oh." I scuff my shoe against the ground. "Just mine, then?"

"Just yours." He sits back against a large rock off to the side of the path.

I scuff my shoe again. "So tell me about your dream last night. What happened on your end?"

"I fell asleep and woke up on the beach. I looked around for you, but you weren't there, so I sat down and waited for a really long time before you showed up."

"And then I disappeared?"

He gives me a small nod, his green eyes filled with intensity.

I cross my arms tighter. "I wish I knew how it worked."

"So do I."

"How about the dreams you had before?"

"Before I met you?"

"Yeah. How do you think those worked?" How could he dream about me before meeting me? How in the world would science or my father explain that one?

He shrugs. "I wish I knew that too."

"Are you sure it was me?" An image of the ordinary looking man who prevented me from freeing my grandmother in last night's dream pops into my head. Apart from the scar, any number of men could pass as him. "I'm sure there are plenty of girls out there with dark hair and blue eyes and freckles."

"It was you, Tess." He takes my hand and pulls me toward him. With him leaning against the rock and me standing between his splayed legs, our noses are at the same height. "Exact same nose. Exact same eyes. Same chin." He traces his thumb over a small white scar along my jaw line. "Even the same scars."

My lungs stop working.

"I don't understand how it worked. All I know is that when you showed up in Current Events that first day, it was like … this huge sense of relief."

"Relief?"

"It seemed crazy to be consumed with thoughts about somebody who wasn't real."

I swallow the dryness in my throat. "Do you think there's anybody else like us?"

"Like us, as in people who see the things we see?"

"Yeah."

"Maybe."

I think about my grandmother and my dread grows. Luka must sense my disquiet because he shakes my palm a little, drawing my attention up to his.

"It's going to be okay."

I wish I could believe him. "We need to find my grandma. The dream I had about her last night? Finding out she's alive? That she tried to kidnap me? I –I need to find her. She might have answers. She might not even be crazy."

"I'll help you. We'll find her."

"How?"

"Could you ask your parents?"

"They'd only get suspicious."

"What about Dr. Roth?"

"I wouldn't know how to go about asking. What if he wants to know how I know?"

"We can figure out what to tell him."

A stick snaps not too far away. Luka stands quickly and pulls me behind him, his posture poised and alert, as if ready to lunge at the first sign of danger. A squirrel hops across the path, into a beam of moonlight, and the tension seeps out of his shoulders. He turns around. "I guess I'm a little jumpy."

I look down at our joined hands, then back up at him. "You're good at this."

"What?"

"This." I lift our hands. "You make it look pretty believable."

"I'm not that good of an actor."

My heart takes off. Short fast little beats, like the hop, hop, hop of a baby rabbit in flight. He pulls me closer and I forget everything. My grandma. My dreams. All the crazy stuff. There's only me and this boy.

"I'm very drawn to you, Tess."

*Why?* That's what I want to ask. But he brushes a lock of hair from my cheek and the word gets lost. My heart is no longer like the quick hopping of a rabbit. It's a jackhammer inside my ribcage. I'm sure he can hear it. I'm sure he can see it pulsing in my neck.

His mouth curves into a grin. "You don't have to look so frightened."

There's another sound, louder this time, as if somebody is crashing up the path. Luka pulls me back again, but there's laughter. It's Summer, and bumbling behind her is Jared, holding her elbow as if to keep her upright. She stops in the middle of the path, reels back, and throws up her hands like a police officer yelled freeze. "I am *so* sorry. We keep interrupting your romantic moments."

Luka's posture stiffens and his grip tightens around my hand, as if the firmness of his grasp might shield me from Summer's poison. She looks from me, to Luka, her expression glazed over, and points her finger from him to me. "I don't get this," she slurs.

Jared hiccups, then cups his mouth and giggles. It's a sound that should not come out of a burly linebacker.

"Jennalee 'n Pete? I get that. Yerbrother's hot. Loner and broody sorta adds to the whole appeal. Plus, he's full of interesting information."

My blood goes cold.

She takes a few belligerent steps toward me, sticks snapping beneath her feet. "I don't know if your boyfriend here knows about it."

Luka doesn't give her a chance to divulge whatever interesting information Pete had to share. He pulls me around Summer and Jared. "Come on, Tess."

"Yeah. C'mon Tess. Why don't you go ahead and tell Luka about your little episode."

I try to turn around.

"She's baiting you," Luka says.

Yes, she is. And I want to take the bait. "I need to know what she knows."

"No, you don't." He pulls me down the path, back to the party.

## Chapter Twenty-Four

# Confrontations

As soon as my brother and I walk inside the door of our home, I grab his arm. He whips around and jerks free.

"What did you tell Jennalee?"

He kicks off his shoes. They thud against the wall. "What do you think I told her?"

I replay Summer's odd threat in the woods, about my *little episode* and I can't think of anything else that could be interpreted as an episode except the séance in Jude. My blood has not returned to a normal temperature since. "What did you tell her, Pete?"

"Don't worry. I wouldn't dream of telling anybody I have a crazy for a sister."

"I'm the crazy one? *I'm* the crazy one? You lock yourself in your room all the time. You listen to obnoxious music. Your entire wardrobe has changed. And you're hanging out with Wren and Jess. *They're* the crazy ones. What did you tell Jennalee?"

"Wren and Jess don't see a shrink. And as far as I know, Wren and Jess have never had to move across the country because they need professional help."

I will not let him distract me. I will repeat the question a million times if it means he'll give me a straight answer. "What did you tell Jennalee?"

"What makes you think I told her anything about you?"

"Because Summer said something to me tonight about an *episode*."

"She asked if I partied in Florida. I told her about the last party I went to."

The blood drains from my face. "You told her about what happened in Florida?" Part of the reason we left was to escape the stigma and now Pete brought it with him? "How could you do that?"

"Relax. As far as she knows, you're just afraid of Ouija boards."

I narrow my eyes—hurt by the resentment simmering in his voice. Sure, the two of us have never been close. But we've never been like this, either. He stands there looking like I'm some sort of pariah, like he is physically uncomfortable being in my presence. "Why are you so angry with me?"

His glower darkens.

"Do you want me to apologize for making you move? Fine, I'm sorry. I'm sorry you have a crazy sister who made you move away from your girlfriend in Jude. Do you think I like it any more than you do?"

Mom hurries down the steps in her slippers, her hair and her sleepy eyes frazzled. "What is going on? What are you two yelling about?"

Pete clasps his hands behind his neck and mutters a curse. "Am I allowed to go to my room now, or do I have to sleep in the living room, too?"

Mom frowns. "Of course you can sleep in your room."

"Am I allowed to shut my door?"

All my fury—at Jennalee, at Summer, at my parents— gathers and swirls and aims itself at my brother. I want to bury my fist in his face, but I'm pretty sure it wouldn't hurt. "You are such a jerk, you know that?"

He doesn't even flinch. He keeps his eyes trained on Mom.

"S-sure," she says.

He stomps up the stairs and slams his door. The sound reverberates through the house. Mom looks at me with wide eyes. "What's going on? Did something happen at the party?"

I bite my lip, fighting back tears. "It's nothing."

"Nothing? Tess, you and Pete never fight like that."

"It's fine, Mom. All siblings fight." But that's a lie. Because Pete and I don't. At least never like that. I walk up the steps and shut myself in my room. When I get there, I shrug out of my sweatshirt and pants, then throw on a tank top and pajama bottoms with jerky, angry movements. I sit cross-legged on my bed and hug my pillow in my lap. My jiggling knees rattle the mattress and the nightstand.

How can somebody like Summer be so popular? Why does anybody like her?

I toss the pillow behind me, fall back, and stare up at the ceiling. Despite all the unexplainable things swirling around me—like Luka and our dreams and Dr. Roth and my not-dead grandmother and Pete's behavior—I'm still just a girl in high school, consumed with thoughts over a mean girl named Summer.

∽

Summer sits on Bobbi's couch, wearing her red devil costume, and she's making out with ...

Luka?

She surfaces from the passionate kiss, her lips swollen, looking more beautiful than ever. Luka drapes his arm over the back of the couch. My stomach cramps. I step away, feeling foolish. But wait a minute. I already left the party. Luka and I left together, with Leela and Kiara and Pete.

*What's going on?*

I scratch the inside of my wrist. It's numb.

Which means this is a dream. My mind races. Why is Luka making out with Summer in our dream? "Luka?" His name escapes like a tiny squeak, no louder than a mouse. I clear the tremor away and try again. "Luka, what's going on?"

But Luka doesn't answer. His eyes feast on Summer as if she is the only girl in the room.

"You don't actually think he likes you, do you?" Her smile makes my skin crawl. I am not a violent person. Martial Arts is all about self-control. Yet the look on her face makes me want to scratch her eyes out. "I mean, look at you and look at him. Why would someone like him be into someone like you?"

Her words fan my insecurity.

"There's only one reason he's been spending time with you." As she speaks, black mist puffs from her lips like frosty breath on a cold day.

I step back, waiting for Summer to shriek or cover her mouth, but it's like she doesn't see the black cloud at all.

"He wants to know how you do it," she continues. "He wants to know how you fight." The mist hovers around her face like cigarette smoke. "He's using you to get information. And then when he has it, he will destroy you."

I shake my head. Why isn't Luka reacting to the mist? Why isn't he moving away? I stare at him, waiting for him to at least acknowledge me. "Why is she here?"

"Who is *she*?" Summer points to herself. "Me? Why wouldn't I be here?"

"Did you invite her to our dream?" I ask Luka.

"Dream?" Summer laughs. "This is not a dream."

"Yes, it is." Now if only I knew why and how it worked. The black mist thins and clears. Luka sits on the couch, rubbing his knuckle up and down Summer's bare shoulder. "I thought you were going to help me find my grandmother. I thought you were going to help me figure out what to say to Dr. Roth."

"Dr. Roth?" Summer cocks her head. "What are you talking about?"

"Luka," I say, raising my voice.

"Don't you get it? He doesn't want to listen to you. He doesn't like you. He likes me. He's always liked me. And he will always like me!"

I squeeze my eyes shut, the sound of Summer's shrill voice ringing in my ears.

The temperature drops. I open my eyes and suck in a sharp breath. Summer and Luka and Bobbi's couch are gone. I'm standing in a closed garage. The air is cold and there's a car inside, running. A woman sits behind the wheel. She looks comatose and standing off to the side, is that man with the gaunt, pale face and unseeing white eyes. Fear strangles my airway. I cover my mouth with my sleeve to protect my lungs from the carbon monoxide and bang on the car window.

The lady doesn't react.

The man disappears into the house. When he returns, he has a car seat with him. A tiny baby sleeps inside. He clicks the car seat into the base in the back seat.

A tremor moves up into my torso. I remind myself that this is a dream. This isn't real. But it feels incredibly real. It feels like the most real thing I've ever experienced. I pound again on the car window, feeling strong. Feeling alert. If she doesn't do something, her baby will die.

She doesn't respond. She doesn't even blink.

The man leaves and comes back again, this time with a tow-headed toddler, tears streaking down his chubby cheeks. Horror expands inside my chest. The small child screams for his mom as the man straps him in his car seat.

I pound again on the woman's window. "Lady, your kids are going to die!"

Her eyelids flutter. She looks at me, but the man shoves me back with hands as cold as ice. I topple into some boxes. The little boy screams in the back seat. The baby sleeps. Desperation consumes me. Like fire doused with gasoline. All that matters is getting these children out. I have to save them. I lurch to my feet and do a roundhouse kick at the window—the way I would break a board on Saturday mornings in the dojo. Only this is not a board. This is thick, unbreakable glass.

To my shock, it explodes into tiny pieces.

I reach inside to unlock the door, open it up, unclick the car seat with the baby, and unbuckle the boy. Before the white-eyed man can react, I bundle the boy in my free arm and hurry toward the door. It must be an exit. I grab the knob and fling the door wide open to a burst of intense light.

My eyes fly open. I sit in bed, in the dark of night, lungs pumping, heart beating wildly. My attention lands on the dream journal on my nightstand, but my body recoils. I don't want to write anything down. I don't want to remember any of that dream. I pull the covers over my head, turn on my side, hug my pillow to my chest and fall back asleep.

## CHAPTER TWENTY-FIVE

# DOUBT

A sound—perhaps a doorbell?—wakes me up. Brightness streams in from the window. I throw the covers over my head and wince against the pain piercing my temple. It feels like somebody has shoved a knife into my brain and twists it around. I groan and try to gain my bearings.

For a moment, I can't remember what day it is or what happened the night before. I just lay there with the pain until last night's dream wiggles in and out of focus. Something about a woman and kids and Luka.

Did we meet again in our sleep? I try to bat away the fuzz in my head. It is Sunday morning. We were at Bobbi's party last night. Luka was there and … it comes in a swoosh of clarity. Luka invited Summer into our dream. They were making out. My heart sinks. If dreams spring from our subconscious, then aren't they more real than our words and our actions? Is it possible that I slipped into Luka's dream undetected and witnessed his true feelings? I try to pull the vague memory into focus. Summer said something about Luka using me to get information. That's twice now that my dreams have warned me against him. Heaviness sits on my chest. How do I know I can trust Luka?

With a groan, I resurface from the covers. The pounding in my head intensifies. I shuffle to the bathroom to relieve my bladder. My body feels weak and shaky, like I'm the one who drank from Jared's flask last night. Black stars flicker in the periphery of my vision as I return to my bed and lay down on my side, cold sweat prickling my forehead.

There's a soft tap at my door. It opens enough for my mother to stick her head inside. "Honey? It's almost lunchtime."

Lunchtime? Already?

Mom steps in my room, her brow etched with concern. "Are you okay?"

"Headache," I mumble.

"Luka's at the door asking for you."

I sit up. The sudden movement leaves me clutching my head.

"I was going to send him away, but he seems very desperate to see you."

"Give me a minute." I swing my legs over the bed. My feet hit the floor and I hurry into the bathroom, ignoring the spots dancing in my vision from standing so fast. I pull my hair up into a messy knot, splash cold water over my face, gargle mouth wash, one-leg hop into a pair of wrinkled jeans and throw a sweatshirt over my tank top. When I come out into my room, I shove the mess on my floor under my bed. Just as I'm tossing a book into my closet, Mom comes up with Luka. I close my closet door behind me.

Mom gives me an odd look, then leaves the room.

Luka stands in the doorway. I can't tell whether he looks miserable or nervous. After last night's dream, I decide on miserable. I was in the dream after all. By now, he has to realize what I saw. What I heard. Summer foiled his plans, whatever they were. I sit down on the edge of my bed. My legs are too shaky to stand.

"I was going to go on a hike." He walks over to the bed. "I was thinking you might want to come?"

I pick at a fray in the thigh of my jeans. Does he really think I don't know?

"You okay?"

"I remember the dream, Luka."

He sticks his hands in his back pockets and cocks his head. "Dream?"

"From last night. With Summer."

"Summer?" He pulls his chin back, his brow furrowing.

"You don't remember?" Is it possible that he really didn't see me? Or is he just putting on a good act again?

"*Remember*? I have no idea what you're talking about."

"We met up last night. We shared a dream."

"No, we didn't."

"Yes, we did. We were at Bobbi's. You and Summer were there and ..." Heat flushes up my neck. I can't bring myself to remind him that they were making out.

"And what?"

"She told me you were using me to get information."

"Tess, I don't know how this dream-thing works, but trust me, I didn't have a dream about Summer last night." His cheeks turn red. It's the first time I've ever seen him blush. It leaves me wondering who he did dream about last night. He sits beside me on the edge of my bed. "It had to be a regular dream."

I want to believe him, but just because I want to doesn't mean I should. Pressing my fingers against my hairline, I glance at my untouched dream journal. I should have written everything down last night so I'd remember the details. There was something about a mother and her kids and a garage, maybe? I close my eyes against the pain throbbing in my temples and a picture of a tow-headed boy swims into focus. My eyes fly open. I stand from the bed.

Luka stands with me. "What is it?"

I hurry over to my desk, plop down on the chair, and open the internet browser.

"What's going on?" Luka asks, leaning over my shoulder.

"I'm not sure." I type words into the search box.

"Why are you searching for carbon monoxide poisoning?"

"It's something from my dream last night." My heart pounds in my ears as a news result pops up on the screen, in a town not more than fifteen minutes from Thornsdale. I click on the link, praying it's not what I think. My dad might think prayers are nothing but a waste of energy, but if angels are real, then God is real. And if God is real, then maybe he's a God who listens to prayer.

A picture fills the screen and my prayer curdles.

"Please tell me what's going on."

"It's them."

"Who's them?" Luka leans further over my shoulder. "Were they in your dream?"

I set my hand on top of my head and lean back in the chair. If the scene in the garage was real, then doesn't that mean Luka and Summer were real too?

"Woman found dead from carbon monoxide poisoning," Luka reads out loud. "Survived by her two children, who were in the car with her. Amazingly, they survived, though doctors do not understand how. The children have no brain damage and no trace of monoxide in their blood system. Doctors are declaring their survival an anomaly."

"I dreamt about them." My voice shakes worse than my

hands. "That same man from the pep rally was there and he had the woman in some sort of trance. I grabbed the children and got them out, but I woke up before I could help the woman. And now she's dead." The shaking has taken over my entire body. It clamps onto my jaw, making my teeth chatter. I couldn't control it if I tried.

Luka swivels my chair around and places his hands on the arm rests. "Tess."

"This is crazy. This is so freaking crazy."

"Tess."

"I did not save those children. Because if I saved them, then that means ..." I picture the mother, sitting behind the wheel, unblinking. I think about those children growing up without her. I think about the guy who shot himself and the two people who died at the fetal modification clinic. Tears spring to my eyes. Could I have saved them too? Are their deaths on my hands?

"Tess, look at me."

His voice cuts through my rising hysteria. I swallow and look up into his eyes, as if he has the power to save me from a truth that is determined to suck me into darkness. "This isn't your fault. Do you understand me? You had nothing to do with that woman's death."

"Then how do you explain the dream?"

He looks at me, long and searching and worried. He has no answer.

∽

I have no desire to go to school the next day. I don't want to face Summer or Jennalee or anybody else who's talking about whatever Pete said about my freak-out at the séance in Jude. As

K.E. GANSHERT

soon as I reach my locker, Leela is there. She looks to have rebounded from Saturday night's party. If only I were as resilient, but then I doubt Leela is being haunted by prophetic dreams or awful headaches or unexplainable white-eyed men.

"I called you twice yesterday, but your mom said you weren't feeling well."

I enter the combination for my locker and shove my books inside. Three girls stand not too far away, whispering and laughing. One of them keeps looking at me. "I had a really awful headache."

"You get a lot of those, don't you?"

"Unfortunately."

"Okay, so," Leela grabs my arm, "Did you hear the rumor circulating about your brother and Jennalee?"

I shut my locker and come face-to-face with her excitement. Her cheeks are rosy and her eyes are bright. "No."

"He rejected her."

"Jennalee?"

Leela bobs her head. "She must not be his type."

"It's Monday morning. Isn't that a little fast for anybody to know anything?" Even for small-town high school?

"I guess somebody saw Jennalee waiting at his locker this morning and he totally blew her off. She walked away looking really upset."

"Good. Pete can do a lot better than Jennalee." At least the old Pete. I'm not so sure about this new Pete. Someone like Jennalee might be this new Pete's perfect match.

Leela's eyes dim.

More laughter from the three girls. More stares. I force my attention away from them and onto my friend. "Leela, *you* are a lot better than Jennalee."

The brightness floods back and her ears turn pink. I'm not sure if it's from embarrassment or pleasure. She fiddles with the edge of one of the folders tucked beneath her arm. "There's something else that's going around and I want you to know, I don't care. I understand."

Dread taps me on the shoulder. "What?"

"Jennalee told a bunch of people that your brother said you freaked out about some séance Ouija board stuff in Florida."

I try to swallow, but my throat is too dry.

"That stuff gives me the creeps too. It always has."

"Yeah. The creeps." If only that's all it was. If only I was a little *creeped out* over the thought of the supernatural instead of actually *seeing* the supernatural.

"And you know what? Who cares if Jennalee thinks it's funny? Her sense of humor has never been kind. You aren't her first target. If you ignore it, people will forget by tomorrow."

I wonder if by *people*, she means the three girls off to the side who aren't even trying to hide the fact that they're talking about me. Sighing, I grab a folder from my locker as a gust of frigid air blows at my back. The hair on my neck prickles. I whirl around and the man from my dream is standing right behind Leela. I gasp and rear back into the locker, but as quickly as he appeared, he vanishes.

"Oh my gosh! What?" Leela darts a quick look over her shoulder.

My heart careens, wild and out of control.

Leela sets her hand against her chest. "You gave me a heart attack, Tess. What was that about?"

"I-I'm not sure." My attention zips around the locker bay. Kids mill around in clumps. The three girls have gone from staring to gawking because they witnessed my freak-out along with Leela. And beyond them, Luka walks toward us, the epitome of perfection with his dark gray V-neck and mussed hair.

Leela spots him too, and understanding erases the concern on her face. "Wow. You sure have a strong reaction to him, don't you?"

"Yeah. I guess."

"I don't blame you. So, are we sitting by each other at lunch?"

"Yes. For sure."

"Are you positive? You're not going to sit with—?"

"We'll sit together Leela, I promise."

"All right, see you at class then." She gives me a wink and a smirk, then leaves as Luka arrives. He leans his shoulder casually against the lockers, standing close, almost protectively so. An onlooker would see him and think him relaxed, but I don't miss the tension in his jaw.

"Please tell me you saw that," I whisper.

He gives a curt nod, then scans the crowd in the locker bay, as if expecting the man to reappear. When his attention lands on the three girls, they quickly look away, their faces red. "I don't understand why he goaded you like that."

"Not exactly a good start to the day," I mutter.

"That's three times now."

"Three times?"

"Three times something …"—he leans closer, so much so that I see each one of his long, dark lashes and the flecks of darker green in his eyes—"supernatural has tried interacting with you. First in Lotsam's class, then in Ceramics, and now this. It's like they are purposefully trying to get your attention." He squints at the floor, as if the answer to this horrid riddle might be found in the fibers of the carpet. "I don't get it."

"They've never tried to interact with you?"

"Never. I see them, but they don't seem to notice me. With you though …" He shakes his head, the tension in his jaw growing more pronounced. "Maybe it's because you have such a strong reaction. Maybe the answer is learning how to ignore them."

"I'm not sure I know how."

"I can help."

"What about the dreams? Can you help with those?"

"I think you need to figure out a way to ignore those too. Shut them out."

A thread of doubt winds itself around my heart. "What if they're real?"

He shakes his head, resolute. "Even if they are, there's nothing you can do about them."

The thread pulls tight. I'm not sure Luka understands. He hasn't had the dreams I've had. He doesn't know what it's like to lunge at that man on the bridge and the next day, discover the girl survived. He doesn't know what it's like to grab those babies from the back seat of a car and find out they survived too. What if the decisions I make in my dreams have a real, profound impact on what happens in real life? How can I possibly shut them out if lives are at stake?

"All this stuff? It's like it's purposefully trying to make you go insane."

I think about Leela's reaction to my mini freak-out moments before. I think about the three girls' reactions too. "Or look that way."

"Neither of those options is safe."

The bell rings. Luka scans the crowd again, then he walks

us to class. In first period, I sit in between him and Leela. Across the classroom, Summer is not at all discreet about her staring. Or maybe studying is the better word. She looks at me like she's trying to figure something out. I keep replaying the things she said in our dream and the more I do, the more I second-guess Luka.

Leela bumps her knee against mine beneath the table. "Stop," she mutters.

I blink several times, as if coming out of a trance. "She was staring first."

"Yeah, well, you're both making me nervous. And by the looks of it, Mr. Lotsam too."

I glance at our teacher, up at the board, and a foreboding drop in temperature settles over my skin. The greasy-haired man is back, standing so close to Mr. Lotsam I jerk in my chair. Luka clamps his hand over my knee, steadying me in place. I close my eyes. I take deep, steadying breaths and tell myself this is not real. When I'm brave enough to look, nothing is behind Mr. Lotsam but a chalkboard. The man is gone.

But the coldness remains.

After Ceramics, Luka walks me to third period and waits with me until the bell rings. As soon as third period ends, he's already out in the hallway. Part of me wonders if he ever left. By the time lunch rolls around, I am exhausted. Turns out, ignoring something takes a lot more effort than a person might think, even if that something is just a coldness only I can feel. Leela waves from our table as I come out of the line with my tray.

"I told Leela I'd sit by her," I tell Luka.

"Mind if I join you?" he asks.

I look at his table of friends, most of whom stare along with Summer. "Are you sure *they* won't mind?"

"I don't care if they mind." He sweeps his hand toward Leela, an invitation for me to lead the way. So I do. Leela fidgets the closer we get. Like me, she is unused to all the eyes. But they come with Luka. The entire student body seems to be constantly aware of his location. It's like he's the moon—a physical force of gravity—and people can't help but shift toward him. I don't blame them. I'm just as guilty. In fact, I feel like his brand of gravity affects me more than it affects anyone else.

He pulls out my chair and sits beside me. Pete, who I've barely given any thought to over the course of the morning, walks past Leela with his tray and flicks her ponytail. He winks at her over his shoulder as he walks off to find a seat, and even though it's with Wren and Jess, a flicker of hope breaks through the oppression that is today. The action was so reminiscent of the Pete I used to know that for the briefest of moments, my heart warms. If only the warmth would stay.

Thankfully, Leela does most of the talking with Luka filling in the gaps. I keep my eyes on my tray and pick at my food, trying hard not to shiver. Luka laughs at something Leela says and takes a swig of his water and I don't understand how he can be *that* good at acting normal. An intrusive thought bullies its way into my head. What if this coldness I can't shake is coming from him? I push the idea aside, angry that it came at all, desperate to forget it altogether. But the question lingers, dredging up another that is equally unwelcome.

If he's this good at acting, how do I know what's real and what's not?

The question fans my doubt into flame.

After the three of us put our trays away, the track coach corners Luka, trying to cajole him into trying out for the team. Luka watches helplessly as I walk myself to my next class. The coldness doesn't follow me. By study hall, it's nothing more than a residual chill. I put my head down on my desk. I don't want to doubt Luka. I hate that Summer, of all people, is the one who placed the doubt there to begin with.

Somebody walks past and shoves my desk. Hard. So hard, in fact, that all my books topple onto the floor.

"Whoops. Didn't see you there."

The class erupts in giggles.

I look up to find the smug face of one of Summer's groupies, her expression filled with such abhorrence, I'm too flustered to respond. Is my association with Luka really cause for such hatred? She steps on my pencil. It snaps in two. The class giggles again while I clean up the mess.

Right before the end of final period, I text Pete that I'll meet him at the car. I need to get out of here, away from all these bodies, away from the whispers and taunts. I'm so spent from the inner battle occurring in my mind and the outer battle occurring with my classmates, I can't imagine going through another day like this one. The bell rings. Mr. Lotsam calls out Luka's name and asks to speak with him. I take off toward the door, but Luka grabs my arm. His fingers are hot, almost feverish. "Can we talk?"

Students file past us, out the door.

Luka pulls me aside. I want to close my eyes and go to sleep, but I'm worried if I do, I'll have more dreams.

"Tess, whatever you're thinking, it's wrong." Saying the words seems to cause him physical pain. He looks as tortured as I feel. "You can trust me."

I've never wanted to believe someone more, but I don't even really know him. "I have an appointment with Dr. Roth."

The last of the stragglers file out of the classroom, but not before I catch one giving me a nasty look. I don't understand what I did wrong. Mr. Lotsam clears his throat loudly and watches us. Luka rakes his hand through his hair. "What are you going to tell him?"

He's talking about Dr. Roth. "I don't know."

"Maybe he'll be able help."

"Yeah. Maybe."

"Everything's going to be all right." He squeezes my hand, bringing warmth to my freezing fingers. "Call me when you're done, okay?"

I nod glumly, then head to the car. Maybe Luka is right. Maybe hope lies at the Edward Brooks Facility.

## CHAPTER TWENTY-SIX

# DRUGS

D r. Roth hands me a glass of water. I hug it between my palms, thankful for the respite. There is no creepy man here in this office. No black mist or flashing lights or unexplainable temperature changes. I want to stay here for the rest of the evening and shut off my brain.

"You don't look well," Dr. Roth says.

I take a long sip. The coolness of the water soothes my throat. Dr. Roth waits, forever patient, never pressing, always waiting for me to reveal something of note. Was it really just last week that he tried hypnosis? It feels like an entire lifetime ago. The clock on the wall ticks away the seconds as I tap my pointer finger against the cup. I count twenty seven of them before I respond. "What do you know about my grandmother?"

He folds his hands over his knee. "Why your grandmother?"

"Because I'd like to know where she is. And I'd like to know what her records say."

"Do you think knowing those things will change your situation?"

"I don't know. It could help." I set the glass of water between us. "I want to talk to her."

"That's impossible."

"Why?"

"She's in one of the highest-security mental facilities in the country. There's no way they would allow you to see her. And even if they did, I don't think you would like what you saw."

"Where is this facility?"

"Why don't you tell me what's going on with *you*?"

I pause, considering. Surely I have nothing to lose. He's not going to report me to the government and have me locked up. If that was his goal, he could have had me committed a long time ago. I'm not worried about my safety with Dr. Roth, not anymore.

"Does it have anything to do with your dreams?" he asks.

I don't respond.

"Did you bring your dream journal?"

I stare at him for an expanded moment, then slowly remove the journal from my bag and set it in front of him.

He raises his eyebrows. "May I?"

I nod.

He puts on his glasses and opens the notebook to the first page. I study his face while he reads, tapping my finger against my wrist while he reads the only dream I've recorded. I printed out the news clipping from the internet—a family man who committed suicide, leaving behind his surviving wife and children—and taped it inside. Dr. Roth finishes reading, his face expressionless, then unfolds the printed piece of paper.

"Hmmm ..." A simple noise. A common one. It could mean any number of things. Or it could mean nothing at all. "Who do you think the man is? The one with the scar."

"I don't know." I jiggle my leg, pinch my bottom lip, shake my head. I'm a fidgeting mess. "At first I thought he was my grandmother's doctor."

"So you believe that woman is your grandmother?"

"Yes."

"Why?"

"Who else would she be?"

"I don't know. Maybe she's a reflection of your fear."

"Meaning?"

"Perhaps she was a projection of who you think you'll become."

"Sounds like psychobabble." I glance around his office, taking in the fancy degrees framed and mounted on his walls. "Is that what you think it was?"

Dr. Roth picks up a pen and taps it against the news article. "You're sure you wrote your entry before you saw this?"

"Yes, but if I'm suffering from psychosis then I guess that could be one of my delusions." I stare down at my hands. They are clenched into fists over my knees. "What would you say if a patient told you that she was starting to believe she could alter reality in her dreams? That the choices she made while sleeping had an effect on what happens in real life?"

He scratches his chin. "I'd probably tell the patient that must feel like a very frightening thing."

Frustration builds. I don't want to be placated. I want him to tell me what he's really thinking. I want to know if I'm crazy. "My grandmother thought the same thing, didn't she? And she was diagnosed with schizophrenia."

"Have you had any other dreams other than this one?"

I take a drink of water, then rest the cup in my lap and stare into the clear liquid. "Yes."

"You didn't write them down?"

"I didn't want to."

"Why not?"

"I didn't want to remember."

"But you do remember?"

I nod and take another drink. "I dreamt that I was in a garage." I skip the part about Summer and Luka. There's no need to drag him into this. Not yet. Especially when Dr. Roth no longer thinks Luka is experiencing symptoms of mental instability. "There was a woman and this guy."

Dr. Roth leans forward. "Go on."

"There was a car too, and it was running. The man went into the house and came out with the woman's kids."

"Where were you in the dream?"

"I was standing off to the side, like a spectator."

He gets out a pad of paper and starts writing. He pauses for a moment to scratch his chin, then writes some more. "What was the woman doing?"

I imagine her blank, glossy eyes. Her expressionless face. "She just sat there. It was almost as if she was in some sort of trance."

"And the man? Can you describe him?"

A shiver runs up my spine. "He looked like a living corpse."

Dr. Roth adds the description to his notes. "What happened next?"

I relay the dream as best I can, including the article I found online the next morning. "So the kids miraculously survived." Although doctors were very careful not to use that word— *miracle*. "I got them out of the car in my dream, and somehow, they are alive in real life."

Dr. Roth writes down every word. When he finishes, he bites the end of his pen and scans the paper, as if checking for missing details.

My restlessness grows. I don't want to be his next project. I don't want my misery and torture to be his next mental illness breakthrough. "Is there medicine I can take for this?"

He sets the pen down. "I'm not sure that would be in your best interest."

"Why not?"

He turns around, opens his filing cabinet and removes a manila folder. He reads something inside, sticks in the notes he took about my dream, closes the folder, and puts it away. "I want you to try something for me, Tess. If it doesn't work, we'll consider medicine."

I narrow my eyes.

"I want you to record every single one of your dreams. I want you to write down as many details as possible. The people. The faces. All of it."

"How will that help?"

"I have some theories, but before I'm comfortable sharing them, more evidence is needed."

My eyes narrow further.

"I need you to trust me."

"How do I know I can?"

"Because I'm a doctor, Tess. And I want to help you." He opens the front drawer of his desk and removes a prescription pad, scribbles something on the first page, tears off the sheet and holds it out for me to see. "If in a month, you still want medicine, then I will talk with your parents and I'll prescribe what's on this sheet."

"I don't understand why I can't have it now."

"I told you why."

"Because it isn't in my best interest?"

He nods.

"That's not an adequate explanation."

Sighing, Dr. Roth folds his hand. "How about we make a

deal, then?"

"What kind of deal?"

"You give me one month. You write down your dreams. Every single one. And at the end of the month, I promise to tell you more about your grandmother."

His words hit their mark. I'm so desperate to know more about her, a month could almost be worth it.

∽

If I wasn't crazy already, Dr. Roth's deal makes me so. My dreams turn into an obsession. The harder I fight in them, the darker my waking hours become. There seems to be a direct correlation—the spiritual and the physical. The fact that I call it spiritual at all may be proof of my insanity.

On November 4th, I dream about an overweight man with bad breath, idling in a rundown van while students file out of an elementary school. He looks like a regular man, except his eyes. They are all white. No irises. No pupils. When a small girl with curly brown hair approaches, he rolls down his window and beckons her over. When she's close enough, he grabs her and drives away. I wrestle him away from the wheel with a strength that shouldn't be mine and the car careens off the road. The next day, there's a story on the news about a kidnapping gone awry in a town nearby. The kidnapper was apprehended by police after his car ran off the road. The child was unharmed and reunited with her parents.

I write everything down in my journal.

Somebody spray paints *Freak Show* on my locker. Luka is furious. Principal Jolly is appalled. Summer and her friends whisper and laugh whenever I walk past. Nobody gets in trouble. My dark circles grow darker. My parents worry. And my headaches get worse.

On November 16th, I dream about a sick woman in a hospital while a man with a receding hairline weeps by her bedside and a doctor shakes his head, as if there's nothing he can do. Neither the doctor or the husband see the skeletal man standing on the other side of the woman's bed, pressing his cold, pale hands against the sick woman's skull. I sweep his legs and fight him away and the next morning, there's a story on the news about a woman suddenly healed from the final stages of brain cancer.

I write it all down in my journal.

Mean things are written about me in the girls' bathrooms. Luka can't see them and I don't tell him. I have a hard time eating. My parents' worry turns into bickering. I hear them at night, their voices escalating through my bedroom walls. I am at the root of each argument. Luka grows increasingly protective. Men with empty, white eyes haunt me during the day—appearing at unsuspecting moments, so I make a fool of myself by jumping or gasping for no reason my classmates can understand.

On November 28th, I dream about a teenager dressed in army combat boots, a trench coat, and a ski mask, with a familiar symbol tattooed on the back of his neck, only I can't remember where I've seen it before. He enters a mall in the middle of Black Friday—the biggest shopping day of the year—and as he's about to open fire with a semi-automatic in a crowded toy store, I jump in front of the gun. Bullets riddle through my body, but I can't feel them. The next morning, it's all over the news. A seventeen-year-old boy tried to wreak havoc in a mall in San Francisco, but his black-market gun locked up and a security guard tackled him before any bullets could escape. Not a single person was injured.

I write it all down in my journal.

Someone starts a rumor that Luka is using me. That his attention is all part of some bet. Pete takes the opportunity to reopen our line of communication. Instead of ignoring me, he goes out of his way to assure me the rumor is true. My parents are at each other's throats, which never happens. Mom wants to move. Dad doesn't think moving is the answer. Dr. Roth cannot contain his fascination.

And for the first time, I die in Luka's dream. He is unable to save me.

Then he does something that surprises us both.

In the middle of the locker bay, right before history class, when the skeletal man nobody else can see lunges at me, Luka steps forward and something bright—like visible sound waves—radiates from his body. The skeletal man's unseeing eyes go wide with shock as the bright, radiating force slams into him. He topples backward and disappears into a shock of brilliant light.

Thankfully, Mr. Lotsam gives us the entire period to work with our partners on our project. Luka and I make a beeline to the library and find a private corner to talk.

"Did you just—?"

"I think so," he says.

"How?"

"I have no idea." He looks down at his hands, as if they, and not the radiating waves, had shoved the man back. "I've never done anything like that before."

"Luka, you made him disappear."

"I know."

My heart gallops inside my chest. Forget a wave of hope.

This is a stampede. "Can you teach me how you did it?"

"I would if I knew. It was like a reflex."

I scoot closer. "Maybe you should try it again."

He looks doubtful.

"You had to have done something. Let's replay it."

"I saw him coming at you, but you weren't looking and I ... I don't know. It just happened."

"Do you remember what you were thinking?"

He turns his hands over and stares at his knuckles, shaking his head. There's a long stretch of silence. The longer it carries on, the more my stampeding hope dwindles away. I want, more than anything, to learn how to do what Luka did. But how can I if *he* doesn't even know?

"You have your appointment with Dr. Roth today," Luka finally says.

I nod.

"It's been a month."

I nod again.

"Are you going to ask for medicine?"

"I can't live like this." Sure, the medicine will not fix my problem in school with my increasingly hostile classmates. But at least I won't be fighting two battles.

Luka takes my hand beneath the table. "You shouldn't have to."

A book drops. We turn around. Summer picks it up, her eyes bright and frenzied, and hurries away. My mouth goes dry, because I'm pretty sure she heard everything.

༄

I plop the journal onto Dr. Roth's desk and sit in the chair, trying to push away the memory of Summer's face. He grabs the notebook like it's a hot meal and he's a starving man. I wait impatiently while he reads my latest.

"May I make a copy of this?" he asks.

"You can have the entire journal. I did your experiment and now I'm done."

He pushes his glasses up his nose. "Are you sure you don't want to continue recording your dreams? We could—"

"No." I shake my head adamantly, appalled that he'd even suggest it. Can't he see how close I am to losing it altogether? "I'd like to go on medicine now."

"What if the dreams are real?"

His question draws me back, because surely he doesn't think any of this is real. I am obviously crazy. I've studied up on schizophrenia. The things I write in that journal—they have to be delusions and I cannot handle any more of them. I'm done with being *Tess the Freak*. Even if it means getting rid of whatever mysterious connection Luka and I share, I have to try if it means a shot at a normal existence. "If the dreams are real, then medicine won't make any difference."

He takes out the prescription he wrote last month with a sigh.

I wipe my palms down the thighs of my jeans. "Will there be side effects?"

"Medicine of this nature has come a long way in the last few years. Side effects have all but disappeared. There is a very, very rare chance of nausea and fatigue, but that's about it."

"How long will it take to kick in?"

"Another perk of medical breakthroughs. It should take effect as soon as the second dose. If not, we'll consider this particular medication ineffective and try another." He holds the prescription in his left hand. I can't take my eyes off of it.

"Of course, I'll need to speak with your mother about this in the front office. There is a specific pharmacy where you will want to purchase it."

"A specific pharmacy?"

"They are not required to report to the state department. They are safe."

Safe. With his own word he has confirmed how vital it is that I get this sickness under control. If the wrong people find out how out of hand it's become, surely I'll be removed from society. "What about the rest? I held up my end of the bargain."

He leans back in his chair.

"A deal's a deal."

Dr. Roth folds his hands beneath his chin. "Your grandmother was diagnosed with paranoid schizophrenia."

"I already knew that."

"She suffered from the same symptoms that you are suffering from."

"Like?"

"Dreams that seemed to come true." He reaches for the folder on his desk—the one with my name on it—and pulls out a stack of photocopied papers all stapled together.

"What's that?"

"You aren't the only person who has kept a journal, Tess."

My eyes go wide. "You mean that's …?"

"Your grandmother's dream journal?" He hands it over. "Yes."

I take the cool pages slowly, reverently. When Dr. Roth promised to tell me what he knew about her, I never imagined this. "How did you get it?"

"Let's just say some rules were bent."

I look up from the pages in my lap. "Where is she?"

"Eugene, Oregon. But I wouldn't get any ideas about going there. It would be a wasted trip."

"Why?"

"She's not allowed visitors. Nobody in that facility is."

Coldness settles into the pit of my stomach. "Why not?"

"Because the patients there are among the most deranged and delusional in the country. The director doesn't believe visitors would be safe."

"Is she really that dangerous?"

"I can't say. She was never my client."

I stand from the chair, shoving the stapled papers into my backpack. The thought of being locked away, not allowed any visitors, permanently separated from my parents, my brother, Leela, Luka? The cold lump in my stomach expands. "I can't end up like her."

Dr. Roth hands me the prescription, his expression solemn. "Don't make this decision lightly."

"There's nothing light about any of this."

## CHAPTER TWENTY-SEVEN

# THE JOURNAL

The pills rattle inside the see-through orange plastic container as I pace in my room. I push down on the white cap, twist, and shake two into the palm of my hand. My pacing stops.

Why would Dr. Roth caution me against taking medicine? Isn't it made to help people like me? For all Dr. Roth knows, I could be two seconds away from kidnapping babies because I think they're in danger, like those kids from my dream—the ones strapped in the back seat of a running car in a closed garage. I shake my head, confused. Dr. Roth is a psychiatrist. Shouldn't he be encouraging the use of medicine? His counsel makes about as much sense as my dad espousing the many dangers of security systems.

I set the bottle on my desk, squeeze the two pills in my hand, and stare at the stapled papers lying untouched on my bed. Opposing desires dual inside me, splitting me into two distinct halves, one of which is dying to read my grandmother's words. That half wants nothing more than to lunge at the papers. But the other half is equally resolute and views those pages like a leper. That half is terrified of having access into the inner workings of a madwoman's brain.

I stand immobilized in the middle of my room, until the curious half manhandles my fear into compliance. I creep slowly to the edge of my bed and sink down onto the mattress.

The springs give a soft squeak. I set the two pills on my comforter and pick up the papers. With my heart thudding heavily, I start to read.

*Last night I dreamt about a plane. I sat in the cockpit, watching the pilot have some sort of seizure. I watched the flight attendants try to keep the passengers calm, their own fear oozing out from their stricken eyes, and I was moved profoundly. Somehow, with immense concentration, I managed to land the plane. This morning, there is news of a plane crashing. There were no casualties.*

I flip several pages.

*A bus full of students died because of me. It was my fault. James insisted I get help, but this medicine is making me weak. I couldn't save them. I wasn't strong enough.*

More pages.

*I can't eat. I can't sleep. He haunts me at all hours of the day. No matter what I do or how hard I fight, I can't escape.*

My heart beats harder. I flip more pages, noting that the further I go, the larger and messier the handwriting becomes.

*Teresa can save me. She can make this stop.*

The shock of seeing my name there, on the page, pulls me back. I blink at the two sentences, reading them over and over, then scan the page, looking for more. How could I save her? Is this why she kidnapped me? But I am not mentioned again. There are more dreams and disjointed stories. The handwriting growing more and more into a child's scrawl. The words become incoherent, as if she's racing a clock to get it all down. Fear and confusion pulse from every line.

I lay the pages down, unable to read any further, wishing Dr. Roth wouldn't have given it to me. Wishing I wouldn't have started to read. Because one thing is clear. Whatever my grandmother had—or has—is the same thing plaguing me. Prophetic dreams. The power to save lives. The belief that what happens in our sleeping hours unfolds in real life. Feeling haunted at all hours of the day.

I shove away from my bed, sit down at my computer, open up my browser, and do what I'm so adept at doing. Googling. Obsessing. Only this time I'm not looking for recent news. I'm looking for news from the past—archived stories. I search for plane crashes and bus accidents until my room darkens around me. My screen glows as I scroll through the different articles, taking meticulous notes.

Finally, I type in *high security mental hospital, Eugene, Oregon.* Dr. Roth didn't give me a specific name, but I can't imagine there is more than one in the city. I hit enter just as a gentle rapping sounds at my door. My mom pokes her head inside. I pull away from the computer as if I've done something wrong.

"May I come in?"

I click out of the internet. "Sure."

She walks inside and runs her fingers through my ponytail. I want to cover up the notes I've taken, unsettled by how much my handwriting resembles my grandmother's.

"Honey, this needs to stop."

"I know."

She runs her fingers through my hair again, her touch gentle and soothing. I wish I could crawl into her lap like I did as a small child, tell her about my nightmares, and let her soothing presence chase the bad things away. Only I'm not a little girl anymore and the bad things are too big, even for her.

I swivel the chair around and the question that tumbles out surprises even me. "Did grandma ever say why she tried to kidnap me?"

Mom bites her lip.

My attention zips to the journal on my mattress. I don't want her to see it. I walk over and sit on my bed, careful to position my body so the journal is blocked from view.

Mom sits beside me, her face softening in that way mother's faces do, as if she would love nothing more than to take my troubles away. She places her cold hand over mine. "Because she wasn't stable, sweetheart."

"So you think that's it—she tried taking me because of psychosis?"

"What other explanation is there?"

"Maybe she knew something we didn't."

Worry expands in Mom's eyes. "Your grandmother was seeing things nobody else could see. She couldn't hold down a job or even carry on a coherent conversation. When I came home from the doctor's office with Pete and found you in her arms ..." Mom shivers. "It was the most terrifying moment of my life."

I look down into my lap. "I'm afraid of becoming like her," I whisper.

Mom picks up the pills lying on my comforter. Their whiteness is impossible to miss against the deep purple. She turns my hand over and places the pills in my palm. "You don't have to be."

With tears in her eyes, she pats my knee and leaves my room.

I sit there, unmoving. For a minute, maybe two. Then, without giving myself time to reconsider, I reach for the glass on my nightstand, pop the pills into my mouth, and chase them down with a big swig of water. Mom is right. I don't have to be afraid of turning into my grandmother. Not when there's something I can do to prevent it.

There's a tap-tap-tap at my window.

I swivel around with my hand against my chest and spot Luka. A puff of breath swooshes past my lips. I hold up my finger, shut my door quietly, and click the lock. Then I hurry to the window and open it. "How did you climb up here?" I ask, looking past him to the shadowed grass below.

"The trellis helped." A cool breeze joins him as he climbs inside and brushes his hand down his shirt, as if smoothing away nonexistent wrinkles. When he looks up, my knees wobble a little. Because Luka snuck into my bedroom. It's late at night. And the door is locked.

"Hey," he says.

I wipe my palms against the thighs of my jeans, wanting to hide the pill bottle, but unsure how to do so without calling attention to the very thing I don't want him to see.

"I wasn't sure if your parents would let me come in this late." He glances at the closed door. "Or if they'd let us talk privately."

"Probably not."

"How'd it go with Dr. Roth?"

I pick up the copy of my grandmother's journal and hand it over. He reads for a bit, flips a page, and reads some more. The longer he does, the tighter I wrap my arms around my waist. When he finishes, he holds the journal up. "Dr. Roth had this?"

I nod.

He looks past me and spots the pill bottle I don't want him to see. "Did you …?"

I nod again.

"Do you feel different?"

"Not yet."

He steps closer, the nearness of his body throwing off heat like a furnace.

"I'm afraid," I whisper.

"Don't be."

"But what about your dream?" I died in it. That has to mean something. "What if I turn into her? What if they lock me up? What if—?"

"Tess," he stands so close I have to tilt my head back to look at him, "I won't let anybody lock you up."

The huskiness of his voice and the nearness of his body and the way his attention drops to my lips has my heart crashing against my chest. I think Luka is going to kiss me. I think Luka is going to kiss me and I have no idea what to do with my hands. He must know, because he looks down, curls one of his pinkies around mine, and draws me closer. So close our bodies nearly touch. He runs his thumb across my knuckles, a feather-light touch that sets every one of my nerve-endings on fire. When he looks at me, his green eyes are like a sea storm and I can't breathe. In fact, I'm quite certain I might not ever breathe again. His attention flickers to my lips. I stand very still. And something creaks in the hallway.

Luka and I break apart.

My lungs spring back into action.

He runs his hand down his face.

There's another creak in the hallway. A definite footstep. Followed by a soft knock on the door. The door handle jiggles. But it's locked. There's a brief pause and another knock. "Tess, are you sleeping in there?" Dad asks from the other side.

I look at Luka with wild eyes.

He takes a couple steps to the window, then turns around, his face a mask of frustrated indecipherability. He looks like he wants to tell me something, but there's another knock.

"Tess?"

I turn toward the door, panicked. Then I turn back to the window. Luka's gone. There is nothing but the fluttering of my curtain and the subtlest hint of wintergreen in the air. Dad knocks again, the sound more impatient this time. I shut the window and hurry over to the door to swing it open.

"Are you okay?" Dad asks.

"Yeah. Fine. Why?" My voice is entirely too breathless for innocence.

His attention lands on the window. "I thought I heard talking."

"Nope. No talking."

His worry turns suspicious. I'm sure the scent of brine lingers in my room. Maybe he even heard me close the window. "You know we don't lock doors in this house."

"Right, I must have done it on accident."

His suspicion remains, but he kisses my forehead. "Sleep well, okay?"

"You too."

Once he's gone, I sit on my bed, scoot under the covers, and flip open the journal.

*They're forcing me on meds again. They don't understand*

*that people will die.*

Unsettled, I turn to the very last page. Her handwriting is that of a small child's.

*Somebody, help.*

## CHAPTER TWENTY-EIGHT

# NORMALCY

When I wake up, my head feels completely normal. No aching. No pounding. I stretch my arms and squint against the sunlight streaming through my window. Somehow, my body feels lighter. I rub the sleep out of my eyes, then touch my fingers against my lips. Was Luka really about to kiss me last night? The question sends a ripple of heat through my belly.

I hop out of bed, feeling well rested for the first time in weeks. No, months. Could the medicine really have taken effect that quickly? I take my time getting ready, marveling at the lightness of my mood. When I step into the kitchen, whatever heated conversation my parents are having comes to a screeching halt. Mom shuts off the morning news. Dad closes the newspaper and pulls it into his lap. They have taken to hiding these things from me, as if doing so would lessen my obsession. Whistling, I unwrap a Pop-Tart and sit at the table, uninterested in the newspaper he's trying to hide. I don't care about it, because I didn't have any dreams last night.

Not one.

"Did you sleep well?" Mom asks from the sink, raising her eyebrows at Dad.

"Like a rock." I pop a piece of Pop-Tart into my mouth.

Dad sets the paper on the table. "You look good."

"Thanks." I wash the Pop-Tart down with a glass of water

and remove the pill bottle from the front pocket of my backpack. I twist off the cap and rattle two into my palm. Funny how something that caused so much angst last night feels like my new best friend this morning. I swallow them happily, give my mom a peck on her cheek, my dad a peck on the crown of his head, shrug my backpack over my shoulder, and meet Pete in the foyer. Even his surly face cannot dampen my mood. Let him be surly.

I don't care. It's not my problem.

With a smile on my face—the first smile I've smiled in weeks—I slide my feet into my shoes, step outside, and spot Luka leaning casually against his car. My left pinky heats with the memory of his curled around mine. He squints at me through the morning brightness. "Wanna hitch a ride with me today?" he calls over.

Carpooling to school? This is new.

Feeling brave, I toss the keys to Pete and change course, no longer heading toward my car but Luka's.

He cocks his head as I approach. "You're looking cheery this morning."

"Is that a bad thing?"

"No, not at all." He opens my door with a grin.

"What?"

"Maybe you should share those pills with me."

"Maybe I will." I wink, then slide into the passenger seat, taken aback by my behavior. Was I just flirting?

Luka walks around the front of the car and gets behind the wheel. Being in such close quarters with him without Pete, especially in light of last night, leaves me feeling all kinds of jittery. "I take it you didn't have any dreams last night?" he asks.

I put concerted effort into thinking back. I remember the shock of seeing Luka framed in my window. I remember him standing very, very close. I remember my dad knocking and Luka leaving and then I remember ... waking up. "Not a single one."

He places his hand on the back of my seat and reverses out of the drive. "Hmm."

"What?"

"Worked fast." He turns onto the highway that will bring us to school, his stare heating the side of my face. It's like a beam of sunshine. "You look good," he finally says.

The words are the same as my dad's, but the effect of them is much, much different. Blood not only rushes into my cheeks, it spreads up my forehead and down my neck. I guess the pills haven't cured my blushing problem. "Thanks."

We ride the rest of the way in charged silence. It's like the medication has made me hyper aware. I notice everything about him—the way the sun falls on his profile, his pointer finger tapping the wheel, his tan arm resting on the console between us, even the rhythm of his breathing. What's crazy? He seems equally aware of me.

The spell isn't broken until he pulls into the parking lot—a hive of teenage activity. Car doors slamming. Music playing. A group of boys kicking around a hacky sack in the front lawn as one of the stoners—too gutsy for his own good—stamps out a cigarette. Students walking in twos and threes, making their way toward another day of high school delirium, taking their sweet time in order to enjoy the rare sunshine and warmth that is so scarce in early December.

Luka pulls into a parking space and turns off the engine. "Wait here."

Sunshine silhouettes his messy hair while he makes his way around the front and waves at a kid who calls out his name. He opens my door. It feels silly. I can open my own door. But I also like it.

We walk side-by-side through the parking lot, our knuckles brushing a couple times. People watch us, like always, but the animosity that was so glaringly obvious yesterday has vanished. Instead, the girls look resigned and the boys, curious. They stare intently, as if searching for whatever they missed the first few times around.

Inside, Leela stands at my locker. I experience a surge of love for this friend who has stuck by my side during one of the darkest months of my life. When she spots Luka, her cheeks flush. She gives me a giddy smile. You'd think after a month, she'd be accustomed to his presence. But then, you'd think I would too. Apparently, Luka is not the type you ever grow accustomed to.

"So," she says, "it's throwback night at the theater. They're playing all these old-school, amazing films. Please say you'll go." Her attention shifts from me to Luka, her hands clasped beneath her chin.

He shrugs. "I'm a fan of movies."

Leela claps her hands and gives a little cheer. "You in, Tess?"

I look around. Students, lockers, a drinking fountain, some windows, and a lot of chatter. No flickers. No pockets of inexplicable coldness. No weird lights or masses of darkness or creepy men with white eyes. I wonder if Luka sees anything. I wonder if anything is there, only blocked by the medicine. If so, I could never tell. Luka is so good at ignoring the things I cannot. I search for the slightest clue, but he leans against the locker looking every inch at ease.

He catches me staring and smiles a smile so irresistible my stomach does a loop-de-loop. And I'm smiling too. Because I feel so normal, so light. I beam at Leela, my best friend, while the popular boy who might have almost kissed me last night stands close to my side. "I think that sounds like fun."

❧

For the first time in my life, I get my birthday wish. I am normal. In fact, I'm better than normal. It's like the medicine has not only fixed my mental problems, it has fixed everything. My parents no longer argue. The rumors at school have disappeared, and somehow, so has the graffiti in the girl's bathroom. If Summer overheard the conversation between Luka and me in the library, she hasn't said anything to anyone. My classmates are actually nice.

Luka and I don't talk about weird stuff anymore. If he's still seeing things, he doesn't share and I don't ask. I'd rather pretend none of it existed. If this bothers him, he doesn't let on. Every now and then, I'll spot a flicker of something—concern, maybe?—in his eyes or I'll catch him watching me in a way I don't quite understand, but overall, he seems relieved that I am happy and my dark circles are gone.

I don't have dreams.

Not bad ones or good ones. My sleeping hours are blank. Sometimes I'll wake up with an inkling of something, but it's all so vague and blurry and easy to forget that I let the inkling float away, despite Dr. Roth's pleas that I at least try to remember.

At school, our lunch table grows. We've jumped from two—me and Leela—to a full house, with extra chairs crammed in between. After Luka joined us, more followed. An artsy girl named Serendipity—formerly on the fringe of the popular crowd—came first. Shortly after, Bobbi followed and with her came Matt and a very repentant Jennalee, whose sugary sweetness makes me want to gag. Beamer, the kid with highlights and skinny jeans, comes too, along with a couple others. Summer stays away, sitting at the old table, head down, Jared faithfully by her side. Sometimes, though, I catch her looking at me. I can never read her expression.

Despite my new-found friends, I spend the bulk of my time with Leela. And Luka. People ask what we are, but I never know how to respond. He hasn't tried kissing me again, if that's what he was trying to do all those nights ago when I took my first dose of medicine. All I know is that we spend a lot of time together and much of that time, there exists this unexplained *thing* between us, this odd sort of gravity, like we are two magnets being pulled together. It would be easy to chalk it up to wishful thinking on my part if not for Leela.

"Sheesh," she likes to say, "the way he looks at you is so intense, even I feel light-headed. And he's not even looking at me!"

Life—at least my life—is better than it's ever been.

There are only three gloomy spots.

My brother remains distant, Luka's mother's disposition toward me does not improve, and the world spins into a bigger and bigger mess. My medicine has not fixed any of those. But it's hard to worry. Luka doesn't seem to care what his mother thinks. Pete's been so well-adjusted up until this point that surely, teenage hormones were bound to hit him sooner or later. It doesn't seem fair for any teenager to pass through these years without at least some measure of angst. And as far as the world? I don't know. The unrest in Africa? The talk of a third world war? The escalating violence surrounding the fetal modification clinics and the massive increase in incarcerations? It's hard to care. All of those things are so far removed from my life in Thornsdale. Besides, the chaos makes my father's job one of the most secure in the country.

For Christmas, Leela organizes a secret Santa and I draw Bobbi's name. I settle on a pair of earrings from this art deco place downtown and a chocolate bar, then sneak a small box of sugar-cookie scented car air fresheners to Leela. I found them while out and about and couldn't resist. Sugar cookies are her favorite. Unfortunately, Beamer picks my name, which means I receive gifts more reminiscent of Valentine's Day than Christmas. And even though Luka got Serendipity, I find a dream-catcher in my locker the last day before winter break, along with a note that says simply:

*Merry Christmas, Tess.*
    *Yours,*
    *Luka*

Something about the word before his signature makes my cheeks warm.

I spend a quiet Christmas with my family and the rest of the break hanging out with our lunch group—going to movies or trying different restaurants in Thornsdale or attending the occasional get-together, most often at Bobbi's. She has a party on New Year's Eve and I'm so nervous about midnight and Luka and kissing that I drag Leela with me to the bathroom the second the countdown begins, then spend the drive home regretting my cowardice.

Luka and I are rarely alone, which is both a relief and a

disappointment. He has not climbed the lattice up to my bedroom window since that first night I took my medicine, but he does make a point of being out on his back deck whenever I'm out on mine, where we spend time talking across a span of too much distance.

On the first day back to school, Mr. Lotsam has us choose an article to read in the New Year edition of USA Today. It covers everything from the upcoming inauguration of our nation's first independent president to a piece on B-Trix's new album and the excitement surrounding her upcoming stateside tour, which (to Mr. Lotsam's disappointment) the majority of class decides to focus on. I pass over a passionately written op-ed about individual privacy verses national security and whether or not the Department of Security and Defense is overstepping their bounds, and eventually settle on a surprisingly upbeat special interest story about life in our country's largest refugee community.

At lunch, Bobbi and Leela regale us all with funny stories from their family Christmas gathering. Serendipity laughs so hard milk comes out of her nose, which makes me like her more than I already do. Afterward, we walk together to Honors English with matching smiles plastered on our faces.

When I step inside the classroom, there's a man sitting at Mrs. Meecher's desk. He has leathery skin, a cleft in his chin, and eyes as dark as his hair. Something about him gives me the creeps. I shake away the feeling and follow Serendipity toward a couple desks off to the right while he writes his name on the chalkboard.

Mr. Rathbone.

"While Mrs. Meecher is away, I'll be your long-term sub."

All of us shift in our seats, my disappointment sharp. I love

Mrs. Meecher, with her flyaway hair and chalked-up blouses. She's so caught up in her passion for literature that she runs the class more like an engaging book club than an honors high school course. Jason Brane—whose last name, pronounced *brain*, is completely appropriate—raises his hand. "What's wrong with her?" he asks.

"She's ill."

We all exchange looks. As far as any of us could tell, Mrs. Meecher looked perfectly healthy before break and that was only a week and a half ago.

"How long-term will you be?" Jason asks.

"Indefinitely."

Wren stumbles into the classroom—her hair shaved except for a strip of neon pink down the center of her head. A new hairdo, apparently. She glares at everybody who stares at her and slides into the empty seat next to me, smelling strongly of marijuana.

Mr. Rathbone either doesn't care or doesn't notice. He takes roll call and when he reaches my name, his gaze is heavy and steady and unnerving. A tiny raincloud infiltrates the sunshine that's been my life and hovers over my head. I wonder if I'm imagining his prolonged attention. I wonder if I'm having a delusion. A wave of panic rolls through my body. Did I forget my medicine this morning? I squish up one eye, trying to remember. No, I took it. Right after I brushed my teeth, like I always do. Another wave of panic follows the first. Is it possible that the medicine is already starting to lose its effectiveness?

I shake the worry away. So what if he's looking at me more than the other students? There could be any number of reasons why. For all I know, I could remind him of a niece who lives somewhere in Michigan.

As soon as he finishes, we get out our books—tattered copies of *Mein Kampf*. Hitler's memoir is both disturbing and enthralling. But the sub shakes his head and tells us to put them away. Then he writes out two words on the chalkboard that elicit a collective groan.

Family Tree.

"Excuse me, Mr. Rathbone?" Jason holds up his book. "We're supposed to discuss the final three chapters of this today. Several of us came to class with discussion questions."

Mr. Rathbone stares at Jason with that same inscrutable face, then jerks his head at the two words on the board. "I'd like everyone to complete a family tree by next week. I want you to look into your genealogy. It's good to know where you come from."

"What does this have to do with literature?" Jason asks.

"I'm the teacher, Mr. Brane."

I'm impressed Rathbone remembers Jason's last name.

Wren raises her hand. "I object to this assignment. It's racist against adopted people."

Jason scoffs. "Racist is the wrong word."

"Whatever. I object. I'm adopted and I have no idea who my birth parents are."

A few students muffle their laughter. Wren isn't adopted.

Mr. Rathbone picks up a stack of papers and begins passing them out. "You can use your adoptive parents, then."

"That's dumb. I don't have any of their *genes*. Isn't that where the whole word genealogy comes from?"

I skim the paper, a groan forming deep down in my chest. A paragraph about each person on our tree—living and deceased, including the legacy they left behind? I think of my grandmother for the first time in weeks. I do not, under any circumstances, want to do research on her or tell anybody about her legacy. The cloud this Rathbone character brought into my life expands.

Wren hits her head against the table. Her forehead makes a loud thud. Several students look over at her, me included. Despite her pink hair and black clothes, I feel a connection with Wren. We are united in our disapproval of this new teacher. I smile, trying to catch her attention, then notice that the small tattoo of the strange symbol on her wrist isn't there anymore.

I lean forward in my chair, checking her other wrist. It's not there either. She whips her head up, her eyes narrowed into slits. "*What* is your deal?"

"Your tattoo is gone—the one on your wrist. Was it henna or something?"

"You are such a freak. I never had a tattoo on my wrist." And as if to prove her point, she holds up both of her arms to show me.

My ears catch fire. I can feel the class staring. I quickly drop my attention to the paper in front of me, feigning interest. Serendipity nudges me and gives me an amused look, like it's obvious *I'm* not the freak. I smile back, but for the first time since taking my medicine, the heaviness returns. I know what I saw before. Wren did too have a tattoo on her wrist.

## CHAPTER TWENTY-NINE

# DISTRACTION

Luka and I sit together at a round table in the library. Mr. Lotsam has given us another class period to work on our project, which means we get forty-five minutes alone, without the expanse of our backyards dividing us. In fact, we sit so close I can feel his body heat. He scratches the back of his head, making his hair stick up in that tussled, fresh-out-of-bed way while he reads from the fat book of world dictators he brought from his house. I peruse one of several library books, all opened to various chapters on genocides throughout history, pretending to focus when really, the words about Mao Zedong blur into a streak of black against the white page.

"Hey, Tess?"

I look up. Luka is staring at me. I don't know for how long. I stop my pencil-drumming. "Sorry."

His mouth quirks in a half-smile. "It's not that."

"What is it?"

"Something's bothering you." He says it like a fact, not a question.

I think about Mr. Rathbone and the way he kept looking at me throughout Honors English. I look around to make sure nobody is close by, then lean closer. "Mrs. Meecher's sub is making us all do family trees."

"What does that have to do with English?"

"No idea."

A flash of worry flickers in his eyes. "Your grandmother."

I nod, my mind wandering to the bottom drawer of my desk at home, where I've tucked away her journal. I haven't looked at it, haven't even thought about it since I started taking medicine. I drop my pencil on the book, plunk my elbows on the table, and dig my fingers into my hair. After weeks of not thinking about her, my brain can't stop now. I want to swallow the entire bottle of pills in my medicine cabinet to make the thoughts go away. I think about her plea for help on the final page. I think about her locked up in some mental institute against her will.

Luka puts his hand over my jiggling knee beneath the table. The warmth of his touch sends my stomach swooping. "Hey."

I look at him.

"You can write the bare minimum. Or you could make something up. This Rathbone guy won't know the difference."

"But *I* do." I bite my lip, look around again. Summer peeks at us from behind a row of encyclopedias, too far away to hear. "She's out there, Luka."

He doesn't respond.

"Isn't that weird? She's out there and I'm not doing anything about it."

"Have you had anymore dreams about her?"

"If I have, I don't remember them. The medicine pretty much takes care of the dreams."

He scratches his jaw, then takes the book in front of me and gives me that grin that is infamous for making females swoon, and not just students either. I've seen him dazzle a few teachers, too. "How about this? We forget about your grandma and focus on our project instead. Surely mass murder will get our minds in the right spot."

"This project is depressing."

"Holocausts and genocides? I don't know what you're talking about." He begins rattling off names of dictators—Hitler, Stalin, Hideki Tojo, Pol Pot. "Cheery fellows if you ask me."

I take his big, dorky book. "I guess in light of these guys, I shouldn't really get this worked up over a silly family tree."

"This is true."

My smile falters. I want to tell Luka about Wren's disappearing tattoo, but I'm afraid of voicing my concern out loud, as if making it audible will increase its validity. Instead, I ask a question I haven't yet been brave enough to ask. "Do you still see ... things?"

His brow furrows. "Rarely."

"And your dreams, about me?"

"Still there."

"Do I ...?"

He shakes his head. "Only that one time."

Confusion settles like a blanket of snow. I know the medicine is helping my psychosis but how does that explain Luka's dreams or the things he sees or our odd connection? Are people who suffer from psychosis naturally drawn to each other? But then I study his profile and decide he can't be ill. He's too perfect. Too flawless. There is nothing wrong with him. So maybe the medicine isn't helping after all and all of this—this entire conversation—is a delusion.

"You know what I can't stop thinking about?" he says.

"What?"

"The way I fought off that guy when he came at you."

The memory is as vivid as if it happened yesterday.

"I've been trying to do it again."

"What do you mean?"

"Anytime I see something unusual. Like the other night when I was out to eat with my parents. There was a guy there—the same kind of guy, at least. You know, with the eyes. He was standing by this table. I got up to go to the bathroom and tried to do whatever I did in the locker bay."

"Did it work?"

He shakes his head. "Nothing happened. Nothing ever does."

I stare at him while his words soak in. None of it makes sense.

Luka's attention drops to my lips. We sit so close, he would only have to lean in a couple inches and…Warmth billows inside my chest. My breath quickens. Unless you count a dare in first grade, I've never kissed a boy. And I really, really want to be kissed by this one.

"Am I interrupting something?" Matt pulls out a chair at our table, smirking at us. "You know, you two should be a little more subtle. Summer's practically in tears over there."

Luka glances over at the encyclopedias. "What are you doing here, Matt?"

"Bothering you, apparently." As if taking the hint, he stands back up and saunters away. "By all means, carry on."

I can't bring myself to look at Luka. My face is much too hot.

❧

That night, I want to think about Luka. I want everything about him to consume me—his touch, the sound of his voice, the impossible greenness of his eyes. But try as I might, my grandmother has taken up residence in my mind—her presence loud and unavoidable.

As much as I don't want to, I can't help myself. I get out her journal and I lie in bed and thumb through the pages, wishing I didn't know about her. Wishing she really were dead. I fall asleep reading an old woman's crazy, unhinged words.

"The pills have zapped your strength, Little Rabbit."

I bolt upright in bed, lungs heaving, unable to press away the sound of gunshots and spraying glass as a black woman with horse teeth wailed and clutched her bleeding son in the front lawn of a rundown apartment complex. The emotionless words, spoken by that man with the scar, reverberate inside my head. I was there. I was in the car while men with empty, white eyes pointed guns outside tinted windows. I sat there unmoving, arms and legs too heavy to lift. I sat there and did nothing while they pulled the trigger.

Cold sweat soaks through my tank top. My heart races so frantically, I press my palm against my chest, as if the pressure might calm it down. My bed lamp casts a circle of yellow onto my ceiling. Outside my room, the hallway is dark.

The house sleeps.

It was a dream. I had a dream. I take a deep, rattling breath and tell myself it wasn't real. But I cannot get that woman's grief-stricken face out of my head or the way she rocked the small boy in her lap. The pair scroll through my mind and the words come back, spoken by that man who calls me Little Rabbit. Where was he in the dream? How did I hear him? What did he mean? And why did I have the dream at all?

I glance at my grandma's journal sprawled open on the floor. And it hits me—my medicine! I fell asleep reading the journal and forgot to take my medicine. I swing my comforter off my legs and stumble, a bit disoriented, into my bathroom.

With shaky hands, I untwist the bottle and tip two pills directly into my mouth. I turn on the faucet, cup water in my palm, and wash the pills down. Then I lie back down and wait for sleep to take me.

∽

I wake up with a niggling feeling in my gut, but I can't place it. My eyes are heavy, my head fuzzy, and I wonder if I'm getting sick. The flu has taken the entire state of California by storm. Maybe I should have gotten the flu shot at school.

I brush my teeth, splash cold water on my face, throw on a pair of jeans and a knit top and go downstairs, unable to shake the sense that I've forgotten something. A female voice from the television mingles with the sound of sizzling eggs that burn on the stove. The morning paper lays open and forgotten on the table in front of my dad. Both of my parents stare at the screen as the news anchor talks about a drive-by shooting in San Francisco, followed by faces of the victims. And all of a sudden, that thing I've forgotten comes raging back.

Last night's dream.

My mom catches sight of me standing in the doorway, flips off the news, and tends to the burning eggs. A haze of smoke lingers above her head and she turns on the oven fan. "This is exactly why I will not tolerate living in a city," she says over the drone. "They aren't safe anymore. I don't even understand how those guys had guns. They're supposed to be illegal."

"It's a black market, honey." Dad reengages with the newspaper. "When we removed the second amendment from our constitution, we didn't eradicate guns. We just ensured that the people who have them are the bad guys."

"I thought you agreed with the gun laws."

Their conversation floats around me, impossible to pin down in light of the chaos spinning inside my head. I forgot to take my medicine one night. One lousy night. And this is what happens? My fingers turn into icicles. I stretch and flex them, but it's no use. They are numb, right along with my heart.

Are people dying because I'm on meds? The words from last night's dream return—*the pills have zapped your strength*. Is this what Dr. Roth's warning was all about? The question is too awful to contemplate. I smash my palms over my ears, as if this might shut out the answer. But it doesn't, because the answer isn't coming from some place outside my ears. It's coming from a place in between them. I close my eyes, wishing I could go back, rewind, and leave my grandmother's journal in the bottom drawer of my desk where it belongs. Wishing I could remember my medication and forget last night's dream with the dead boy in that woman's arms and his face on my television screen.

"Tess, are you okay?"

I open my eyes.

My parents are staring at me.

My hands slide down the sides of my face and before I can answer, my cell phone chirps from my back pocket. Saved by the bell. I pull it out. It's a text message from Serendipity, inviting me to a bonfire tonight at her house—a timely reminder of how normal my life has been lately. This medicine has given me friends. This medicine has given me a social life.

Mom sets a plate of blackened eggs in front of Dad, her attention unwavering. "Tess?"

"Yeah, I'm fine." I show her the text, evidence that everything is okay. That nothing has to change. "Can I go to a bonfire tonight?"

She smiles. "Of course."

# CHAPTER THIRTY

# RUMORS

I call up the stairs to Pete, wanting to get out of the house before Mom can ask any more questions, but he doesn't answer. So I stomp up the steps and open his door. He's still in bed, a mass under the covers.

"Are you coming?"

"I'm sick," he mumbles. His voice is scratchy—whether from sickness or sleep, I can't tell. I shut his door and make my way down the stairs. Mom stands in the foyer, looking up into the stairwell.

"Where's your brother?"

"Sick in bed, apparently." I swing my backpack over my shoulder and head out the door to a cloudy, cool day. I glance over the hedge into Luka's yard, but he's not leaning against his car like he usually does, waiting to drive us to school. Instead, his front door flies open and he stalks outside. Even across the distance, I notice the rigid set of his jaw and the deep furrow in his brow. His shoe makes contact with a rock—not by accident—and he swears beneath his breath. When he reaches his car, his eyes meet mine and his expression softens.

I approach hesitantly.

He meets me at the passenger door, but avoids eye contact. "Hey," he says, shoving his hands into his pockets.

"Hey," I say back.

He glances over his shoulder, toward his house. His mother

peeks through the drapes of the front window. When she sees us looking, her face disappears and the drapes swing back and forth. Luka opens my door, a muscle in his jaw ticking. It would appear his day is starting off much the same as mine.

I duck inside and clasp my seatbelt, unsure if I should tell him about last night's dream and this morning's news. How is it possible that everything came rushing back after one lousy missed dose of medicine? Is my mental illness really that close to the surface, itching to escape and ruin my life? And if I don't have a mental illness, what's the medicine doing? I shake that last thought away and the shudder that follows it.

Luka slips inside and starts the car, tension radiating from his body. I wait for him to say something, perhaps explain what's bothering him. Instead, he reverses out of the drive while I nibble my bottom lip, stewing over my grandmother. She won't leave me alone. Neither will the face of that grieving mother from my dream. For once, I'm thankful for Luka's mom and the highly suspicious way she acts toward me. She serves as a nice diversion. "Is everything okay between you and your mom?"

"She likes to worry."

"About?"

Either he doesn't hear me, or he's choosing to ignore me.

"She doesn't like me." It's the first time I've said the words out loud to him. I wait to see if he'll deny them.

His knuckles whiten as he grips the steering wheel and pulls the car out of our gated community—one that is safe from drive-by shootings. "She knows you go to the Edward Brooks Facility."

The words scrape against my already frazzled nerves. All my anger—about last night's dream and my forgetfulness with the medicine and my messed up mental problems—somehow, they are Luka's mom's fault. "Does she forget that you went there first?"

The muscle in his jaw tightens. "I know. But I'm her son."

I cross my arms and look out the passenger side window. Even in January, a mass of dense green whizzes past. We drive in stony silence, which gives me plenty of time to reach some conclusions. Like the fact that my mother is more understanding and forgiving than Luka's. If my mom knew he went to the Edward Brooks Facility, she wouldn't care. Which means she is the better person. And if, on the off chance she did care, I wouldn't justify her behavior. Luka shouldn't defend his mom. Not about this.

He pulls into the high school parking lot, finds a spot, and turns off the car. The stony silence remains. Well, I'm not going to be the one to break it. Eager to get away from him, I swing the door open and step out into the nippy air. I know my level of irritation is misplaced. I know that this wouldn't be such a big deal if last night hadn't happened. But it did and my emotions will not be reasoned with. Luka's car door slams shut and he catches up with me. As much as I want to look at him, as much as I want to gauge his thoughts, I keep my attention pinned on my Converse All Stars.

He opens the door to the hum of high school. "I need to use the restroom," he says. "I'll meet you in class."

I stand inside, staring after him. Abandoned.

I turn toward my locker. Leela leans against the one beside mine, staring off in the opposite direction, her hands unusually fidgety considering Pete is nowhere to be seen. I try to bolster my spirits for her benefit. She doesn't deserve my dark mood. I stop in front of my locker, slide my backpack off my shoulder, and twist the lock to the first number of my combination. "Hey." I twist to the second number. "You might want to stay away. Pete's sick today. I could be contagious."

"Is it true?"

My fingers stop twisting. "Is what true?"

"That you go to the Edward Brooks Facility?"

Leela's blunt question hits me like a sucker punch. The shock of it steals my breath. All I can do is blink at her with my mouth ajar.

Her face lengthens. "It's true."

"Leela ..." I want to erase the betrayal and hurt in her eyes, but I'm too stunned to do much of anything.

"And I defended you against Summer."

"Summer?"

"Does Luka know?"

I don't know how to respond.

"He does." Leela shakes her head. "I thought we were best friends."

"We are."

"Best friends don't lie to each other. They don't keep secrets from one another." She turns around and makes to walk away, but I grab her elbow.

"Wait." Why should it matter? The question bulges in my throat. I mean, really, how conditional is her friendship if she ditches me because of my once a week appointments with Dr. Roth? Maybe Leela and Mrs. Williams should get together for lunch. "I didn't want anyone to know. It's not exactly the kind of thing you go around telling people."

"I'm not *people*, Tess."

"Right. You're the first best friend I've ever had. I was afraid if I told you, this—whatever we have—would change.

Obviously I was right."

"You didn't even give me a chance to prove you wrong." Leela yanks her elbow from my grip. "This whole time, you told me you were taking piano lessons." Tears build in her eyes as she turns and stalks away.

Scott Shroud gapes at me, his pointy Adam's apple bobbing in his throat. I quickly look away, only to find other students staring too. Small huddles of them fill the locker bay, whispering and darting furtive glances. When I spot Serendipity and Jennalee peeking at me sideways, my heart sinks. I finish the rest of my locker combination and attempt to hide inside.

Summer must have finally told everyone what she overhead in the library all those weeks ago, vanquishing any headway I made into a life of normalcy. But why now? Why did she wait so long? I recall Matt's words yesterday in the library. Maybe Summer finally snapped.

My heart thuds against my eardrums. Somehow, I always knew this would happen. The last several weeks were too good to be true. My life never really felt like my life. There was this feeling of transience undergirding each blissful moment. I just didn't expect it all to flip inside out and upside down so quickly.

I want to climb all the way inside my locker, shut the door, and never come out again. Or better yet, I want to slam the locker shut and leave. But I can't do that, because I drove with Luka, and Pete is home sick with my car in the driveway. So instead, I head to Current Events, shrinking more and more into myself with every step. Funny how fast I turn into the old me—*Tess the Freak*. Tess, the girl who wants to be invisible.

I reach for the door that opens into the stairwell, but before my hand finds the handle, Beamer swings it open for me, smiling in a way that makes me think somebody forgot to give him the memo. "Where's your boy?"

"I'm not sure." Realization hits, followed swiftly by dread. What if Luka's sullenness in the car had nothing to do with his mother? What if Matt or Jared called him this morning to tell him what the student body is buzzing about? What if Luka decided I'm more trouble than I am worth? And then like an idiot, I came outside and climbed into his car and he was too nice to tell me to drive myself. A groan rumbles deep inside my chest.

"Did he ditch you because of the rumors?"

Okay, so Beamer did get the memo.

He drapes his arm around my neck as we reach the second story landing. I want to shrug him away, but I can't bring my body to work properly. "Hey, I think it's cool," he says. "Freaky is the new sexy, if you ask me."

We come out of the stairwell. Summer leans against the wall beside the drinking fountain with Jared and a couple guys on the basketball team. When she spots me, her face glows with triumph.

*Ignore her, ignore her, ignore her…*

I wiggle out from beneath Beamer's arm and walk quickly with my head down, and as I do, Summer mumbles, "Cuckoo, cuckoo."

The guys in her group snicker.

Something inside me snaps. Luka's mom has nothing on this girl. I whip around and dagger her with my eyes. "What is your deal?"

"Please tell me there's going to be a cat fight," Beamer says.

The door opens and Leela steps out of the stairwell. She looks between me and Summer, her eyes wide. I'm momentarily distracted, hopeful even. Until Leela presses her lips together and hurries past us into Mr. Lotsam's classroom.

"Tut, tut. Looks like Tess has lost all her friends."

I glare up at Summer, hating that she's taller than me.

"No Luka. No Leela." She shakes her head, like this is all an unfortunate tragedy. "Have they all abandoned you?"

"If they have, it's because of whatever lies you're spreading."

"Oh, I'm the liar? No, that's you. All this time you've been hiding who you really are." She sneers. "Does Luka know? Maybe somebody should tell him that his girlfriend is a total psycho. Because only major whack jobs go to the Edward Brooks Facility."

My hatred swells. I've been trained never to hit unless it's in self-defense, but in this moment I want nothing more than to sink my fist into her face.

"In fact," she says, raising her voice so that everybody walking past slows and looks. "I think everyone should know. Hey everybody! In case you don't know, the beloved new girl Tess Eckhart goes to the Edward Brooks Facility!" Her proclamation hiccups over the final word. She snaps her mouth shut and stares over my shoulder.

Everybody watches, so silent and still, I'm positive the blood whooshing past my ears thrums into the silence. I can't handle it. If I don't leave right now, I will either haul off and smack Summer, or worse, start crying. I whip around and collide with something hard and warm. It's Luka—his hair a mess, his green eyes raging. Only his wrath is not directed at me.

"Did you know your girlfriend is a mental case?" Summer asks the question boldly, but the slant of her shoulders looks diminished, less confident. In light of Luka's smoldering stare, I don't blame her. She takes a small step back, toward Jared. "She's going to end up like her grandmother."

The words ring in my ears. My grandmother? There's no way Summer can know something like that. "What are you talking about?"

"Play dumb all you want." Summer peels her attention from Luka and pins her vindictive face on mine. "It won't change the fact that she's locked up in an insane asylum. With any luck, it won't be long before you follow."

*How does she know? How does she know? How does she know?* This is all I can think.

Luka steps in front of me. "You need to back off."

Jared steps forward in kind. "No, *you* need to back off, Williams. You and your crazy girlfriend."

It happens so fast. One minute Luka and Jared are facing each other. The next, Luka throws a mean-looking left hook and Jared topples back. Summer screams. I jump away, but not far enough, because Jared recovers and lunges at Luka's waist and they tumble into me. I fall with a sharp thud on my butt and scoot away quickly while Luka and Jared grapple on the floor, throwing punches and knees. Students mob around them, cheering and chanting.

Mr. Lotsam charges out of his class and throws himself between Luka and Jared. He manages to tear them apart. How, I have no idea. Mr. Lotsam is a skinny-looking tree hugger, probably more acquainted with peace signs than fists. He holds the two boys apart by their arms and yells at the crowd, "Break it up. Get to class!"

Luka wipes at a trickle of blood on his lip. Jared cups his hand over what I'm sure is a swollen eye. Leela peeks out from

Mr. Lotsam's class, catching sight of me before ducking back inside.

Mr. Lotsam looks at me on the floor and Summer standing shell-shocked by the drinking fountain. "All four of you. You're coming with me."

## Chapter Thirty-One

# FORBIDDEN

M rs. Finch answers phones and types into her computer while Summer and I sit in uncomfortable chairs outside the principal's office, glaring at one another. I refuse to look away first. Luka is behind the closed door, telling his side of the story to Mr. Jolly. Jared already went.

I scratch my wrist, wishing this whole day was one giant nightmare. But my eczema burns with agitation. I sit there, waiting for my turn, trying to figure out what to say, wondering if Summer will tell Mr. Jolly about the Edward Brooks Facility. How long before my parents find out everybody in school knows? How long before we pack up our bags and move again?

Away from Luka.

A strong, sudden sympathy for Pete overwhelms me. Because what if this is how he felt about Elliana? With a flash of clarity, I get it. I understand why he hated me for moving. At this moment, I hate myself. I hate this problem I have. I hate that I need medicine. I hate that missing a dose makes my world go haywire. I hate that I am *Tess the Freak* again. And I hate—really, really hate—this girl across from me.

Not able to bear the unanswered question any longer, I shift into the seat beside her.

Summer leans away from me.

"How did you know about my grandmother?" I hiss.

She lifts her nose, the epitome of snob. "You wouldn't believe me if I told you."

I narrow my eyes. Now that was an interesting answer.

The door to the office bursts open, severing my glare-down and distracting me from my intrigue. It's Luka's parents. His mother enters first, prim and proper, beautiful as ever. His father follows close behind. I've only seen him a couple times, but each encounter leaves me newly intimidated. He's a man who exudes authority, commands attention. Where Luka's good looks are attractive, Mr. Williams' good looks only make him more intimidating.

Summer's scowling face morphs into sweet innocence and for a second, I think I might throw up. She straightens in her seat. "Oh hi, Mr. and Mrs. Williams."

Mrs. Williams gives her a smile much warmer than any she's ever given me. The unfairness of it crawls under my skin. The woman is an awful judge of character.

"Luka should be out in a second," Mrs. Finch says.

As if on cue, the door opens and Principal Jolly appears. Luka steps around him. He spots his parents filling the bulk of the office and looks at the carpet.

"Mr. and Mrs. Williams." Mr. Jolly nods at them both, tugging at the waist of his khaki slacks. "This isn't like your son. In fact, I was shocked when Mr. Lotsam brought him into my office. I believe he's remorseful, but protocol needs to be followed. Which means Luka will go home today and can return tomorrow."

Mr. Williams looks at his son, then at me, and the disapproval painting his face makes me shrink back in my chair. "I can assure you, Principal Jolly, that this will not happen again."

"I don't think it will."

"Come on," Mr. Williams puts his hand on the back of Luka's neck, "it's time to go."

I will Luka to look at me, but his father guides him out of the office and Luka keeps his attention glued to the floor. My heart plummets. I can't shake the feeling that everything is ruined. Everything.

Principal Jolly waves Summer into his office. "You first."

Great. Summer first.

She'll put on her sweet, fake mask and tell him all about how dangerous I am and how students have the right to know. I won't stand a chance. She steps into his office and the door closes with a definitive click. It's me and Mrs. Finch, who doesn't seem to notice my presence at all. She stands from her desk and starts punching buttons on the copy machine.

I crane my neck and stare at Luka, flanked by his parents, growing smaller and smaller down the hallway. The urge to eavesdrop overwhelms me. With one final glance at Mrs. Finch's back, I make my escape. I need to know what Luka's parents have to say. I close the door silently behind me and hurry after the trio, my back sliding against the wall. Once outside, I keep close to the building, behind some hedges, careful to stay out of sight.

Luka jerks away from his dad's grip and I duck behind some bushes.

"I'll drive myself home," he says.

"No, you won't." His dad's voice exudes as much authority as his presence. "I think it's best if you lose your car privileges for a while." He looks around, as if making sure nobody's within hearing distance. I flatten myself against the ground, desperate to stay hidden. Mr. Williams leans closer to Luka. "You're obviously not listening to your mother, but you *will* listen to me. You are not to see that girl anymore."

"*That girl* has a name."

*That girl*, I assume, is me.

"I don't care about her name. All I care about is that this ends today. No more, Luka. You *will* obey us."

Luka glares.

Mrs. Williams twists the silk scarf in her hands. "She's dangerous, honey."

Me? Dangerous? I'm five-foot nothing. Barely more than a hundred pounds, soaking wet. Sure, I'm strong in my dreams. Maybe even dangerous in them. But that isn't real life. In real life, I can break some boards. That's about it.

"I won't have my only son throwing his future away on a crazy girl," Mr. Williams says.

Luka squares his shoulders. "You forget that she's not the only one who's gone to the Edward Brooks Facility."

His father shushes Luka's words. "All the more reason why you can't be associated with her. Do you think if it gets out about her that it won't get out about you? Listen to me, it ends here. Crazy people are not tolerated in this society. They are a burden. I will not have you labeled a burden. You are to have nothing to do with her, do you understand?"

His words are like a blast that rock me to my core. Mainly because of their truth. Mr. Williams is right. I shift, trying to get a better look at Luka. He stares back at his father in defiance, the back of his neck red.

I want to jump up from my spot behind the bush and tell him to agree. His dad's right. I'm not worth the trouble. A boy like Luka—he has a whole world of possibilities stretching ahead of him. A world I will only ruin. My quick descent from normalcy is proof.

"I'll take drastic measures, Luka. Don't test me."

Mr. Williams clamps his hand on Luka's shoulder and leads him across the parking lot. I lay there in the gravel, making the decision for us. I won't let Luka drown with me. As much as my heart breaks over losing him, I know what I have to do. If he won't stay away from me, then I'll stay away from him. Because this psychosis or whatever it is? It's not going away. I refuse to let Luka ruin his present and his future for a girl headed to an asylum.

# CHAPTER THIRTY-TWO

# THE PILE UP

I don't return to Principal Jolly's office. All day I hide behind my hair, ignoring the whispers and the laughs and the occasional overt point, dreading the moment Mrs. Finch will call my name over the intercom, asking me to report back to the principal's office. But it never comes. Principal Jolly either doesn't notice my absence or doesn't care.

By the time the final bell rings, I realize that getting home will be tricky. Leela won't speak with me. Luka's already gone. So I call my mom and tell her a lie—that Luka went home sick. When she pulls up to the curb, I slip into the car and tell her I'm coming down with something, hoping this will keep her questions at bay. It's only a matter of time until my parents hear what is happening. Thornsdale is not a very big town. I plan to ride out their oblivion for as long as possible.

As soon as I'm home, I change into a pair of sweats and crawl under my covers. I reject dinner. I take my medicine. Luka calls. Every half hour his number lights up my cell phone. He texts a few times, but I stick to my resolution. I will not be his demise. I let his calls go to voicemail and his texts go unanswered. My loneliness grows, like I'm slipping into some deep dark rabbit hole that leads to the inevitable.

I will end up like her. My grandmother. Alone, locked in an asylum.

I wonder if Pete will be upset when we move again. Perhaps it's for the best. Despite making friends with Wren and Jess, he doesn't like it in Thornsdale. The move has turned him into a different kid. Even though I don't want to be away from Luka, even though the thought of it whaps at my brittle heart, I know it would be for the best. I lay in bed, eyes wide open, begging sleep to take me. I want oblivion, but my eyes refuse to cooperate.

So I slip into my bathroom and take two sleeping pills—at seven thirty in the evening. I lie back down, counting time in the half hour segments between Luka's phone calls.

∽

I wake up on a familiar stretch of highway. The one I take every weekday to school. Only there is a pileup and greasy-haired men stand in the middle of the road, causing more and more cars to slam into one another. It's as if they control the direction and speed of each vehicle with the movement of their hands. And a thought hits me, in this moment, like it's the most obvious thing. My father is wrong. We are more than physical. These *men*, who aren't really men at all, are proof.

I watch it all unfold—the crushing of metal, the car alarms and the screams—from the shoulder of the road, with the detachment of one watching a poorly-produced movie on TV. I look into the cars, seeing adults and children unconscious or desperate to escape, and I know I should care. But I don't. I stand there, unaffected, while horns blare and sirens wail and people bleed and cry.

None of it matters.

Not even when the strange men start lighting cars on fire.

But then, in the distance, I see something that pings at my indifference. Somebody up the road is fighting the white-eyed men. Somebody is fighting like I used to fight before the medicine and I want to see who. Who is this person—this fighter? I shift and squint to get a better look, but more tires screech against pavement. Brakes squeal.

As if in slow motion, my attention moves toward the sound and my eyes go wide, because the car is mine and my brother is behind the wheel, his face twisted in panic as he tries to avoid the collision. A few paces to my left, a man aims his out-stretched, spider-like hands at Pete in my car. I could fight him if I wanted, like that person up the road. He's not too far away. But I don't move. I stand there as my car smashes into the pile and my brother's unbuckled body flies into the windshield and the glass bursts apart and he lies motionless on the pavement, a trickle of blood seeping from his mouth and I scream and scream and scream until it turns into a shrill ring and I bolt upright in bed.

There is motion in the hallway. I hear Mom's frantic voice and Dad's deep rumble, telling her to calm down, it will be okay. The door across the hall flings open.

I sit up straighter.

"He's not in here." Hysteria swallows my mother's words. "He's not here."

I jump out of bed, groggy from the sleeping pills, and open my door wide. "What's wrong?"

Mom's face shines pale white in the dark. Her terror awak-ens my own. "It's your brother," she says, clutching her chest. "He snuck out. He took your car and there was an accident. A horrible, horrible accident." Mom's chest clutching turns into mouth clutching. "That was the hospital. He's in the ICU."

Dad takes Mom's elbow. "It will be okay, Miranda. It will be okay." He looks at me, his face every bit as white as Mom's.

"Get dressed, Tess. Quickly."

I hurry into my room and grab a wrinkled sweatshirt from the floor. I glance at my clock. It is five fifteen in the morning.

## CHAPTER THIRTY-THREE

# BREAKTHROUGH

M om and I drive home in silence. She didn't want to leave the hospital, but after a full day of fretting in the waiting room, Dad insisted we go home. He will be there, right by Pete's side and he promised to call if anything changes. We should try and get a good night sleep, he said. As if that could happen with Pete in critical condition in the ICU.

We don't talk. I drive, because Mom's nerves are too frayed, her mind too consumed, her body too close to collapse. On the contrary, I am eerily steady. Which makes me wonder if I'm in shock, if this numbness is a sign that the day's events have yet to sink in. If that's the case, I'm secretly hoping the shock remains indefinitely, because I don't want to feel. I need the protection from feeling. I'm not sure I can handle any of it.

When we step inside our dark, empty foyer, Mom gives me a lifeless hug and says we should go to bed. She walks up the stairs and shuts herself in her room, but I'm not fooled. She isn't sleeping. I sit on my bed and listen to her pace two bedrooms away—back and forth, back and forth, wearing out the floor. I kick off my shoes, wondering if my mother is praying. In a world where God does not exist, where science has done everything to systematically remove any sort of deity from society, does she turn to one anyway? Despite all its answers and logic, science offers no comfort, no hope. Not at times like these.

I stare blindly at my carpet, remembering that I didn't take my medicine this morning. I look toward my bathroom, where the pill bottle sits in the medicine cabinet and I shrink back, as if whatever's inside has sharp teeth and claws. My mind replays last night's dream and the way I stood there and did nothing while those monster-men made the cars crash and lit them on fire. The way I stood there and did nothing while my brother flew through a windshield. Did the medicine steal my ability to care? To react? To fight?

I scratch my eczema. The pain is dull and distant, but there. I'm not dreaming. And the thought squeezes my muscles. I want to crawl outside of my skin. Never mind waking up, I don't want to be me anymore. I'm afraid to go to sleep. I'm afraid to be awake. I'm afraid of taking my medicine. I'm afraid of *not* taking my medicine. I'm afraid of returning to school and I'm afraid of what will happen to Pete. I'm just afraid. And in the midst of my fear, I find myself wanting to pray too.

A light rap, rap, rap against glass brings my head up.

My bedroom window frames Luka's face, and as much as I've resolved not to bring him down into this dark spiral I am spinning into, I hurry over and open the window. He climbs inside and does something I don't expect. He pulls me into a fierce hug. The shock encasing my body splinters apart. I breathe in the scent of clean cotton and the feel of his warm, strong body and squeeze my eyes tight, unsure if I want to let myself feel what Luka is making me feel or hold onto the numbness for everything I'm worth.

"My parents are idiots. They don't know what they're talking about." The warmth of his hand pressing against the small of my back splinters my shock further. "I was going to talk to you at school today, but you didn't show. And then Principal Jolly announced what happened over the intercom. How's your brother?"

I don't answer. I can't. My emotions swell so close to the surface that if I open my mouth, I'm afraid they will burst out, shattering my numbness into fragmented bits.

Luka grips my arms and pulls me away from his chest, his face filled with so much concern that I have to bite my bottom lip to keep it from quivering.

His eyes widen. "Is he …?"

I shake my head quickly. "No."

*At least not yet.*

I want to banish that thought from existence. Pete will not die. My brother will live. He has to. I take a few steps back, sit on my bed, and stare at my chipped nail polish—a pale blue color Leela painted on a few days ago, when life was still good. "It's my fault," I whisper.

"How's it your fault?"

"I dreamt about it. Last night. I watched everything happen. I could have stopped it. I could have fought. But I didn't. I didn't care." I squeeze my eyes tight against the accumulating moisture, fighting to regain the comfortable numbness I had downstairs in the foyer. "And then I woke up and now Pete's in the hospital."

"He's not in the hospital because of you."

"Isn't he?" I look up at him. "The other night, I had another dream. I was reading my grandma's journal and I forgot to take my medicine. I dreamt about that drive-by shooting. And then the next morning, it was on the news."

"Why didn't you tell me?"

"Because you seemed to have other things on your mind

and then we got to school, and well ..." I let the explanation fall away. He knows what happened at school.

"Dreaming about something doesn't make it your fault."

"You don't understand. I couldn't stop those men from shooting their guns. I couldn't move. That guy—the one with the scar—he was there. He said the medicine made me weak. But the next morning, I took the medicine anyway and then Pete was in my dream and I couldn't save him. I didn't even try." A memory shifts through the mire. "But someone else was there. Someone else was fighting."

"Who?"

"I don't know. I couldn't make the person out, but whoever it was, they were fighting and I wasn't." I dig my face into my palms. "I wish I could turn all of this off."

Luka sits beside me on the bed, his desperation this tangible thing. He wants to fix all the broken parts. I can tell. But he can't. I'm not sure anybody can. "Tell me what to do."

"I don't want to be by myself."

"Then you won't be," he says.

I look over at him, confused.

He scoots back and leans against my headboard. "I'll stay here. With you."

My stomach tightens. If my mom comes in to check on me and sees Luka, she will freak out. She doesn't need anything else to freak out over. I listen for the sound of her pacing, but somewhere along the line of Luka climbing in my window, it has stopped. I wonder if she took some sleeping pills.

"I won't leave you alone, Tess. Not tonight."

His words crumble the last of my resolve. Even though it's against the rules. Even though I promised to distance myself from Luka, I lock the door and slip into bed beside him. We don't touch, but I can feel him as if he were trailing his fingers over my skin. His presence is strong and steady. Closing my eyes, I tell myself that once this is over, I will take back the resolution I made in the high school parking lot. I will stay away from Luka Williams. But right now, in this moment, his nearness makes me feel warm. It makes me feel safe.

⌘

I awake to the sound of seagulls and waves crashing against rock and a breathtaking sunset. Rubbing my eyes, I sit up.

Luka sits beside me, smiling. "I was wondering if you'd show up."

I scratch my wrist and feel nothing. "Are we …?"

"Dreaming? Yes."

It's been so long since we shared a dream that it takes me a second to acclimate. "How long have you been waiting?"

"A while. I come here every night."

"Why?"

"Hoping you'll show up." A blip of sadness flickers in his eyes, then disappears. "This is the first time since you started taking medicine."

I wrap my arms around my knees and breathe in the peaceful surroundings. "I wish we could stay here forever."

"Yeah, but it's not real."

A wave rolls up onto the shore. The water stops just short of my toes. "I don't want to be crazy."

"I don't think you are." He reaches over and takes my hand, threading his fingers with mine. "I never thought you were."

"Then why did you let me take the medicine?"

"Because it made you happy and I like seeing you happy."

I look down at our clasped hands and something tugs at my body. I can feel myself being dragged away. Only I don't want to go anywhere. I'm not ready to leave Luka, not yet. So I squeeze his hand as tightly as I can. I will not let go, even as the pulling grows stronger and the beach disappears. White walls replace the sunset, beeping monitors replace the crashing waves, but Luka's hand is still in mine. Somehow, I dragged him with me.

He stands by my side, in the middle of the hospital room, eyes wide with disbelief, then alarm. He nudges me and I look. My brother lies in the hospital bed, hooked to machines. Only he's not alone. There's a presence beside him—a presence with empty, white eyes. This one is short and burly. And by one of the machines, with his hand casually propped on top, is the man with the scar. He steps to Pete's bedside, picks up his limp arm, and presses his finger against Pete's wrist.

I step forward. "Get away from him."

The man with the scar cocks his head. "But he invited us here."

My attention darts from him to the other. I'm not sure which one is the bigger threat.

"Your brother has been seeking us out ever since the séance in Jude." He moves the tip of his finger over Pete's skin, carving a symbol that looks very much like Wren's disappearing tattoo. The same symbol on that seventeen-year-old gunman from a dream I had months ago. It finally clicks that the two symbols are the same, and now this man with the scar is marking my brother with it. "He's been very intrigued. Very curious. If people aren't careful, that kind of curiosity leads to us."

"What are you talking about?"

"He didn't even notice what was happening. We have the upper hand that way. You see, people have a hard time fighting against something they don't believe. Their denial makes our job easier. Your brother didn't honestly think he was involving himself in anything dangerous until it was too late. Our only roadblock was you. At least until you started taking medicine."

Fear builds in my lungs.

"Once you were no longer aware of our presence, getting to him was a piece of cake." He finishes the symbol and drops Pete's arm. "I think he's ready."

"What are you going to do?"

"We're going to give him his wish. He's going to be ours."

"No!" I lurch forward, but the movement is clumsy.

"You made your choice, Little Rabbit. Just as Pete made his. I'm afraid it's too late."

No. It's not too late. It can't be too late. I try to move, to stop the white-eyed man from pulling the cords away from Pete. But my legs are so sluggish and my frustration swells and with it comes memories. They ping, bright and vivid, in my mind. Dad tossing Pete into the air. Pete and I picking up starfish off the beach and throwing them back into the water. Pete and I building tents in the basement. Pete's little-boy hand squeezing mine in the dark, as if I had the power to protect him from the things that go bump in the night. That little boy lies in bed, unconscious, his vitals plummeting.

A surge of love—white and hot and intense—sears through my medically-induced stupor. I lunge at the man with the scar and his eyes widen with shock. With all my strength and training, I sweep his legs out from under him and take him to the ground. Ice-cold fingers grab my elbow. I twist my arm up and spin around and with all the force I can muster, I shove my palm toward the skeletal face before me, connecting with his nose, shoving the cartilage up and in. He collapses onto the ground.

There is a quick movement behind me, like something swinging for my head. I duck and cover, prepared for the blow, but waves of light shove Scarface back. It's Luka. Light shoots from his palms, his face a mask of determination and concentration and powerful beauty. The light hurtles Scarface toward the wall, only instead of slamming into it, he sinks through the solid mass as if he's nothing but smoke and vapor.

Doctors swarm into the room—a whole team of them. They shock my brother's heart while the mark on his wrist fades away and the shrill ring of the telephone startles me awake. Luka sits beside me in the bed, our breath rising and falling in unison. Darkness surrounds us, but even so, I can see the wideness of his eyes.

The phone lets out another shrill ring.

Through the walls, my Mom mumbles a groggy hello, followed by a pause, some unintelligible mumbling, then footsteps in the hallway. Luka hides in my closet. I hurry to the door, unlock it, fling it open, and come face-to-face with my mother, who is smiling. Beaming. Tears streaking her cheeks. She wraps her arms around my neck and squeezes so tightly I can feel her trembling. "He's going to be okay, Tess. Pete's going to be okay. That was your father. Your brother woke up." She releases me from her vice-like hug. "I'm going there. Right now. I have to see him. Do you want to come?"

Every inch of my body melts with sweet relief. My baby brother is going to be okay. He's going to make it. "You go. I'll come in the morning."

She hugs me again, then hurries down the steps. Luka

doesn't come out of his hiding place until the front door slams shut. I flip on my light and hurry out into the hall, into Pete's bedroom, my legs weak. As if fighting in my dream has zapped my strength.

Luka follows, and from the look of his face, he's feeling weak too. "What's going on?"

I shake my head and dig under Pete's bed, pulling out books about the occult and dark magic, Tarot cards, and a Ouija Board. All of it needs to go.

"How did you bring me with you like that?"

"I don't know."

"Is that what used to happen in your dreams—before the medicine? Did you always fight like that?"

I nod, transferring the pile from my arms to Luka's. I open Pete's laptop and pull up his search history. What I find is incredibly disturbing. I delete it with one click of the mouse and push away from his desk. "My brother's okay, but we have to make sure he stays that way. We have to get rid of all this stuff."

We carry it down into the living room and throw it into the fireplace. Luka douses it with lighter fluid, lights a match and tosses it in, then turns to me. "I did it again. That man came at you and I—I stopped him."

A shiver takes hold of my jaw. What would have happened if Luka wouldn't have been there to protect me?

"You brought me with you into that dream," he says.

"I know."

"How?"

"I have no idea, but I'm glad it happened."

The fire flickers and bursts and there's an awful screeching, so loud I clamp my hands over my ears and Luka steps back.

"Whoa," he says.

The screeching stops and the fire goes dark in the grate.

He stares at me with bright, almost wild eyes. "I have no idea what's going on, but I don't think you should go back on that medicine."

I want to plug my ears. I don't want to hear what Luka is implying. As much as I know he is right, my life was miserable before the medicine. A hair away from unbearable. "I didn't ask for this."

He steps closer.

"I just want to be normal. That's all I've ever wanted."

"Tess."

"You don't get it. All those people in the pile up? That boy in the drive-by shooting? If what you're saying is true, then those deaths are my fault." Never mind the weeks spent not dreaming at all. Never mind the weeks I spent on medicine while the world grew darker.

"No, they aren't."

"Yes, they are."

"Listen, Tess. The past is the past. It's done. It's over. It only has power if you let it keep you from making the right choice in the present." He dips his chin, pulling me in with his eyes. There's calmness there. Strength. And fire too. "I didn't get it before. I didn't understand. But after what I saw tonight. The way you fought? You can't run away from that."

Luka is right. I don't want him to be. But he is. No matter what happened before, I can't let people die. Taking a deep, rattling breath, I walk up the stairs, pour my medicine into the toilet, and flush it away.

"What now?" Luka asks.

"Now we need to go to Eugene. I need to speak with my grandmother."

## CHAPTER THIRTY-FOUR

# SHADY WOOD

My car is totaled. Luka's dad confiscated his keys. Both of which makes getting to Eugene trickier than planned. Thankfully, it's the middle of the night and his parents are asleep. So while he sneaks into his home with plans to snag his car keys and some other important items that might help us break into one of the highest-security mental institutions in the country, I make a beeline for my dad's office, searching for anything that might prove useful.

First place I look? Bottom drawer of his desk. With trembling fingers, I remove a jewelry box squished all the way in the back and find the small key tucked inside the lid. Looking over my shoulder, half expecting the police to barge in with guns and handcuffs, I hurry over to the polished armoire standing innocently in the corner of the room, slide back one of the panels to a hidden safe, and jam the key inside the lock. I open the lid to the jackpot—Dad's work iPad with important passwords. I slip it into my backpack, along with his work identification card, and my attention lands on a couple of tasers. I really hope we won't have to use them, but better safe than sorry. I slide them in beside the iPad, shut the safe and the panel, return the key to its hiding place, and leave his office exactly as it was.

In the kitchen, I scrawl a hurried note, assuring my parents that I'm okay. That I needed to get away with Luka for a breather and will be back soon. It sounds so lame. Why would I abandon my parents when my brother is in the hospital? Surely they will see right through it. They will know I'm up to something, but what other choice is there? I leave my cell phone next to the note on the counter because I don't have the energy to see their names flashing on the screen every other minute.

Zipping my coat, I double-check that all the lights are off and pray Luka accomplishes his goal, because without a car we are screwed. I pace the foyer until an idling car purrs softly from my driveway. I fling open the door and race out on silent feet. I climb inside and buckle my seat belt, panting as if I just ran a mile while he reverses with his headlights off. We don't say a word until we're past the gates of our neighborhood.

"This is all I could find," he says, holding up his father's ID card. I have to imagine as the owner of a mental facility—albeit private—the card will come in handy.

"That's plenty." I show him my father's iPad, the identification card, and the tasers. He raises his eyebrows at the tasers, then turns onto the main road and flips on his headlights.

I lean back into the seat. "This is crazy. We don't even know what the facility is called."

"Google it."

I power up the iPad. Finding the name isn't difficult. The place is called Shady Wood. We enter the address into Luka's GPS and stop at a gas station on the outskirts of town. We each get a coffee, even though neither of us need the caffeine, and spend the five-hour drive shooting questions at each other like popcorn, trying to piece together the puzzle that's become our lives. The dreams. Why they came back after I stopped taking the medicine. Why the medicine made them stop in the first place. How Luka fits into the picture. How Summer found out about my grandma and what she meant when she said I wouldn't believe her if she told me. Once we've exhausted our sparse list of half-baked theories, we turn to more pressing matters. Like how we're going to reach my grandmother. Each plan we devise sounds more reckless and foolish than the one before. There's no way we're getting in without an incredible amount of luck.

Thankfully, we have some on our side. Because of my dad, I have a lot of useful information conveniently tucked inside my head. For once, I'm grateful for his position and my lack of popularity. Up until Thornsdale, I spent plenty of Saturdays shadowing him on the job, learning the ins and outs of security systems. Plus, we have identification cards that might get us in a few back doors. At first, we considered walking up to the front desk and asking to see Elaine Eckhart, but quickly tossed the idea aside. Not only would our request arouse suspicion, we trust that Dr. Roth was telling the truth when he said she isn't allowed visitors.

With all the plotting and theorizing, the drive goes surprisingly fast and before we know it, the sun is up and Luka's phone has rung three times, each call from his parents. I don't let myself think about how livid my father will be when we return, or how much worry I'm putting my mother through. My brain is already waterlogged with worry and what-ifs. It doesn't need anything else to process.

Once we reach the outskirts of Eugene, we pull into a gas station to rinse our faces, use the bathroom, and buy breakfast—a couple bottles of water and a cinnamon roll to split. Luka eats most of the roll while I break into my dad's work site using a password I've known for a couple years. I type Shady

Wood into the system. The place is a mental rehabilitation center, which is a socially acceptable way of saying insane asylum. Even so, their tagline promises rehabilitation and healing so patients can rejoin society as healthy contributors. We learn that there is a gate to get through up front and several security doors on the east and west wing, only accessible with key cards. We fine-tune our plans, then drive the rest of the way in silence. Luka turns off onto an obscure road that winds through the woods. The facility is so well-hidden I wonder if the people of Eugene even know it exists.

Luka parks behind a thicket of trees and turns off the car. We lean against our seats and stare at one another, the silence bloated with every single one of our unspoken words. Truancy. Trespassing. Identity theft. Breaking and entering. And who knows what else. The amount of trouble we will get into if we're caught is overwhelming, but neither of us can go there. So we take deep breaths and Luka squeezes my hand. "You ready?"

"I think so."

We step outside and walk toward the iron gate. I can't decide if their purpose is to keep people out or keep patients in. It's a Saturday morning and the place is deserted. You'd think there would be visitors, but there's not a person in sight. Apparently, my grandmother is the norm, not the exception.

Luka removes his father's identification card from around his neck and steps up to the scanner. "Here goes nothing."

I hold my breath as he slides the card in front of the red beam. The scanner emits a series of different pitched beeps and then a female, robotic voice announces, "Voice activation required."

Already prepared, Luka holds his cell phone up to the

speaker and his father's voice plays into the system. "Luka, call me now."

"Identity accepted. Thank you."

There's a loud clanging sound and like magic, the iron gates slowly begin to open.

We look at each other, shocked. I'm not sure either of us expected to get past the gates. Luka grabs my hand and we hurry across the grounds, eager to escape the wide-open space and whatever surveillance cameras are surely scanning the area. He pulls us away from the front doors, heading for the west wing, and I don't think I let out my breath until we have our bodies pressed against the outside wall. We slink forward and stop in front of the exit. My attention darts from one direction to another as Luka holds his dad's ID card up to the red scanner. Only this time, nothing happens. No beeps. No voice. I'm quite certain only hospital staff can enter these doors.

I remove the iPad from my backpack and hope this little trick will work. I press the back of the iPad against the scanner, marked with Safe Guard's logo. Shady Wood's account pops up on the screen. I click on a tab marked *employee access* and punch in my father's work password. I've watched him key it in enough that it is ingrained in my brain. Once I'm in, I hold up the iPad to the scanner again and all of Shady Wood's security system information pops up on the screen. With shallow breaths, I type in *west wing code.*

E6bs*9zx%

I punch it into the key pad above the scanner and like a miracle, the red light turns to green and the lock clicks. Luka grabs the handle and slowly pulls it open to a deserted hallway, lit with fluorescent lights. We stand close, our hearts beating so fiercely I can hear Luka's. After a short beat, we step inside. I can't believe we're actually in or that my grandmother is somewhere close by. The impossibility of finding her presses against my shoulders. This place is a labyrinth of rooms filled with who knows how many patients and we don't have the slightest clue where to look. Luka taps my shoulder and jerks his head for me to follow. We slink against the wall, quickly but silently, desperate to get out of plain view. Luka grabs the handle of the first door we reach and pulls me inside. Our breaths escape in quick, nervous puffs as we stare at one another inside what appears to be a supply closet.

"Now what?" All our plans in the car involved getting inside. We never considered what to do if we succeeded.

Luka looks around, as if something inside will help us find my grandma. He digs out some scrubs from a box and we both put them on over our clothes. I have to roll my sleeves and my pants several times when the sound of whistling outside stops my movements. My eyes go wide. Luka puts his finger up to his lips, then cracks open the door the tiniest bit and peeks through. He motions for my backpack. I hand it over. He removes one of the tasers and points for me to creep toward the back of the closet.

"What are you going to do?" I half-whisper, half-mouth.

"Get in the back."

The footsteps and whistling grow louder. With my heart in my throat, I obey Luka's command. As soon as the whistling reaches us, he bangs on the supply closet door. The whistling stops. I duck behind a mop bucket, picturing the doctor or nurse or whoever it is standing on the other side with a cocked head, wondering at the loud, unexplained thump.

"Is somebody in there?" The feminine voice sounds more

confused than frightened.

Luka twirls his hand at me to speak.

I clear my throat. "Help, please!"

The door knob twists and the woman appears, but before she even knows what's happening, there's an awful, screeching zap and she falls to the ground. Luka tasered her.

I blink dumbly as he drags her into the closet. "What are you doing?"

"Getting her key fob."

"What voltage did you use?"

"A very high one, apparently." He nods to a shelf with duct tape and rope. "She's not going to stay unconscious forever and we can't have her alerting people that somebody knocked her out and shoved her in a closet."

Together, we tie her hands and feet and put duct tape on her mouth. I keep muttering apologies, even though she can't hear me. I remove the key fob from around her neck. Luka takes her charts and we peek outside again. With the coast clear, we leave the closet and the woman behind.

"Slow down," he says from the corner of his mouth. "Act natural."

So easily said, so hard to do. But I force my legs to decelerate and keep pace with Luka, who carries himself with such a sense of authority I'm reminded of his father. He walks with the folder open in front of him, his head down, as if studying the notes on one of his patients. "Do you see her name anywhere?" I mutter.

He shakes his head.

A nurse comes out of a room. Besides the lady we knocked unconscious in the hallway, she's the first person we've run into. I'm certain she will hear the hammering of my heart, the quickness of my breath, but Luka pretends to engage me in a deep discussion, pointing at something in the file, and the nurse passes right on by. We pass several more people, but nobody speaks to us. As far as I can tell, nobody even looks at us. Luka and I keep our heads bent together, like two doctors consulting. We step inside the first stairwell we reach and head up to the second floor. It's obvious there are no patients on the first.

When we come upon a room, I use the key fob. The door unlatches and what we find inside is beyond disturbing. So disturbing that we forget ourselves for a minute and stare with gaping mouths. Rows upon rows of beds, exactly how I've always imagined eastern European orphanages. Only instead of babies in cribs, these are full grown, emaciated adults hooked to IVs. Every single person is unconscious. Gravity pulls at my shoulders, until I'm not sure I can stand beneath the oppressive weight of what I'm seeing.

"What is this?" I whisper.

"It isn't rehabilitation, that's for sure."

Swallowing my horror, I force myself to walk up and down the rows, looking at each face, hoping to find my grandmother. The more I look, the more my nausea grows. "I don't see her."

"Didn't you say your grandmother was constrained?"

"Yes, she was." And these people aren't. They don't need to be.

Eager to get away from this place, I hurry out the door after Luka only to find the same thing in the next room. A room filled with the living dead. By now, it's late morning, almost lunch time, yet nobody is awake. The silence is eerie. "Luka, in my dream, my grandmother was in her own room."

We head back into the stairwell and climb another flight of

stairs, only to find the same thing on the third floor. The fourth feels different. We peek into the window of a room and see a man inside, rocking back and forth, bound in a straitjacket. Luka points to a pair of initials on the outside of the door and snags the chart. Jonathan Becket, diagnosed with Dissociative Identity Disorder.

We go from door to door, searching for the initials E.E. When we can't find them, we head up another flight of stairs and continue our farce, wondering how long before the woman in the closet downstairs comes to and starts flailing around for help. Panic and urgency throws us into fast forward, our desperation growing as we climb yet another flight of stairs to the last floor. Five doors down, we finally find it.

E.E.

Luka opens her chart—Elaine Eckhart. Diagnosis: Paranoid Schizophrenia. Threat to Society. Uncooperative. Highly delusional.

My pulse throbs erratically as I hold the key fob up to the door and the small red light turns green. Without giving myself time to think, I open the door and step inside.

It is exactly like my dream. A white box, barren, with that same awful fluorescent lighting. And there she is with her long white hair, shackled to the bed like a prisoner. She stares up at the ceiling, unresponsive to our presence, until I take another step closer and her head jerks around. She blinks, then strains away from me as far as the restraints will allow.

Approaching slowly, I bend down to her eye level and look into eyes that are like my dad's but nothing like my dad's, because his are always so logical and sane. Never this wild or unhinged.

"Do you know who I am?" I whisper the question, as if the

walls have ears and at any minute a team of doctors will swarm into the room and lock me up in the room next to Elaine.

Her face flickers with the smallest hint of recognition. I can almost see her fighting for clarity, but whatever medicine they have her on seems to be winning the battle.

I hold my hands up, fingers spread wide. "We aren't going to hurt you."

She squints from me to Luka, from me to Luka, her terror slowly subsiding. "Who is he?" she finally asks in a dry, raspy voice.

"He's my friend. We came to help you." This is a lie. We came so she could help us, but the notion is hopeless, because how in the world can she help us? She doesn't even know me. What did I expect—a flood of love and recognition? Answers upon answers? How could I expect any of that when she's been locked up in this place for the past fifteen years?

"My name is Teresa Eckhart," I say. "Does that name mean anything to you?"

Nothing.

"A long time ago, you tried to take me. You thought I could save you."

Her fingers flutter.

I reach out and take hold of them, as if my touch might offer her comfort. "We don't have much time." I glance over my shoulder at the door, then back at her. "I'm having dreams. Dreams like you used to have."

"Help." The whispered words send a chill through my bones. They are the same ones I read all those months ago in her journal, before I went on medicine and let innocent people die.

"We can't help you without information. We need to know

what you know."

"Help," she says again, louder.

"I want to help you, but we don't know what's going on."

She lifts her head off the pillow. The tendons in her neck bulge. "Please, help me."

"Why did you try to kidnap me all those years ago?"

She shakes her head and closes her eyes and a wave of despair crashes over me. Despair and panic. Because all of this was for nothing. She's incoherent. Whatever she used to know has slipped away in the years upon years she's spent locked in here. I jiggle her fingers, my final plea for answers.

Her eyes pop open, filled with terror again. The digital number on the heart monitor in her room jumps several paces and the monitor begins beeping—a loud, alarmed beep, as if notifying the nurses and doctors that one of the patients is about to have heart failure. "You are the key," she rasps.

Luka grabs my arm. "We need to get out of here."

"I'm the key? The key to what?"

"Come on, Tess," Luka urges.

The beeping grows louder, faster. And my grandmother nods, as if agreeing with him. I want to tear away her restraints. I want to take her with us, far from this place. But we aren't equipped for that.

Luka grabs my elbow, but I jerk free. "We can't leave her here!"

"We don't have a choice!"

"You're the key!" she yells.

With my grandmother's odd words ringing in my ears, Luka yanks me out of the room and we sprint toward the stairwell, afraid to look behind us. We leave her, in this madhouse of a prison. We race down the stairs, and as soon as we reach the first floor landing, Luka stops us both. He motions for us to slow down, to walk. So we do, until we get to that stretch of deserted hallway. Something about finding the place we started propels us into panic-mode. I race toward the supply closet, positive the woman will no longer be there. Positive somebody has to be on to us. I glance at my watch and am shocked to discover we've only been inside for twenty-five minutes. The woman stirs on the floor and moans. I toss the key fob at her and we take off toward the exit. We throw open the door and come face-to-face with a woman on the other side.

She rears back and clutches her chest. "Oh my goodness, you scared me half to death!"

"We're so sorry." Luka grabs my elbow. "She's not feeling well. Needs some fresh air."

The woman lets her hand fall away from her heart, gives us both an odd look, then walks inside. Once the door closes, we run. We run like we've never run before. We use his father's ID to get back out. This time a voice is not required and as soon as we're past the gates, we sprint to his car and collapse against the seats. We did it. We got to my grandmother. We accomplished our mission.

Only instead of feeling victory, I feel defeat.

Without saying anything, Luka starts the car and drives away. The more distance we put between ourselves and Shady Wood, the more our breathing returns to normal. And the more my sense of defeat grows.

"We didn't learn anything," I say, tears burning my eyes. "It wasn't worth it."

"That's not true." He pulls onto the main road, his attention glued to his rearview mirror, as if waiting for police lights and sirens, some sort of sign that we've been caught. "We learned that something is seriously wrong. Shady Wood says they're taking patients in for the purpose of rehabilitation. What we saw back there? That wasn't rehabilitation. That was messed up. They're all in medically-induced comas."

"We can't leave her there, Luka."

He reaches across the console and squeezes my hand. "I know."

His phone rings. His home phone number flashes on the screen. Luka powers it off and throws it in the back seat. "What do you think she meant when she said you were the key?"

I shake my head. "I have no idea."

Luka merges onto the highway, toward home.

"We are in so much trouble," I say.

He doesn't respond. Really, what is there to say?

## CHAPTER THIRTY-FIVE

# TROUBLE

Luka threads his fingers with mine as we pull through the gates into Forest Grove. He squeezes my palm. "We're in this together."

"Maybe we shouldn't be."

"What?"

I pull my hand from his. "I don't want to drag you into my problems."

"Tess, you didn't drag me into anything."

On the contrary. I dragged him into last night's dream.

"I'm part of this whether you want me to be or not."

"Even if it means being grounded for the rest of our lives?"

"Even if." Luka pulls into his driveway. The front tire is barely over the curb when both of our doors open and our parents march outside. It's as if they've been watching for us out the window. Mr. Williams stalks toward the car.

Luka grimaces. "I apologize in advance for anything he says."

His father raps the driver's side window with his knuckle. "Out!" The glass muffles the word, but not enough to snuff out its sharpness. "Now."

Luka grabs the handle and does what his dad says. So do I.

A vein in Mr. Williams' temple throbs. His eyes are so dark, foreboding settles in my stomach. And I'm not even the object of his wrath. He pins every ounce of that on Luka. His mom? Not so much. She glares at me like this is my fault. I can't help but think that she's right.

My parents race over to my side. Mom wraps me in a hug, then grips my arms and pulls me away, her face a perfect storm of bewilderment and relief. "How could you do that to us? Your brother is in the hospital, on the brink of death, and just when we find out he's okay, you go missing?" Before I have time to respond, she crushes me against her chest and squeezes. "Where did you go? What were you thinking?"

I look at Luka over her shoulder, feeling like a strangled frog.

He steps forward. "It was my fault, Mrs. Eckhart. I thought Tess needed to get away."

It sounds so lame. But we're not telling them where we went. No way. Not ever. Mom lets go of my neck. "You thought she needed to *get away?*"

Obviously, she's not buying it.

Mr. Williams grabs Luka's arm. "I couldn't have made it any clearer," he says through clenched teeth. "You are not to be associated with her."

Luka jerks free.

Dad narrows his eyes at Mr. Williams. "Who's *her*—my daughter?"

"She's a bad influence on our son," Mrs. Williams says.

Dad's eyebrows shoot up his forehead. "I believe you have things mixed up. Our daughter never made a habit of running away from home before she met your son."

"Mr. Ekhart is right." Luka looks at his mom. "This was my idea, not hers."

"Luka," I interject.

He shakes his head sharply at me and finishes. "Her brother was in the hospital. She was having a hard time. I made the suggestion. I snuck in the house and got my car keys. It was all me. So if you're going to be mad, be mad at me."

"Oh, you better believe I'm mad at you." Mr. Williams holds out his hand. "Keys."

Luka hands them over.

"Phone."

"It's in the car."

"Then I'll get it later. Let's go. Inside."

Mom puts her hand on my back and nudges me toward our house. "You too, Tess."

Walking across Luka's front lawn into our own, my parents flanking me like body guards, I look over my shoulder at Luka. He's looking at me too—confident, passionate, fire in his eyes. Like there's no way our parents can keep us apart.

Until my dad slams the front door shut and Luka is gone. "That's it. We've had it. Your brother's a mess. And you? This?"

Mom holds her head, as if the same headache plaguing me plagues her as well.

"We're not staying here anymore. We're moving."

"What? No! We can't move." I grab Dad's arm, panic crowding my lungs. "I'm sorry, okay? It won't happen again. I promise. We can't move. I ... I ..." I scramble for a reason, an explanation as to why we cannot move. Needing Luka won't fly. "I need Dr. Roth. He's been helping me." I look at Mom, searching for an ally. "You know he has. You've seen it with your own eyes. I'll only get worse if we move. I'll—I'll turn into Grandma."

This does the trick. Mom's eyes go round. Dad's face goes pale. And his resolve deflates. He pushes his hand back through his thinning hair. "If you ever do that again, you will leave us with no choice. Do you understand?"

I nod, quickly. Emphatically.

He slides my phone from his back pocket. "This is ours. Your car's out of commission and we will not be replacing it. At least not until you can earn back our trust. Now go up to your room."

My obedience is immediate. Dad follows close behind. He steps inside my bedroom, unplugs my computer, and tucks it beneath his arm. I have no way of contacting the outside world. No way of contacting Luka.

"We're going to the hospital in thirty minutes. Pete's doing well."

He shuts the door with a loud thud. My imprisonment is complete.

Visiting my grandmother? Despite what Luka thinks, it accomplished nothing.

$$\infty$$

We spend the rest of the day at the hospital. Pete is wide awake and more like his old self than I've seen him in a long time. It's like the car accident snapped him out of a long-standing depression. After my road trip debacle with Luka, seeing Pete's clear eyes and boyish smile is a much-needed breath of fresh air. My parents don't tell him about my disappearance. In fact, they specifically ask me to keep the whole fiasco to myself. I have no problem with this arrangement.

Now that I'm not taking my medicine, I expect to see the things I saw before. I brace myself for the white-eyed men, the temperature fluctuations, the beings that glow like miniatures suns. The bracing is for naught. I don't see anything at the hospital but doctors and nurses, visitors and patients.

That night, I reread my grandmother's journal. Three times through, searching for clues about me and her and these dreams we both have and why she might have thought that I— a mere toddler—could save her. My parents don't know I'm not taking my medicine anymore. I wish I could confide in them. I wish I could tell them about everything that has happened. But I can't. Dad will think I'm nuts, and Mom? I'm not sure what she will think. She's not as staunch in her convictions as Dad, but this is so far out there that all they will see, all they will hear is that their daughter is just like her grandmother. And I am. I'm exactly like her, but it's not what they think. This isn't psychosis.

My dreams are disjointed. I try finding the beach and Luka, but I can't. Instead, I end up back at the hospital. Not Pete's, but Shady Wood, staring at rows upon rows of comatose bodies. I'm not sure if the machines are keeping them alive or keeping them from living. I want to unhook them. I want to set them free from this dark, oppressive place. But when I try, nothing is solid. It's all vapor.

When I wake up, I write everything down, then spend the rest of Sunday visiting Pete, yearning—no aching—for Luka. That night, my dreams are the same. Me, trying to get to Luka but ending up at Shady Wood instead. Me, trying to free those people. Me, failing at both. I'm happy and relieved when I wake up. It's Monday morning, which means school. While my parents will go to many lengths to keep me from Luka, robbing me of my right to an education is not one of them. I pray that Luka's parents are the same.

Mom drives. As soon as she pulls up to the front entrance, I fling open the door and hurry toward the school, brushing off the looks and the whispers. As soon as I step inside the building, Luka is there. He grabs my face between his hands and kisses me. Full on the mouth. The shock of his lips on mine turns my kneecaps to putty. Luka is kissing me. He's kissing me, right there in the locker bay in front of everyone. And I'm so stunned by it all, so caught off guard, that my body has morphed into a ragdoll. A really hot, tingly ragdoll.

When he pulls away, my head spins. My lips throb in the best possible way.

Several students gape.

He takes my hand and pulls me out of the locker bay, right outside the bathrooms, a space that is relatively empty. "You have no idea how good it is to see you."

I blink like an idiot, unable to get past his greeting.

He pushes his hand through his hair. "I couldn't get to you in my dreams. I could hear you calling out for help. But I couldn't get to you."

I point toward the locker bay, dumbstruck. "You-you just kissed me."

A grin pulls at his lips—the very lips that were on mine seconds earlier. And then he does it again. He cups the side of my face and kisses me. His fingers move up into my hair. His other hand moves to my waist, pulling me closer. I grab onto his shirt front to keep myself upright. Luka is good at this. Much, much too good. But the kiss ends as abruptly as it began. He groans and leans against the wall.

My head spins. I've never been kissed by a boy before. I don't really know how these things work, but I have to imagine groaning is not a good reaction. I must be bad at it.

"I am so pissed at my dad," he says.

Luka's sudden shift in the conversation is not helping the

head-spinning situation.

"C'mon. We should get to class. If I get a tardy on my record, I'm going to be home-schooled." He takes my hand, laces his fingers with mine, and doesn't let go. "How's Pete?"

"Really good." I try to elaborate. I try to say more. Like how the doctors keep telling my parents how lucky Pete is. How they have a few more tests to run and if everything pans out, he'll be released tomorrow. But my brain is mush. Because Luka kissed me. He kissed me twice and I have no idea what it means.

"That's great."

"I dreamt about Shady Wood."

He doesn't look at me. He doesn't respond with a question or a comment. If not for the darkening of his expression, I might think he didn't hear me at all. But he heard. I can almost see the cogs spinning in his brain. I just wish I knew what they were spinning over.

When we get to Mr. Lotsam's classroom, Leela stands outside the door, her eyes puffy and bloodshot. I try to give her an encouraging smile. Either to apologize or to say it's okay. I understand why she was so upset, why she felt betrayed.

"I heard about Pete," she says.

"He's going to be okay."

She nods, her chin quivering. "I'm glad."

"Thanks Leela."

She gives me a weak smile. I think she might sit next to us—Luka and me—but she walks to the other side of the classroom. Even so, a sliver of hope works its way into my heart. Our friendship might take time to mend, but at least it has the potential of mending.

The bell rings and Mr. Lotsam begins a discussion about

the latest goings-on in Egypt and whether or not the United States should send troops. The class is engaged. The debate is lively. Luka and I don't chime in. We sit close—shoulder-to-shoulder, and stay quiet. I find myself relaxing a bit. Letting my guard down. Something about Luka's presence calms my nerves.

Until the door bursts open.

I jump, then sit up straight in my seat.

Two burly men stand in the doorway on either side of Principal Jolly. For a second, I wonder if I'm seeing things again. If the medicine has finally worn off all the way. But the conversation has come to a screeching halt and every single student stares at the same place I am staring.

Mr. Lotsam's brow knits together. "Is something the matter?"

One of the men—with a square jaw and flecks of gray in his dark blonde hair—flashes a badge. "We're here for Teresa Ekhart."

All eyes turn to me.

I shrink back in my seat.

Luka comes forward in his.

Did they find out I broke into Shady Wood? Did they identify my fingerprints on that woman's key fob? Did my grandmother rat me out?

"Are you Teresa Ekhart?" the man with the badge asks me.

I nod.

Luka stands. "Who are you?"

Principal Jolly frowns. "Luka, please sit down."

"Government officials." The other burly man flashes a badge of his own. "Teresa Eckhart, you have officially been declared a danger to society."

A danger to society?

Before I can process what's happening, one of the men starts reading me my rights. I'm being arrested in the middle of Mr. Lotsam's Current Events class.

Luka steps in front of me. "You can't do this."

"There have been multiple reports that Teresa Eckhart has been resisting treatment for her mental illness. She has stopped taking her prescribed medication. And she has been making irrational, reckless decisions."

My eyes go wide, because how could anybody know? The only person who knows I've stopped taking my medicine is ... Luka? My heart squeezes. Did he tell someone?

Before he can explain, one of the men shoves him aside and takes my wrist. My training kicks in. When a man grabs me, I've learned to throw my thumb straight up and jerk away. His grip falters, but the other man wraps his fingers around my bicep as I struggle to break free.

"Let her go!" Luka strains against Principal Jolly, who is trying and only partially succeeding in holding him back.

My face burns underneath everybody's stares. I feel light-headed. Dizzy. Because no way is this happening. I see Leela, looking frightened. And Summer, looking delighted. And Luka, looking panicked.

"You can't take her!" he shouts. "Tess, I'll find you."

Escape is impossible. No amount of self-defense will make up for the sheer muscles on these men. Fear strangles my trachea as they drag me away. I can't breathe. I can't call out for help. I can't ask them where they are taking me. Outside, a black police car waits. The man with the square jaw opens the back door, his grip bruising my arm. "Stop fighting us."

I don't listen. I jerk and pull and strain away. I'm not getting in that car. I want my mom. I want my dad. I want this to be a dream, but their grip won't even allow me to scratch the inside of my wrist.

The other man, who has icy blue eyes, removes a needle from his coat pocket, along with a syringe. And my fear surges into full-out panic. I thrash and kick and try to claw, but it's no use. With an evil glint in his eye, he jabs the needle into my neck and pushes me into the car. "Don't forget to buckle up, Little Rabbit."

My vision blurs.

Little Rabbit? That can't be right. That's what the man with the white scar calls me. I flop my hand toward my patch of eczema and scratch at it with heavy, fumbling fingers. It burns. Which can only mean one thing.

This is real. This is all very, very real.

# CHAPTER THIRTY-SIX

# ESCAPE

I wake up in a white room. My wrists are bound like my grandmother's. It takes a minute before the panic that engulfed me before my world went black comes back in full force. I fight and strain against the cuffs. I scream at the walls. I arch up my body, only to discover my ankles are bound as well.

I'm in Shady Wood. Surely this is where they've taken me. I call out for help, over and over and over again, until my voice is hoarse. Until I fall back into a restless, dark sleep. When I wake up, there is an IV in my wrist and a woman dressed in scrubs by my bedside.

"Please, help me," I croak.

She smiles brightly and pats my shoulder. "Don't you worry, honey, that's exactly what we're going to do." She removes a cap off a syringe and injects it into my IV line.

"Whadiz that?" My heart gurgles—uneven and lazy, as if detached from the fear flooding through my body. Whatever *that* is, I don't think it's my first dose.

"This is what's going to help you."

I try to shift away.

She tsks, like I'm a naughty, uncooperative child.

"Where'm I?"

"You're right where you're supposed to be." She dumps the needle into a nearby waste basket. "This is what happens when you stop taking your medicine. You become violent and disoriented. We can't have you attacking people, Teresa."

"Attacking people?"

"You attacked one of the men who brought you here."

My eyelids flutter. "No, I din attack anyone. I don't even know how I got'ere."

"You need to settle down or we'll be forced to give you more medicine."

Settle down? But I'm not doing anything. I can't do anything. It's like there's me, the Tess inside, who is flailing and screaming and clawing to get out. And then there's Tess on the outside, heavy and lethargic in bed. "Please, I need Luka."

She shakes her head sadly, like I'm in denial. Like I have no idea what I'm talking about. "Sweetheart, there is no Luka."

What? No. I shake my head. "Whadare you talking about? I was with him ..." We drove here together. Broke in here together. He kissed me in the locker bay and then he kissed me again outside the boys' bathroom. We shared dreams. I try to think how long I've been here, in this place. But time no longer exists. It could have been hours or it could have been days. I have no way of knowing. "Where're my parents?"

"They want you to get better just like the rest of us."

I try to grab for her, to make her really listen to me, to wipe that false cheery smile off her face. But I can't move my arms. "What about my grandmother?"

"Your grandmother is dead. She's been dead for years."

"Thas not true." It can't be. I saw her. With my own eyes. I held her hand.

"Honey, this is all part of the illness. The delusions. The hallucinations. You've been going downhill fast. You're here to get better."

I think about the rows of people in beds. Is that getting

better? Surely this woman is lying. Confusion engulfs me. I don't know what to believe anymore. I don't even know which way is up and which way is down. It's as though I've fallen into Alice's rabbit hole. The Tess on the inside—the one clawing to get out—surfaces. I strain against the leather straps on my wrists and ankles. I strain with everything I have.

The nurse shakes her head, like she's disappointed, and pulls out another needle from her pocket. Only instead of injecting it in my IV, she jabs it into my neck. There's a sharp burn and then nothing.

<hr />

I am weak. So weak, I can't lift my arms. I can't even lift my head. The same nurse is in my room. I lick my dry, cracked lips with a tongue that feels too thick to be my own. The whiteness of the room hurts my eyes. "How long have I been here?"

"A while," she says serenely.

"Are you going to shoot me with that needle again?"

"That depends."

"On what?"

"You." She picks up a glass of water from my night stand and holds out two pills in her palm. "I can make you take your medicine, or you can take it willingly."

I stare at the two white capsules. "What will they do?"

"They will help you get better." She holds the glass closer to my lips. My restraints smart against my wrists. My entire backside throbs with numbness. "Your parents are rooting for you. Your brother Pete is rooting for you. We're all rooting for you, Tess. We want you to get better. We want you to take your medicine so you can go home and become a productive member of society."

"My parents." My voice cracks over the word. The swell of emotion is intense. I want my mom. "Can I see them?"

"Soon. If you take these."

"And Luka?"

She sighs. "Luka isn't real. He's never been real. He's a figment of your imagination."

Tears well in my eyes. What if she's right? What if everything—Luka, our shared dreams, his insistence that I am not crazy, this quest to get answers from my grandmother—what if it was all a coping mechanism devised by my deranged mind? A way for me to deal with my psychosis and make sense of this messed up world that is mine?

The nurse studies me. "It's either the pills or the needle."

I have no choice. None. Except maybe I can fight. "Can you let me out of these restraints so I can take them myself?"

She seems to consider and the weakest flicker of hope taps against my wrist like a barely-there pulse. If she lets me out, maybe I can overpower her and escape. She purses her lips, then shakes her head. "It's not time for that yet."

A tear slips out of the corner of my eye and rolls down my temple.

"Stick out your tongue."

There's nothing for me to do except obey. She places the pills in my mouth and the cup to my lips. I swallow them down because I don't want whatever's in that needle in my bloodstream. My only chance to escape is to cooperate until they let me out of these restraints and then I can fight ... if I have any fight left.

"Now say *ahhhh*."

I didn't think it was possible to hate somebody more than Summer, but I do. I hate this woman. Like an obedient child, I open my mouth.

"Stick out your tongue, please."

I do.

She checks to make sure the pills are gone, smiles satisfactorily, then leaves me alone in the room.

I float in and out of consciousness, unaware of my body. Unaware of time. There's no window in my room, so I don't know when it is night and when it is day. I imagine this is what solitary confinement feels like. I stare at the white ceiling. I take my medicine. I can't tell if I'm coming into clarity or slipping away from it. Nothing feels real anymore. Not Dr. Roth. Not Luka. Not my parents or Pete. Not even me. Perhaps my whole life has been one giant hallucination.

I wonder if this is going to be my life now—this white box of a room and this IV and these restraints and this saccharinely sweet woman who makes me take medicine but never brings me food. I wonder if I will starve to death. I wonder why I'm not hungry.

My door opens.

I don't bother looking. There are footsteps. Somebody bends over me. It's not the nurse. I squeeze my eyes shut, positive I am dreaming or hallucinating. The person staring down at me is Luka. Wonderful, gorgeous, perfect Luka—his eyes flooded with equal parts horror and fury. And then there's somebody else too. On the other side of my bed. Dr. Roth. Only he doesn't look nearly as horrified as he does livid.

Dr. Roth unbinds my wrists and ankles and just like that, I am free. I rub my wrists and try to sit up, but dizziness blurs my vision and the world fades to black. Luka places his hand gently on my back and helps me sit upright.

"We have to get her out of here," he says.

"They told me you weren't real," I mumble. "They said I imagined you."

Luka takes my hand and flattens it against his chest—solid and warm—and I remember an eternity ago, when he did the same thing in a hallway outside of ceramics class. "Do you feel that?"

There's a faint *thud-thud, thud-thud* against my palm.

"I'm very real, Tess."

Dr. Roth removes my IV and examines the label on the bag of fluid. "They've been pumping her full of sedatives."

"Can you stand?" Luka asks.

I try, but my legs collapse beneath me. It's like I have no muscles at all. Luka puts one arm behind my back and the other beneath my knees and sweeps me into his arms like I weigh nothing. I rest my head against the place he put my palm moments earlier, relishing the sound of his heart. If this is a hallucination, then I'm going with it. For as long as it lasts. I will cling to it if I have to. Reality is overrated.

"Come on," Dr. Roth says. "Quickly."

"What will happen if they catch us?" Luka's voice rumbles in my ear.

"I'll lose my license. We'll both be arrested."

"Then it's hopeless," I say, remembering the labyrinth of hallways and rooms and expressionless doctors. There's no way we're getting out of here with Luka carrying me in his arms. "This is Shady Wood."

"We're not in Shady Wood, Tess," Dr. Roth says. "This is the Edward Brooks Facility."

"It is?" I'm having a hard time keeping my eyes opened.

The adrenaline that should be coursing through my veins refuses to make an appearance. This is my escape. Luka and Dr. Roth—potentially two figments of my imagination—are busting me out. Yet all I feel is lethargy.

A door opens. I force my eyes to open. Dr. Roth peeks out into the hallway.

"How long have I been here?"

"Two days," Luka whispers.

Two days? That's all?

Luka carries me out into a dark hallway after Dr. Roth. I open my mouth to ask a question, but Luka shushes me. "I'll explain everything later."

He holds me tight to his body as we hurry down two flights of stairs in the dark. I hear the *thump, thump, thump* of Luka's heart, the quickness of his breath. And all of a sudden, there is fresh air on my cheeks and we are outside beneath a full moon and sure enough, there it is. The looming, ominous Edward Brooks Facility. All this time, I've been a few blocks from home.

"Your parents have been trying to get to you," Dr. Roth explains as we hurry across the grounds. "Mr. Williams assured them they'd be able to see you tomorrow, but you were going to be moved by then."

"Moved where?"

"Shady Wood."

Luka shifts me in his arms, his warm, minty breath tickling my ear as we trot toward a car—Dr. Roth's, I'm assuming. "You're free, Tess. It's going to be okay."

I smile and give in to the heaviness dragging at my eyelids.

## Chapter Thirty-Seven

# The Gifting

Luka lays me down in a warm, comfortable bed—so much softer than the one I was shackled to for a lifetime, even if that lifetime was only two days. He rubs a cool salve onto my wrists while Dr. Roth encourages me to drink a really disgusting-smelling drink that steams inside a mug.

"It'll help counteract the medicine they were pumping into your system."

That's all the convincing it takes. I gulp it down, then I curl into a ball on my side. Luka pulls the covers over my shoulder and sits with me until I fall asleep. When I wake up, he sits in a chair by my bedside, glaring at the red welts on my wrists. But I smile, because my head is clear and there is strength in my limbs.

"I'll never forgive him for this," he says.

"Who?"

"My dad." He leans forward in the chair and rests his elbows on his knees. "He's the one who did this. He's the one who reported you to the authorities."

So it was never Luka. Of course it wasn't. I don't know how I could have doubted him. I sit up in bed. A little too fast. The room tilts. I cup my forehead with my palm.

Luka sits up straighter, concern etched in the corners of his eyes. "Here, you should eat this." He picks up a bagel off the nightstand and hands the plate over.

I place it on my lap, rest against the headboard, and eat small bites, taking equally small sips of the disgusting tea Dr. Roth had me drink before I fell asleep. With the sustenance, comes fear. I cannot be locked up again. Not like that. Not ever. "They're going to come back for me."

"I won't let them get to you."

"Luka, why did your dad have me locked up like that?" How could he—especially since his own son went to the very facility he locked me up in. For crying out loud, his dad bought the place in order to protect his son.

"It's a long story."

"I have time."

He cracks his knuckles, one at a time, that muscle I've grown to know so well ticking in his jaw. "It all goes back to that screening."

"Your mom's pregnancy screening?"

He nods grimly. "The government didn't approve of her decision. I guess the only way my dad could protect me was by striking a deal."

An ominous feeling clamps onto my muscles. "Protect you from what?"

"That was the same question I asked my dad. He never gave me a straight answer."

"What was the deal?"

"They knew my father was in the mental health field. They wanted him to do some screening. Look for crazy people. *Dangerous* people. Specifically, people who claimed to have prophetic dreams. Then report them to the proper authorities. If he agreed to do that, they'd forget about me. But my dad didn't do it. At least not everyone. He went out of his way to hide as many as he could. Even more so when my symptoms began. That's when he bought the Brooks facility. But then you moved to town and the rumors started circling and I was hanging out with you so much. My parents, they freaked out, and well ..." His eyes narrow. "They made a really stupid decision."

None of it makes sense. How could the government use a failed pregnancy screening as blackmail? And why did they want Mr. Williams to weed out people who were having prophetic dreams?

"You have to tell me everything you know. What's been going on while I've been locked up? I don't even know whose room this is. What happened after they took me from school?"

"I'm not sure; I left too." He drags his hand down his face. "I watched them drive you away."

A burst of clarity hits me like a sudden, bright flash of light. "One of the men. He called me Little Rabbit."

Luka's brow furrows.

"That's what that man in my dream calls me. The one with the scar. The one you fought off in the hospital."

He squints at the floor, as if trying to piece it together. I finish my bagel and the last of the tea, trying to put some pieces together myself. Only nothing fits. The man who called me Little Rabbit looked nothing like the man from my dream.

"Where are we?"

"Dr. Roth's apartment."

"Does anybody know we're here?"

Luka shakes his head. "My dad warned me he'd take drastic measures if I didn't obey him. He didn't know I'd take drastic measures right back."

"You mean like soliciting the help of a psychiatrist to break me out of a mental facility?"

"I knew your parents were getting the runaround by the police. The authorities were no help. They wouldn't let them see you, even when your dad wielded his influence. I didn't know where else to go. So I went to Dr. Roth. Something in my gut was telling me I could trust him." Luka leans closer. "Tess, he knows everything. When I showed up, he had me come into his office, almost as if he'd been waiting for me, and he locked the door and turned up some music and he told me to meet him back here with a bag for you and one for me. He'd already been planning on breaking you out."

"Dr. Roth?"

Luka nods. "So I went to your house and I told your mom."

"My mom?" My voice pinches over the word. I want to hug her, but I'm not sure when I'll see her again. I'm not sure *if* I'll see her again.

"I told her everything. About you and me and your grandma."

"Did she believe you?"

"I think she believed that you were in serious danger. She made me promise that I'd take care of you. That I wouldn't let anything bad happen to you." He takes my hand, his own hot. "It's a promise I won't break. Your safety means everything to me."

His words and the way he says them makes my stomach quiver. But beneath the fluttering warmth, my fear grows. "What are we going to do? What if they find us?"

Before Luka can answer my questions, Dr. Roth flings open the door and steps inside. "We don't have much time." He hurries over to my bedside, listens to my heart with a stethoscope, sticks a thermometer in my mouth, flashes a light into my eyes. "I'm afraid you have to leave."

"Already?" Luka asks, standing.

"It's not safe. For either of you."

I stand up too and notice for the first time that I am wearing a hospital robe. Luka hands me a bag. I pull out a pair of jeans and pull them up under the robe. He and Dr. Roth turn around, giving me privacy while I pull a t-shirt over my head and a sweatshirt too. "How did you get this stuff?"

"Your mom packed it for you."

They turn back around as I get to work pulling my hair into a ponytail, shoving my feet into tennis shoes. The energy from the bagel works its way into my blood. "Why are you helping us?" I ask Dr. Roth. I can't quite figure out where his piece fits in the puzzle. "Aren't you supposed to be one of them?"

"I will never be one of them," he says.

"Who are you, then?"

"I'm a Believer."

"A believer in what?" Luka asks.

Dr. Roth goes to the window, peeks outside. To my surprise, it's dark out. I'm not sure if I slept through another day, or if this is the same night of our escape. "I've been doing research for years. Taking notes. Keeping journals. Once I had sufficient proof, my plan was to find more of you. After this, I believe I have all the proof I need."

"*More* of us?"

"Proof of what?"

Luka and I ask our questions at the same time.

Dr. Roth looks through the blinds again, and addresses Luka's question first. "Proof that you're all in danger."

The hairs on the back of my neck stand on end. I bend

over and tie my laces, my gaze never leaving Dr. Roth.

"What do you mean *all?*" Luka asks.

"There are other people out there. People like you."

I stand. "Who are we?"

"You are The Gifting."

There's a loud pounding at the door, followed by a deep shout. "Thornsdale police!"

My heart jumps into my throat.

Dr. Roth shoves Luka's bag against his chest. I strap mine over my shoulders.

"Quick, come with me." Dr. Roth leads us to the back door of his apartment. "Come back tomorrow morning. I promise to tell you everything I know."

More shouting from the front. "Open up or we'll let ourselves in!"

Luka grabs my hand and pulls me out of the apartment, down the fire escape. We sneak into the dark of night, Dr. Roth's words reverberating inside my mind.

*You are The Gifting.*

And there are more of us.

Tomorrow can't come soon enough.

———

# About the Author

K.E. Ganshert was born and raised in the exciting state of Iowa, where she currently resides with her family. She likes to write things and consume large quantities of coffee and chocolate while she writes all the things. She's won some awards. For the writing, not the consuming. Although the latter would be fun. You can learn more about K.E. Ganshert and these things she writes at her website at www.katieganshert.com. You can also follow her on Twitter, where she goes by @KatieGanshert.

Want to stay up to date on The Gifting series? Visit K.E. Ganshert's website and subscribe to her mailing list. Book 2, The Awakening, is available now for purchase. Read on to enjoy a complimentary excerpt.

# Excerpt for *The Awakening*

## CHAPTER ONE

# DEAD MAN HANGING

D arkness has never been a friendly thing. Not to me. But now, huddled behind a dumpster in the alleyway behind Dr. Roth's apartment building, I burrow into its protective arms, pulling it around myself until I'm wrapped up as tightly as a swaddled infant.

Perhaps we should make a run for it. Sprint as far away from here as possible. But fear paralyzes me. I'm pretty sure it has the same effect on Luka, too, because we crouch there—me and him, this boy who has come to mean so much—holding our breath as if the police might hear the sound of breathing five stories up.

Raindrops begin falling from the sky—fat, cold globs of moisture that plop against the dumpster's top and soak into the cotton of my sweatshirt. Luka wraps his arm around my hunched form and pulls me so closely to him I am unsure where he ends and I begin. It's not enough. I want more. I want the things he makes me feel to carry me off into oblivion, some place where this reality we're facing now no longer exists.

The clank of footsteps on the fire escape forces us to duck further back. A beam of light slices through the darkness, searching. My heart hammers against my chest. I'm sure Luka can hear it, maybe even feel it. They are looking for me, those people upstairs. They want to take me away and lock me up in Shady Wood with my grandmother, where I will never see my family or Luka again. I don't breathe until the light finally goes away and the footsteps retreat.

The police are not coming down here, at least not right now. Dr. Roth is a smart guy. Surely he will find a way to throw them off our scent. Even so, we stay where we are, as still as statues, afraid to blink, afraid to think, until my legs cramp and the chill in the air turns my fingers numb. Northern California in January is not an ideal time for a night spent outdoors. For the first time since moving to Thornsdale in September, I find myself wishing for the balmy Florida heat I'd taken for granted back in Jude. But as cold as it might be out here, what other choice do we have?

We can't go home. I'm sure mine is under surveillance and Luka's isn't safe. His father would hand me over the second we arrived. The two of us can't be seen at all. I'm sure by now, my escape from the Edward Brooks Facility has been splashed on the news, along with my face. Nowhere is safe. Which means we will have to wait out the night behind this dumpster. Dr. Roth gave us specific directions to come back in the morning. He promised to explain everything.

The raindrops thin out into a misty drizzle. Luka loosens his grip around my waist and we stare at one another through the dark. He straightens his legs, as if his muscles are cramped too. I want to tell him to stop moving, but I'm doing the same thing.

"Are you okay?" he whispers so softly I have to strain to hear.

It's a silly question. Of course I'm not. He knows it. I know it. Over the course of six days, my brother almost died, we broke into a high-security psyche ward and discovered rows upon rows of patients in medically-induced comas, my deranged grandmother said I was "the key", I was dragged out of school against my will by government officials, locked up and drugged in the Edward Brooks Facility, then rescued by Luka Williams and my psychiatrist, who turns out, isn't who he claimed to be. All I can manage is an almost-silent, "I can't feel my fingers."

Luka takes my hands between his own and rubs until they are slightly warmer than frozen.

"Do you think they're still up there?" I whisper.

"I don't know."

A shudder takes hold of my body and convulses through my limbs. Even in the thick of night, I can see the concern pooling in his green eyes. "I have so many questions."

"Me too," he says.

"What do you think he meant about there being 'more of us'?"

"I'm more concerned about the part where we're all in danger."

A shudder ripples through my arms.

Luka sits against the brick wall of the apartment building. He pulls me beside him and wraps his arms around me. "Is this all right?"

I nod against his chest, too frightened and cold to be self-conscious.

"It's going to be okay, Tess." My body rises and falls with his breath. "We'll get answers from Dr. Roth tomorrow. You can go to sleep. I won't let anything happen to you."

Despite the chilly nighttime air outside and the cold fear inside, something about his nearness warms me. I am not alone. Luka is here—brave, handsome, confident Luka. I can almost believe it's true—that he has the power to keep me safe. That I might really be able to go to sleep.

I curl up against him and wrestle my fear into submission. I don't let myself think about my family or how much I miss my mom. I don't let myself think about what my life will be now. I take deep, even breaths. I borrow Luka's warmth. And I force all my attention onto one thing.

I'm not suffering from psychosis. Neither is Luka.

Dr. Roth gave us a name. We are The Gifting.

Movement awakens me. It's a twitch at first. Then something bigger, like a jolt. My eyelids flutter open. I am wrapped up with Luka, tangled into a knot on the hard cement. We are face to face, our bodies pressed together. Only his eyes are closed. His face twitches. Then his eyes fly open. Before he can make a sound, I cup my hand over his mouth, trapping the noise inside.

His nostrils flare.

"Shhh, Luka. You were having a nightmare." Something I know all too well. My nightmares are what put us in this position. He stares down at me with pupils so large, his irises are nothing but the thinnest ring of green. Slowly, his breathing regulates. His pupils shrink.

I remove my hand.

And without the slightest warning, his fingers twine into my hair, he pulls my face close, and his lips crush mine. A quick burst of intense passion before he pulls away and hugs me to his chest, where his heart crashes against my ear. The whole thing happened so fast, I barely had time to register it, let alone kiss him back. Three times now he has kissed me and three times now, they have come as complete surprises. He springs them on me when I least suspect, like in a crowded locker bay at school or on the dirty ground behind a dumpster. Perhaps this is a good thing. His method leaves no time for agonizing over how awful I must be at it.

He untangles himself from my arms and sits up, propping his elbows on his knees, digging his fingers into his hair, staring at some arbitrary spot on the ground. A white-throated sparrow lands on one of the fire escapes and lets out a wavering whistle.

"Do you want to talk about it?"

He avoids eye contact.

I should probably push him, but honestly? I'm afraid of his answer. Luka has had dreams about me long before we first met in September. In every one, I'm in danger. In one of his dreams, I actually died. I'd rather not know if it happened again. I sit up beside him. The faint glow of early morning filters into the alleyway, softening everything around us—the dumpster, the trash cans, the brick walls. The night has given way to dusk. And I am desperate for answers. "Do you think it's safe to go up now?"

"He said the morning. He never said how early." Luka stands and pulls me up with him.

His grip tightens around my hand as we tiptoe toward the fire escape and climb the metal stairs on silent feet.

One flight.

Two flights.

Three.

Four.

We stop before landing on the fifth. Luka holds up his finger, his meaning clear. I am to wait here while he pokes his head inside the open window. We have a wordless argument with hand gestures. I don't want to stand by while he puts himself in jeopardy, not when I've already put him in enough. But he refuses to let me go first. So Luka wins and I wait. When the coast is clear, he waves me over. He climbs through the window first, then helps me inside Dr. Roth's apartment.

It's too quiet. Too still.

Goose bumps march up my arms. My palms turn cold and clammy. What if this is a trap? What if Dr. Roth was arrested and the minute we open our mouths, the police will descend and the two burly men who dragged me out of Thornsdale High School will drag me away again. Only this time Dr. Roth and Luka won't be around to break me out.

Luka pulls me forward, toward the bedrooms. I want to dig my heels into the carpet. Fear claws about inside my chest, scrapping and scratching for an exit. I have no idea why I don't want to see whatever it is we are about to see. Until we round the corner and find him—the man with all the answers.

Hanging from a noose at the end of the hallway.

## CHAPTER TWO

# CLOSE CALL

Footsteps sound outside Dr. Roth's apartment door. Luka clamps his hand over my mouth to muffle my scream and wraps his arm around my waist. There's a knock. Something like a squeak issues from the back of my throat. Luka tightens his grip around my waist and half-drags, half-carries me up the hallway, toward the still, hanging body, and into a room. The same one I woke up in not more than twelve hours ago.

Another knock at the door. "Rise and shine, Dr. Roth. It's the police."

The room looks untouched and unruffled. Nobody would suspect somebody had slept in the bed recently. In fact, it looks as if the guest room is perfunctory and really, the doctor hasn't had a guest in years. Luka pulls me toward the bed and the two of us hide underneath. I cup my hand over my mouth to mask the sound of my breathing.

"All right, I'm coming in," the voice says. There's a pause, then a loud bang. I jump. Luka tucks me closer. Another bang, followed by a thud, as if the door has swung open and crashed into the wall. "You awake in here?"

Footsteps draw nearer, then stop. Whoever it is clucks his tongue. "Well now, Doc, why'd you go and do a thing like this?"

Luka cups his hand over mine, whether to provide an extra sound barrier or as a gesture of comfort, I'm not sure. The frayed hemp of his bracelet bites into my skin. With eyes buggy and unblinking, I stare at the police officer's shoes in the hallway. He pivots and walks out of eyeshot.

"Hey-a Manny, it's Jake. Patch me through to the Chief, would ya?" Officer Jake is on his phone, calling the chief of police, which happens to be Leela's uncle. How long before this place is swarming with cops? The floor creaks. It doesn't seem possible, but my eyes grow wider. "Yeah-a, Bill? Looks like the doc offed himself ... No, he's hanging right here in front of me. Apparently, the threat of losing his license did a number on him."

I picture Dr. Roth's limp body hanging from the noose, his neck bent at a weird angle. I'm not sure I will ever be able to scrub that memory from my mind. He's dead. The man with all the answers is dead.

More floor creaking. Officer Jake's shoes come back into view. "Suicide's a pretty safe bet, but the medical examiner will need to verify."

Another pause, longer this time.

My mind buzzes in the silence. It doesn't make sense. Dr. Roth would not have hung himself. He was waiting for us to return. He told us to come back. He called himself "a believer". He said he had been gathering evidence.

"So now what? I can't exactly question a dead man ... No, there's no sign of the girl, but I'll look around. See if there's any evidence that she's been here."

I swallow another squeak and press back into Luka. His grip tightens.

"A national alert, huh? I don't understand why she's so important. Have to imagine a teenager can't be much of a threat ... Right, I understand ... I have a jump drive. I can copy all the files and bring it into the station. Hold on a tick." His shoes shuffle past the doorframe. Beneath this bed, with my hand cupped over my mouth and Luka's cupped over my hand, sound seems to be magnified. A chair groans. Computer keys clack. He's accessing Dr. Roth's computer files.

Luka nudges me, then points toward the nightstand. A crate holding two thick manila folders sits on the ground, as if Dr. Roth had been preparing for our visit.

More computer clacking. "Bill, there's nothing here. His computer's wiped clean."

A memory floats to the surface. It all feels like a lifetime ago, back when my biggest problems came in my sleeping hours and Dr. Roth was nobody but a psychiatrist at the Edward Brooks Facility. I had questioned his archaic record keeping.

*"Pen and paper doesn't crash. It's not nearly as accessible, either."*

A flood of gratitude toward the man washes over me. He knew all along that something like this could happen. That digital files were not safe or indestructible. He was protecting me from the very beginning. But as soon as the relief comes, so does the panic. Because all Officer Jake has to do is walk into this room and he'll see the files that are not more than five feet from our heads. Not only will he come into possession of extremely confidential information, he'll see us as soon as he bends down to get it.

"Either he erased them or somebody else did ... Yeah-a, I'll look around ... is the medical examiner on his way?" Something snaps shut, like a laptop. "Ten-four. I'll be waiting here. See ya at the station."

A chair squeaks, followed by a stretch of silence.

I feel immobilized, paralyzed. Even my thoughts are frozen. I wonder if Luka feels the same way, because he does not move behind me.

"Tut, tut, Dr. Roth. Just what were you hiding?"

My heart thuds so loud I'm terrified Officer Jake will hear it. I can cup my hand over my mouth to silence my breathing, but there's nothing to silence my heart.

"You don't mind if I use your bathroom, do you? I didn't think you would."

The man is having a conversation with a dead body. A psychiatrist, to boot. If I weren't having a silent panic attack, if Luka and I weren't in such horrible danger, if our only ally wasn't the one hanging out in that hallway, the situation would be laughable.

"Now, you stay there. Don't move. I'll be out in five and we'll see if I can't find where you hide your secrets."

Officer Jake's shoes appear in the doorframe again.

*Please don't see the crate ... please don't see the crate ...*

His shoes keep going, followed by a soft click of a door latch and a tuneless whistled melody from the bathroom beside us.

Luka goes from statue-still to a flurry of silent motion. He releases my waist and my mouth, then quickly and silently shimmies out from under the bed. I want to pull him back under, because—is he nuts? We can't be seen. If we're seen, we're dead. I will be locked up in Shady Wood and he will be put into prison and our keys will be thrown away. There will be no escaping this time.

"Luka," I hiss.

But he pulls me out alongside him, grabs the two manila folders, takes my hand and leads me out into the hallway. A strip of light shines beneath the bathroom door, the man's whistling muffled by the droning of a fan. Without hesitating, Luka pulls me toward the window. We climb out. I hold my breath while Luka shuts it as quietly as possible and we tear off down the steps.

Away, away, away ... as fast as we can.

∽

Not until the entire length of the alleyway is between us and Officer Jake do I dare talk. I huddle against the brick façade of a building, my words escaping in huffs and puffs. I'm not used to sprinting. "We need ... to get ... out of here." And by here, I mean Thornsdale. In five minutes that apartment is going to be crawling with police, which means we need to put as much distance between us and this place as possible. Much easier said than done when all we have is our feet and our backpacks, and now, these two folders containing who knows what.

Luka swings his backpack off his shoulders, unzips the zipper, and pulls out two baseball caps and a pair of sunglasses. "Hide your hair in there and put these on." He pulls his hat over his hair and stuffs the folders inside his bag.

I do as he says, stuffing my hair up in the hat and putting on the glasses. I try not to think about Officer Jake's words about me and a national alert. I can't process that right now. Or Dr. Roth's death. All I can think about right now is making it to safety. Wherever that is.

"All we have to do is make it across this street. Walk normally. Do you see that alley over there?" Luka points to the other side of the street, toward an alleyway between an insurance building and liquor store.

I nod.

"I'm pretty sure it will lead us to some more. Once we're out of Thornsdale, we can find a motel and figure out what to do next."

"What if somebody recognizes us?"

"They won't. Not if we stick to the alleyways." He grabs my hand. "And not if we hurry."

"Luka," goose bumps march across my skin, "that wasn't a suicide."

"I know." He squeezes my hand and we step into the hazy sunlight.

---

CPSIA information can be obtained at www.ICGtesting.com
Printed in the USA
LVOW07s0552250916

505972LV00002B/156/P